The River Rolls On

DIANE GREENWOOD MUIR

Cover Design Photography: Maxim M. Muir

Don't miss all of the books in
Diane Greenwood Muir's

Bellingwood Series

A short story based
on the Biblical Book of Ruth (Kindle only)
Abiding Love

CONTENTS

ACKNOWLEDGMENTS

The world has exploded with life and color. Spring threw off the browns and greys of winter and summer arrived with lush tree canopies and thick grasses. Farmers planted their crops and perfect rows of corn and beans popped up from dark, black earth. I am grateful every day for the opportunity to pour out my stories while living in the midst of Iowa's beauty. If I can give you just a small look at why I love the Midwest, that's momentous for me.

A quick note. You will read a scene in Chapter Twenty-Two that happens under a bridge. The photograph on the cover was taken one day this spring by my photographer husband, Maxim Muir, from that bridge. How fun is that?

Thank you to Rebecca Bauman, Tracy Kesterson Simpson, Linda Watson, Carol Greenwood, Alice Stewart, Fran Neff, Max Muir, Edna Fleming, Dave Muir and Nancy Quist for all they do to make these books happen.

These people will never know how much they mean to me. I trust them with my words and they make me better. They encourage me, while also correcting my work and asking me to rethink what I've written. With each edit, unique issues are discovered and my books get better and better. I appreciate their gift of time and attention.

CHAPTER ONE

Polly tried opening her eyes, but her eyelids were so heavy. What time was it? What was wrong? Why was she lethargic? She had no memory of falling asleep. The last thing she remembered was dropping Rebecca off at school. It was starting to rain and she'd watched Rebecca run to the front door, lower her Marvel Avengers umbrella, and turn to wave before going inside.

But what happened next? Polly concentrated. She had nothing. What in the hell was wrong? She wanted to bring her hands up to rub her eyes, but found that she couldn't move. Something held her wrists to her sides.

Trying to quell rising panic, Polly attempted to lift her legs. Those were held down as well. When she tried to lift her head, pressure on her forehead allowed no movement.

"Help me," she said softly. She'd seen enough movies and television to know that if someone had her strapped in and she wasn't gagged, no one outside could hear her. Screaming would be a waste of energy. Everything inside her clenched up and she began to cry.

Was she going to die? Why was she here? Who would do this

to her? What if she never saw Henry again? Had she told him that she loved him? And Rebecca? Who was going to take care of Rebecca when Sarah died? And Jessie and her new baby. She'd just moved into an apartment. Polly was in the process of helping them find furniture. Last weekend they'd gone to antique stores and thrift shops. Oh god, what was happening?

Polly's lower lip quivered. It flashed through her mind that this might be some awful practical joke, but none of her friends would take it to this level.

If only this made sense. But it didn't. Actually, she was having a difficult time thinking much beyond her immediate memories of the morning. Things were foggy. She must have been drugged. But how? And where?

"Is anyone there?" she asked quietly.

When no response came, she relaxed. Unless they were watching her from another room, she was alone. She didn't know what time it was or how long she'd been here, but someone would come looking for her.

Polly pulled her arms against their restraints. Not too tight, but not loose either - her fingers were free, so she patted around, trying to figure out what she was attached to. She took a deep breath and reached out, trying to sense her immediate surroundings.

She was on a mattress with no pillow. What was holding her wrists? She moved her hands and realized she could feel the outer edges of the bed. She was attached to metal posts. Maybe a hospital bed. What was holding her wrists? Polly bent her hand back in on itself to touch the restraint. Leather, tight enough to keep her in place. She wasn't planning to break her thumbs in order to escape them, no matter what the tough guys in the movies did.

A door opened, someone took a deep breath and she heard gas escaping a container.

"Hello, Polly," a voice squeaked, like he'd breathed in helium.

"Why am I here?" she asked.

"We'll get to that. Are you comfortable enough?"

"No. Not at all. Who are you?"

Another breath and the voice squeaked again. "Oh, not yet, my sweetheart. We have lots of time."

The voice pitch started to lower back to its normal range. After another loud intake of breath, the person said, "I'll release your head. I want you to be comfortable."

"What about going to the bathroom?"

Another intake, "Come now. It's not been long enough for that. You'll be allowed to use the facilities and have food and water in a while. For now, you might as well relax."

The restraint on Polly's forehead dropped away, but the blindfold remained with pads pressed against her eyes. When she could turn her head, she did so and stretched her neck.

Another intake of helium. "Try to sleep. We'll be back later." The person drew his finger down Polly's face, hesitating at her lip, then he gently brushed across it. A sharp breath and the finger yanked away.

The door opened and closed again.

"Why?" Polly asked out loud. "I don't understand. Why?" Tears filled her eyes, burning when they had no place to fall. Polly twisted her head, rubbing it against the bed. Maybe she could push the blindfold off. She twisted and turned and felt it move. She pushed her head up and down, adjusting so that it would loosen as she twisted. It began to work when she heard the door open again.

"Oh no," a deep voice said. "That will never do. Not if you want to live."

This new man reached up and lifted away the blindfold, but she was still in darkness. "It looks as if we'll need duct tape."

"Not on my face," she whimpered.

"You made the choice."

"Why?"

"Because you tried to remove the blindfold. Our little friend wasn't thinking when he removed the brace. I'll just fix that."

"No. Why am I here?"

She heard the duct tape rip from the roll and tried to shake her

3

head. Before she could make anything happen, a strong hand clamped down on her head, then tape was applied from temple to temple.

"No," she whimpered. "Tell me why."

A foul odor passed over her nose and she felt him get closer to her. He smelled horrendous. His breath was overwhelming - onions and garlic and sausage. He whispered in her ear. "Because it's about time."

"Time for what? Why are you doing this?"

"Patience. Patience."

The door opened and closed and in a few moments the scent of him dissipated. Polly was alone again. She felt the burning sensation of tears in her eyes again and wondered how in the hell she was ever going to get free.

This was Iowa. How could this be happening in the middle of Iowa? People didn't do these types of things here. What had she ever done to anyone that would cause them to hurt her like this?

"Wait a minute," she said out loud. "You aren't hurt. No one has hurt you. Quit feeling sorry for yourself and start thinking through this. Pay attention. The only way you're getting out of this is to be smarter than whoever it is outside the room."

She took a deep breath. What would the tough Polly do? Probably not lie here and whimper. She'd think and plan and be aware.

Polly started thinking about the television shows she watched. She loved a good mystery and the heroes were always solving problems because they observed, not because they screamed and threw tantrums. In fact, she couldn't bear it when they portrayed women as screamy little stupid things. Any woman worth her salt would only use screaming if it was going to do her some good.

She slowed her breathing, trying to relax, listening for anything that might tell her where she was. A few quiet moments passed. There. A car started. She might still be in town. She listened for sounds inside whatever building she was in. There was a television playing somewhere but it was only background noise. If they'd turn that off, she could hear so much more.

4

What else could she do? She tried to sit up. It was awkward, but she tried. That was bad. Dizziness and nausea forced her to lie back down. If that had anything to do with the drugs they gave her, it would soon pass. She wished they had given her something to drink. Her mouth felt like cotton.

Polly took a few moments to salivate, concentrating on bringing relief to her dried out tongue and throat. She still couldn't get past how strange this was. This only happened to actors who were about to be killed in a scene. Maybe it happened in big cities or to people with money who were being held for ransom.

Wait. Ransom? She and Henry didn't have that kind of money. They might if everything was liquidated. Did Henry know yet that she was gone? Was he worrying? Had these kidnappers called him? Did they tell him not to contact law enforcement? What about Lydia? She'd be beside herself. She was always trying to protect Polly.

Sal. They had just started construction on the coffee shop. Sal couldn't do this on her own. Nobody out here knew Sal like Polly did. What would she do?

And Jason. Polly's eyes burned with tears again. She loved Sylvie's boys. They filled her days with life and so much joy. Jason was deep and brooding while his brother, Andrew, was outgoing and filled with energy. She didn't even have to ask him and he'd know what she needed and was off to take care of it. Every day after school, he tore up the steps to get Obiwan and Han for a quick walk outside. He watched over Rebecca, worrying about her more the closer her mother got to the end.

At the thought of her dog, Polly lost all control. How could she ever leave her animals? She was just getting to know them. Sure, it had been a couple of years, but this was when it was getting fun. Luke and Leia were comfortable in the house no matter how many people or animals came and went. Obiwan was her heart and soul. She loved him so much. He'd never understand why she wasn't coming home again. Sweet little Han had turned into a wonderful companion for Henry. He loved traveling to job sites and never got more than ten feet from his master. If he lost sight of Henry, he ran to find him. Even at home, he lived for Henry. At least they'd have each other.

"Stop it," she said. "You have to quit feeling sorry for yourself. Think."

Polly hitched herself on the bed, wondering if it was on wheels. It moved, but there were brakes in place.

She wondered exactly what was around her wrists, so she scootched down in the bed until her face was against her right hand. She touched her cheek with her thumb and started to cry again. Maybe she could rip that tape off and finally see.

After twisting and contorting, Polly finally snagged a corner of the duct tape and began to pull. Everything in her clenched. There was no way to rip it off, she didn't have leverage or enough turning radius ... unless she could twist her head so she got the other side of the tape. It took a few minutes, but finally she had another corner. She peeled enough back to get a good grip and then, steeling herself, took a breath and flung her head away from her hand, ripping the tape away.

She shuddered and then put her face back in her hand so she could brush away the pads covering her eyes.

Leather bands were strapped to her wrists and ankles. Damn it, she wasn't going to let them keep her here. She twisted and contorted herself again and couldn't manage to get into a good position to wrap her teeth around the strap. The collar bone she'd broken last fall rebelled at the pressure she was putting on it while pulling herself into these strange positions. She relaxed and tried to think.

Polly looked around the small bedroom and saw nothing except for the bed she was on and a tank which she assumed was the helium. A door to the right and a much smaller door on her left - probably a closet. There was a window at the other end of the room, but dark, black plastic had been taped to the window sill, covering it completely.

Polly took a deep breath and contorted herself until she couldn't move any longer, finally reaching the strap of the restraint on her right hand. She put her teeth on it and pulled, but found that it was thick and resistant to the small tugs she was able to make. Then she saw the metal brace that had been snapped down to keep it from moving and her eyes filled with tears.

Slumping back in the bed, Polly allowed the tears to flow. Now that she could see, the tears weren't of loss, but frustration. There had to be a way out of here. She had to be able to find it.

She heard the television turn off and a front door slam shut. She went rigid, but soon a car engine roared to life. Polly waited as she heard it shift gears and drive away. Now was as good a time as any to fight through the restraints. She gathered her resolve and contorted herself again to try to reach the snap holding the leather strap closed. Her tongue reached it, but she didn't have enough strength to make it do anything.

Polly continued to twist her wrist and head until she felt her top teeth scrape against the metal. Just another few millimeters and she could. Ahhh! She got her mouth around it and pulled back, releasing the strap. More tears leaked from her eyes as she pulled the strap through the buckle. She tugged back on it, releasing the prong.

One wrist was free. She scrambled to release the other wrist and then bent forward to unbuckle her ankles. She jumped out of bed and ran to the window, peeling back the tape to look outside.

Her heart sank. She was in the middle of nowhere. She had no idea where she was and no idea how to get out of here. There was nothing in the room that she could use as a weapon, so she grabbed one of the heavy leather straps that had bound her ankles. Maybe the buckle would hurt someone bad enough for her to escape.

And where were the rest of her clothes? She was dressed only in her panties and bra, everything else was gone. Rain was still pouring down outside, but today was supposed to get up into the mid-sixties. She'd live through cold rain if necessary.

With the buckle in her right hand, Polly gently turned the door knob, praying she could be absolutely silent. Fortune was on her side and the door didn't squeak. She stepped into a darkened

7

hallway and held her breath, listening for sounds and movement. There was nothing.

She tiptoed down the hall and peeked around a corner into the living room, not at all surprised to see that it was filthy. Pizza boxes and empty food containers, beer and soda bottles littered every flat surface.

Desperate to find her clothes, Polly considered going back and checking the two rooms she'd passed in the hall, but worried that if someone was sleeping in one of them, her escape would be over. There had to be something here. A pair of men's boots sat beside the front door. At least those would give her protection on the ground. She grabbed them up and took one last look, then ducked into the kitchen and looked through the cupboards. There. Black trash bags. That would be enough. She pulled three of them out of the box and rather than open the front door, gently turned the handle on the kitchen door. It led out onto a rickety stoop and stairs. If anyone was in the house, they would certainly hear her on that.

The only solution was to step toward the outside of the stoop. She placed a foot down and slowly lowered her weight, then did the same with the other foot, moving forward. Looking around, Polly saw trees and grass. She had to find a road, but out here, the first person she saw on that road could be her kidnappers.

"Okay," she thought silently. "Everything in Iowa is on a mile long grid. All I have to do is walk a mile and I'll find a road. I can do that. Even if I have to walk two miles. I can still do that."

She ran for the tree line, swearing and cursing as her feet hit every rock and tree root. As soon as she felt that she had some protection from the house, Polly stopped to put on the boots. Her feet were bleeding and a gash on the ball of her left foot hurt like hell. The boots were much too big, so she stuffed a trash bag into each of the toes and pulled them on, then laced them up. It was uncomfortable, but at least she could travel without further cutting herself to pieces.

She ripped a hole in the bottom of the last trash bag and drew it over her head, poking her arms through holes she ripped in the sides and feeling much better at not being quite so exposed. Polly looked down at herself. This was better by far than the feeling of helplessness she'd had while strapped to that bed. She still had no idea who had kidnapped her or why they'd done it, but they'd screwed with the wrong woman today.

Running through the trees, Polly hesitated when she heard a vehicle pull in at the trailer. She only had moments before someone would look for her. She took off at a dead run, stopping at a creek separating the trees from an empty field. Farmers were just starting to plant crops and what she needed to find was someone out here with his tractor. She scrambled down the bank and decided to run through the water, hoping to throw them off. The creek turned back on itself several times and she came to a spot where the bank wasn't quite so steep. She grabbed a root sticking out and pulled herself up, then sat to catch her breath.

She needed to keep going straight, not zig zag through a creek. There had to be a road. There had to be a farmer's house. How long was this going to take?

A sound from where she'd run from spurred her into action and Polly took off, dashing for another copse of trees. This ran along the creek for a distance as the bank got steeper and steeper. Polly finally came up to a fence line and stopped for another breath. The fence would lead somewhere. She climbed through the barbed wire to the other side and then took off running along the fence.

It seemed to take forever before Polly saw a house above a rise. Silos and barns filled the horizon as she continued to run. Tears began again. Salvation was just ahead. All she had to do was get there. Her calves and thighs burned with exertion and her side was beginning to ache. Now that she had found civilization, everything that had happened to her filled her mind and she slowed to a walk, crossing the field one step at a time.

When she reached the fence, Polly ducked through it and wanted nothing more than to collapse, but kept going until she reached the house. She looked for vehicles to give her a clue as to which door she should approach, but there weren't any there. A blue pickup truck was parked in front of one of the barns, but that didn't help.

Back door it was. The way she was dressed, she wouldn't want to walk across anyone's living room floor anyway. She shook her head. After what she'd been through and she was worried about a farm wife's living room?

Polly climbed up the steps and looked for a doorbell. Finding none, she rapped at the door.

"Hello?" she called out. "Is anyone here? Hello?"

She waited and when she realized that no one was coming to help her, sank down on the steps and put her head in her hands. Where were they?

"Can I help you?" A man in a ball cap and denim jacket came around the corner of the house. He took one look at Polly and backed up, then stepped forward again.

Polly stood, "Please help me. I was kidnapped. Can you call Sheriff Merritt?"

"Uh. Okay." He pulled a cell phone out of his pocket. "Do you have his number?"

Polly thought about it. She had no idea. He was a preprogrammed number in her cell phone.

"Just call 9-1-1. Tell them I'm here and I need Sheriff Merritt. We're in Boone County, right?"

He nodded and pressed the digits on his phone and waited.

"Who are you?" he asked her.

"Polly Giller."

He relayed the information to the 9-1-1 operator and then looked at Polly in surprise. "*That* Polly Giller?"

She nodded and dropped her head back down into her hands.

"Let's get you inside," he said after hanging up. "They'll be here soon, but you don't need to be sitting outside dressed in whatever that is."

He slipped past her and opened the back door. "I'm sorry Marian isn't here. She's shopping in Ames today." He waited for Polly to come inside and then took her into the kitchen and pointed to a chair. "I'll get you a blanket. Can I make coffee for you? Something warm? If you're hungry, I think there are leftovers in the fridge."

"No that's fine, but a blanket would be great," she said. "Thank you."

As soon as he left the room, Polly started shivering. He was gone for less than a minute and when he returned and saw her body shaking, quickly wrapped the blanket around her, then turned on the oven and opened the door. "This will warm you right up. Let me boil water for tea."

"Thank you," she said, feeling as if every moment was surreal. This truly couldn't be happening to her. She watched him move in the kitchen, uncomfortable, as if he didn't really belong there. It took him a couple of tries at cupboard doors to find the mugs and even longer for him to find a box of tea bags. She was glad that Henry was as comfortable in their kitchen as she was.

He filled the mug with water and put it in the microwave. Before he turned that on, he asked. "How long?" giving her a slight grin. "I don't ever do this."

"That's okay. Just give it a minute."

"Tea bag in or out?"

"Leave it out. That's fine."

Just having someone speak normally helped to relax Polly. "What did you mean, *that* Polly Giller?" she asked.

"Aren't you the one who finds all the bodies?"

"I was afraid of that," she said. "So that's my reputation?"

"We all know that you own Sycamore House in Bellingwood, but yes, everyone knows the rest about you, too." He popped the microwave door open and touched the mug, then brought it over to the table, setting it down quickly. He handed her the box of tea bags and after opening two drawers, found a spoon and set it on the table beside the mug.

"I'm sorry I'm not a better host. I wish I could do more for you. You look like you've had a rough time of it. When were you kidnapped?"

"I think it was this morning. I don't actually remember anything until I woke up, strapped to a bed."

A sharp rap at the back door made Polly jump.

"It's probably the Sheriff," he said. "I'll be right back."

Polly tensed up, hoping he was right. When she heard Aaron's voice, she relaxed again. He strode into the kitchen, saw her sitting in the chair and knelt in front of her.

"Oh Polly," he said and reached out his arms.

She fell against his chest and began to sob.

CHAPTER TWO

Until Henry could get to her with clothing, Polly sat quietly on her hospital bed. She wanted someone ... anyone to tell her that she could leave. Polly told everyone who happened to walk into the room that she was fine, that they hadn't had time to hurt her yet, but no one listened. They'd taken blood and then taken everything she was wearing. She felt like she had nothing left to offer.

A soft tap at the door and Henry poked his head around the corner. "Can I come in?" he asked.

She felt her throat close up and tears rose in her eyes. They hadn't had time to talk yet. From the moment Aaron took her out of Cecil Levitt's house, she'd been caught up in a flurry of activity. Aaron had promised to call Henry. Now, here he was.

He rushed in and took her up in his arms. As he did so, she felt his chest heave and huge sobs come up out of him.

"Honey," she said. "I'm okay."

Henry didn't release her. He just held on and cried, his face buried in her neck.

The door opened and Aaron looked in, then stepped back out and quietly closed the door.

"Henry," Polly said. "Really. I'm okay."

He stepped back, looked at her, and pulled her in for another tight hug. Polly held on, letting him deal with the emotions that had to have been raging for the last couple of hours.

Finally he pulled back and wiped his eyes with the sleeve of his shirt. "I've never been so worried in my life. They wouldn't let me see you. Are you sure you're okay? He didn't hurt you?"

Henry picked up her wrists and gently touched the bandages that were there, covering the scrapes that came from Polly twisting in the restraints.

"I'll be fine," she said softly. "Will you?"

"No. I want to leave town right now with you. Go somewhere far from Bellingwood."

"You know we can't do that."

"Why not? What's stopping us? If there is someone intent on hurting you, let's get out of here."

Polly took the plastic grocery bag Henry held in his hand. "I'm feeling exposed here. Let me get dressed before we go too far down this conversation path." She went into the bathroom and changed into the clothes he'd brought her. The shoes weren't going to go on over the bandages she was wearing on her feet, but she could put socks on. That would help.

"I feel like a human being again," she said, opening the door into the main room. "It's amazing what real clothes will do for a person."

"Is it true that they took your clothes?" he asked. "Were you really running across fields in a black garbage bag?"

"I don't want to talk about it," she said, waddling across the floor to the chair on the sides of her feet. "At least not right now. Anyway, I think Aaron is waiting. He's in the hall. Would you tell him that it's okay now?"

Henry sighed deeply, gave her a worried look and went out into the hallway. She heard his voice rise and fall. This wasn't going to be easy for him. She knew that. But now was not the right time to leave Bellingwood. She just couldn't.

Sarah Heater was in true hospice care. She and the doctors had decided to stop all chemotherapy about a month ago. The cancer was moving too quickly and her time was limited. Rebecca was handling it as well as possible. She was sleeping in Sarah's room. It was a matter of weeks, if not days.

No matter what happened, Polly wasn't leaving her. Nothing else was quite as important as taking care of that family.

Aaron and Henry came into the room.

"Can I go home now?" Polly asked. "I promise I'm not broken."

Aaron nodded. "They'll be in with paperwork for you to sign and you can leave. But Polly, you need to be careful. I don't want you to be alone until we know who took you."

"You have no idea?"

"By the time we got to the trailer, they'd cleaned up and cleared out. You said there were pizza boxes and trash in the living room?"

"Yes."

"Everything was gone."

"Do you think I'm crazy? That I made it up?"

"Oh no," he said, trying to reassure her. "It was just cleared out. And the worst of it was that they'd wiped down surfaces, too. We haven't found a single fingerprint. Not even yours. But we won't give up. No one is that good. They have to have made a mistake."

"So did they rent this place or what?"

"Pretty sure they squatted."

"But the electricity was on. Why would it be on in an abandoned building?"

"There's a generator out back. All it needed was gas to get started."

"Oh," she said, dejected. "So nothing to tell you who this was?"

"Not yet. Can you remember anything from this morning?"

"Stu and Jim and Will have all been in and asked me those questions. I don't remember." She pulled her knees up in front of her, adjusting her feet until they didn't bite with pain on the lip of the chair. "Where's my truck?"

"We haven't found it yet. Maybe they're driving it. Maybe they just hid it."

"They took my damned truck? Damn it all to hell," she spat. "Who is doing this to me? Why? I'm a nice person. I help people. I try to treat people with respect. I don't deserve this crap."

"It's losing your truck that makes you angry?" Henry asked.

"That's my freedom. I can't pick the kids up or take them to school. I can't visit my friends. I can't do anything because some jerks out there want to have their fun terrorizing me." She dropped her feet to the floor and stood up, startling both Aaron and Henry. "Screw them. No one gets away with this. I want to smack something."

Polly stood in front of Aaron and looked up at him. "Give me something to smack. I'm mad as hell."

He backed up a step. "Please don't hurt me." Aaron looked at the door as a nurse came in carrying a clipboard. "It looks like they're going to let you leave."

"I don't have a phone anymore," Polly said, as tears threatened. "They took my phone. How am I supposed to live? I can't go anywhere or do anything and now I can't even text my friends. Henry ..." she fell apart.

"We'll stop at the phone store. I'll go in and take care of it."

"What if they have my contacts and know who my friends are? What if they're so mad that I got away that they go after someone I love?" Tears flowed down her cheeks.

The nurse glanced back and forth between them and Henry finally reached out. "Paperwork for us to sign?"

"Yes. Do you need anything else?"

"Just to get out of here," Polly said, then she looked up. "Not that you haven't been wonderful, but I want to go home."

"I understand."

They went over the checkout procedure and finally, Polly was in Henry's truck and he was driving away."

"Phone?" she asked.

"Aaron told me I couldn't leave you alone in the truck. Do you want to go in with me?"

"I want a phone. I'll do whatever I have to do."

"You kinda look like hell. Are you sure?"

Polly pasted a huge fake smile on her lips. "There. Is that better? Don't make me beg."

"I wouldn't dream of it."

~~~

Polly was huddled under a blanket in front of the television with both dogs trying to crawl into her lap. Han kept getting bigger and bigger. He was nearly as tall as Obiwan now. What had happened to the sweet little puppy that she'd found with his just-as-sweet mama? That female wasn't very large, but a big dog had certainly gotten to her. Polly had found a DNA kit online that would identify the breeds in Han. Maybe one of these days she'd just go ahead and do it. She scratched his head and he climbed closer to her face, reaching up to give her a lick.

Leia wasn't too happy with that. She was curled up on the back of the couch at Polly's shoulder and reached out to bat at Han's nose. He pulled back, but then came in anyway. Polly pushed him back down so he was settled with his head in her lap. Obiwan had taken his position on the inside of the couch along her legs. He wasn't moving. It was as if they all knew something was wrong.

The house was quiet. Rebecca didn't know anything had happened. She had enough to worry about with her mother. When Evelyn Morrow thought the little girl had had enough, she sent her upstairs for time with the animals. For the last three days, though, even that hadn't happened. Rebecca made it to school in the morning and then when she got home, headed right back to sit beside her mother.

Polly and Rebecca's teacher had spoken several times. The girl had difficulty concentrating, but she'd managed to get her grades to a point where these last few weeks of school wouldn't damage her too much.

Andrew and Kayla had become better friends just because they were thrown together. Kayla loved spending time in the barn with the animals and dragged him down there as often as possible. Polly thought that maybe she ought to offer Eliseo babysitting money. The barn was filled with kids. Jason was bringing some friends with him after school. They loved working with the horses. Eliseo was teaching them to drive the team. He made a deal with each of them. They helped put his garden in and he taught them to ride and to drive. Sam Gardner and Ralph Bedford had also been tapped to help with projects at Sycamore House once spring arrived. The kids, the horses, and the three men had cleared several acres in a field on the other side of the creek and planted sweet corn and potatoes.

Obiwan and Han both jumped down from the sofa and ran to the back staircase. Henry must be back from picking up supper. He hadn't wanted to leave her and for a few minutes after he drove away, Polly had found herself absolutely terrified. Aaron had warned her to never be alone, but once she thought about it, there was no place safer than Sycamore House. The outside doors were locked and Henry had checked the inside doors before leaving.

"You're the talk of the town again," Henry said, dropping the bag on the coffee table.

"The kidnapping?"

"Yep. Everyone is worried about you. You have your own personal security service if you want it. Four different people told me that if you needed anyone to be with you when you had to go somewhere, all we had to do was call and ask."

"That's sweet," Polly said.

"Mom called. She's worried. Aunt Betty called. She wanted you to know that she could be here in five minutes if you need to go somewhere. How about your friends? Have you talked to any of them yet?"

Polly looked down at her phone. They'd remotely bricked her old phone so no one could use it, but she hadn't finished setting this one up the way she liked it. And she hadn't made any calls on it either. She wasn't ready to explain what had happened over and over again.

At some level, she was surprised that no one had reached out to her, but at another, she was relieved. All she wanted to do was sit quietly with Henry and her animals tonight and be thankful that nothing worse had happened today.

Her mind went back over the events of the morning. She wished she could remember, but there wasn't anything there at all. The doctor told her that between the drugs they'd used to knock her out and the trauma of the experience, it wasn't any surprise that she'd lost that bit of her memory. He also told her that it might return. She hoped so. There wasn't much she hated more than having a chunk of her memory go missing.

Henry brought forks and napkins from the kitchen. "What do you want to drink?" he asked.

"Water's fine." Polly was thankful for the interruption. In her mind's eye, she had just woken up on the hospital bed and found herself restrained again. She closed her eyes again and found herself back in the little room, struggling to get out of those leather bands. She unconsciously touched the bandage on her wrist and all of a sudden it was too much.

She scrambled off the sofa and tore for the bathroom, then unloaded what little she had in her stomach into the toilet. Tears burst from her eyes and she hovered there, sobbing.

Henry came in and turned the water on in the sink. He knelt down next to her and wiped her forehead with a cool wash cloth and then her lips, cleaning her face.

"I'm so sorry, honey," he said. "I'm so sorry."

She collapsed into his lap and cried, unable to stop fear from overwhelming her. He held her and stroked her hair, murmuring quietly that he loved her and she was safe.

All four animals had joined them in the bathroom. Obiwan tried to lick her face, but Henry pushed him away.

"S'okay," she said, reaching for her dog. He climbed over her legs and squeezed into the little bit of space between her and the toilet, and then put his head on Henry's knee beside her face. A tentative lick and Polly put her arms around him and held tight.

Han, on the other hand, tried to climb up her side. He knew a puppy pile when he saw it and wanted to join them. Luke paced behind her, trying to avoid the puppy, yet wanting to know what was happening. Leia had taken a perch on the back of the toilet, keeping an eye on everything.

Polly smiled to herself. What a crazy family she had.

"Why don't you all go back to the couch? Let me brush my teeth and I'll be right out," she said, sitting up.

"I really am sorry," Henry said. "I wish I could take this away."

"I know you do. But that isn't realistic. We'll get through this."

"They're still out..." He stopped himself. "I'm sorry. It isn't like you don't know that."

Polly nodded. She'd like to think that since they'd failed at whatever their plans were, they would leave town and leave her alone. But she wasn't naive. This wasn't over yet.

"Go on," she said. "I'll be right there."

Henry left the bathroom and Polly pulled herself up. She bent over the sink and looked at herself in the mirror. She was a sight. Her face was splotchy and her eyes were bloodshot. She wet another washcloth and giggled. Leia had taken up residence beside the sink and was batting at the running water.

"I'm not very pretty tonight," Polly told the cat. Then she whispered. "It's embarrassing to have your sweet husband help you while you're puking your guts out. It's a good thing he loves me."

Leia glanced up as if she understood Polly's words, then went back to batting at the water. Polly opened a new toothbrush and turning the water to cold, brushed her teeth. Leia stood up and tried to snag the end of the toothbrush as Polly moved it.

"You're not helping," Polly said after she spat. "But then, that isn't your job." She dried her face, picked Leia up and carried her out to the media room.

"Are you hungry at all?" Henry asked. "I can put this in the fridge for later."

"It isn't that my stomach is upset. I just started picturing what happened to me this morning and everything rebelled. I'm sorry."

"No apologies, please," he said.

She dropped Leia onto the sofa and sat down, then opened the bag of food. She'd ordered a pasta primavera and actually, it sounded good. "What about some wine?" she asked.

"Are you sure?"

She nodded and jumped when her phone buzzed with a text.

"Mom just called and told me what happened to you. Can Billy and I walk your dogs tonight? I don't want you to go outside."

"It's Doug," she said with a smile. "He wants to know if they can come take the dogs for a walk so I don't have to go outside."

Henry grinned. "You have great friends, but they don't have to do that. I can."

"What if I let them? I wouldn't mind if you stayed here with me. Is that okay?"

He bent over the back of the couch and kissed her forehead. "Of course it is."

"If I know my friends, they're going to be overly helpful the next couple of days. You may want to run away."

"I'll be fine with all of it. As long as you stay inside and safe, I don't care how many of your friends show up."

Polly texted back to Doug. *"That would be awesome. Thank you. We're locked up pretty tight over here, so text me when you get to the back door."*

"Gimme three minutes," he responded. *"And we'll come get them in the morning, too. Tell Henry it's cool."*

"They'll be downstairs in three minutes," she conveyed to Henry. "And you're supposed to let them take the dogs out in the morning, too."

He nodded and put a glass of white wine on the table in front of her. "I can learn to accept their help. Come on, dogs. It looks like you're going to spend time with someone else this evening."

He walked through the office to the back steps and let out a whistle. Obiwan and Han ran after him and followed him down the stairs.

CHAPTER THREE

Sleep had been elusive, yet Polly didn't want to get out of bed. She knew today would be filled with friends asking too many questions. She didn't want to have to relive yesterday over and over.

Henry had sent the dogs downstairs with Doug, and Sylvie was stopping by to pick Rebecca up for school. There was no reason she had to go anywhere. Her bed was going to be just fine.

"Polly, honey," Henry said, as he sat down on the bed beside her.

"Don't make me get up."

"I'm not going to. You were up all night. I was worried."

"You didn't sleep either?"

"Not much, but that's okay. You should have said something. We could have watched television." He took a breath. "I need to spend time at the coffee shop today. Who do you want to come over and stay with you?"

Polly pulled herself into a seated position. "You have to go? I thought you'd be able to take time off."

"I'll be in and out all day long, but I need to work."

"You're fine. I'm just being a wimp. Why do I need a babysitter?"

"Because I'm not leaving you alone. Not even here."

"You left me alone last night to go get supper."

"Not really," he said with a chuckle.

"What does that mean?"

"That means that Stu Decker kept an eye on you while I was gone."

"That's ridiculous. I'm safe up here with everything locked down."

"Too late," he said. "It happened. Nothing you can do about it."

"So, I'm not going to be allowed to be alone? This is going to get old fast."

The thing was, Polly would have been fine with Henry spending days at home with her. She hated the idea of putting anyone else out. They didn't need to see her be so afraid of the world.

"I've heard from your friends. Any one of them will spend the day with you. In fact, all of them would if that's what you want."

Polly slid back down in the bed and pulled the covers over her head. "I don't want anyone here. I don't want this to be real. Tell me it's not real, Henry. Tell me that my little utopia in Bellingwood, Iowa, hasn't failed me."

"You need to give me a name," he insisted.

She pulled the blanket down below her chin. "I don't want to have to answer everyone's questions today. It's just too much. I know I sound like a whiner and that drives me crazy, but I'd give almost anything to ignore yesterday."

"I know you won't believe this, but the more you talk about it and own what happened to you, the less of an emotional impact it's going to have on you. If you internalize it, all that's going to do is make it bigger and bigger in your mind."

"When did you get so smart?" she asked with a small snarl in her lips. "I don't want to."

He bent over and put his arms around her. "I don't want you to have to. If I could take this all away and deal with it myself, I would. But your friends love you and they're worried. Each one of them texted me last night to tell me that they were leaving you alone until you were ready to talk. These are your friends, sweetie. Remember that."

"I know. You're right." She sat up again. "Would it be strange if I said that I wanted your mom or your Aunt Betty here today?"

He sat up and looked at her, his brows creased. "Really?"

"If I can't have you, I'd just as soon have one of them stay here with me. Would they do it?"

"In a heartbeat. You'll probably make Mom cry, asking her to do this."

"They're family and I guess that's who I feel the most comfortable with."

"What would you like me to tell your friends? You know they're going to ask about seeing you."

"Anyone can come any time. I want to see them. That's not it. But if someone is going to spend the day with me, I want it to be your mom. And your aunt too if she wants to come."

He leaned back in and kissed her cheek. "I'll call Mom. She'll be over in a flash. We might have trouble keeping Dad away, too. Is he okay?"

"Sure. That's fine. I feel like I'm being turned into an invalid. Can I go downstairs? I'd like to spend time with Sarah today. I need to explain this to her." Polly closed her eyes. "How is she ever going to trust that I can keep Rebecca safe when these terrible things keep happening?"

"Don't worry about that. She'll understand."

"I don't know what I think I'm going to explain to her. I wish I had some inkling as to why this happened."

"It will reveal itself soon enough," Henry said.

"That scares me too."

"Are you ready to get up or do you want to sleep?"

"I won't be able to sleep if you aren't in the bed."

"You didn't sleep with me *in* the bed last night."

"It would have been worse if you weren't. I'm sorry I kept you up."

24

"I'll try to get through as much as I can this morning and come home early. Maybe we can try to take a nap."

"A nap?" she asked with a grin. "A real nap or a different kind of nap?"

"You're really asking me that question? Now? After all that happened?"

"Well..."

He smiled at her. "We'll make time. I promise."

"Knew you would. Now go make your calls. I'm taking a shower."

"Another one?"

"Yep. Call me Psycho-Polly. But I think this one will just about do it. I almost have all of yesterday's yuck showered away." She patted her head. "And besides, my hair has to be a complete wreck after sleeping on it when it was wet last night."

He tilted his head and looked at her. "It's interesting. Not a complete wreck, but interesting."

Polly swatted at him. "Go call your mom. I'll be out in a few minutes. Is there coffee?"

"Of course."

~~~

Polly startled awake and looked around to get her bearings. Marie Sturtz was on the couch across from her, quietly knitting.

"Are you all right?" Marie asked.

"How long was I out?"

"About forty-five minutes. As soon as Leia curled up in your lap, you dropped off to sleep."

"I'm sorry I'm not better company."

"Oh Polly, don't think about that. Henry told me that you didn't sleep last night. I don't think I'd sleep for a week after what you went through." Marie put her knitting down on the table in between them. "Can I get you anything from the kitchen? I need a glass of water."

"I can do it," Polly said.

"Don't be silly. I know where things are."

Polly followed her out into the kitchen. "I feel ridiculous. I can't believe I need a babysitter."

"None of us want to think about what could happen to you if those men got their hands on you again, so let your friends and family take care of you. You do enough for us every other day of the year."

"I still feel ridiculous." Polly poured the last of the coffee into a mug and took the time to set it up for another pot. So far it wasn't helping to keep her awake, but who knew how many people would be by this afternoon.

"What would you like to do for lunch?" Marie asked. "I could start something."

"I'm not even sure what I have. I was going to go to the grocery store yesterday." Something flashed through Polly's mind. It was a tiny piece of a memory of an image in her side view mirror. Rats. She almost had it.

"Then we order out. Bill can pick lunch up and bring it to us. I know he'd love to say hello to you. He's been worried sick. Do you want a tenderloin from the diner?"

Polly shook her head. That didn't sound good at all. "I don't know what I want." She took a sip of coffee and looked out her kitchen window. There were people working in the garden on the corner. It was so good to see green grass and bright colors. She had promised herself that she was going to appreciate that every single day after the winter they'd just been through.

"Who's that woman?" she asked.

Marie joined her at the sink and looked out at the garden. "Which one?"

"The woman in the red plaid jacket. Do I know her?"

They watched for a few minutes until the woman turned.

"That's Lillian Dexter," Marie said. "I'm surprised she's here. She owns the flower shop uptown."

"Lily's Flowers?"

"That's the one."

"We use her all the time. She does beautiful work."

"Yes she does and she's quite proud of it." Marie grimaced. "I'm sorry. That was rude of me. She does do beautiful work. I should just leave it at that."

Polly chuckled. "That's funny. So, she's not usually a dig in the dirt kind of girl?"

"She doesn't dig in someone else's dirt unless there are stories she can spread." A light went off in Marie's head. "That's why she's here. She's looking for gossip about yesterday."

Polly laughed out loud.

Marie ducked her head. "I'm horrible, aren't I? I should be ashamed of myself. Why don't we return to the fact that she is very talented and does beautiful work?"

"And she's a gossip."

Marie rolled her eyes. "Just like me, I guess. Would you allow me to retract everything I've said?"

"Nope. I like it."

Polly's phone rang. "It's about time," she said. "I was beginning to wonder if this new phone even had a ringer on it."

She swiped it. "Hello?"

"Hello there, dear. I couldn't wait any longer. I had to hear your voice. How are you?"

She mouthed the word, "Lydia" to Marie and said, "I'm fine, Lydia. I wondered how long it would take you to call me."

"I wanted to give you plenty of time to recuperate before I started bothering you. Henry tells me that Marie is staying with you today. Would you two like lunch?"

"We were just talking about that."

"Have you made any decisions?"

"Other than deciding that we want some, nothing is set in stone yet."

"I've sliced a ham and a roast for sandwiches. Sylvie has your favorite bread and Andy made potato salad and cole slaw. Could we come over and hug on you for lunch?"

"No Beryl?"

Lydia laughed. "She'll be there, but made me promise that she didn't have to bring anything."

"That makes sense. If you want to come over, I'd love it. The place is locked down. I think you and Sylvie are the only ones with keys."

"I'll pick the others up. If we're there right at noon will that be okay?"

"It would be lovely. Thank you, Lydia."

"Dear, all I want is to hug you so tight that you pop. Thank you for letting me come over."

"Lydia is bringing food," Polly said to Marie. "If Bill wants to join us, that would be wonderful."

"I'm not sure how he'd react to being surrounded by all of those women. I'll ask," she said. "But I doubt that he comes over today. Maybe another day this week."

"Before they all get here for lunch, I'd like to run down and see Sarah Heater. Can I get away with that?" Polly asked.

Marie took a breath. "I've been given strict orders not to let you out of my sight."

"Today isn't a day that I'm going to give anyone any trouble about keeping an eye on me," Polly said. "Would you mind going with me, then? If you don't want to see her, that's fine. But I'm afraid that once this day gets moving, it won't slow down. I need to talk to her about what happened."

"I can knit anywhere. I'll just sit in the hallway while you have your conversation."

"Are you sure that won't be too far away?" Polly teased.

"Don't get sassy with me, young lady," Marie said with a laugh. "I'm old enough to be your mother."

Polly reached out and hugged her and felt tears come back into her eyes. "I'm so thankful you're here."

"Oh sweetie," Marie said, drawing her arms tight around Polly. "I love you."

"I love you too, Marie."

Polly opened the door and shooed the dogs back into the living room as Marie walked through and they went down the steps together. She waved at Stephanie in the office and crossed over to the addition.

"This might take a few minutes," she said. "Make yourself comfortable in the lounge. I'll be back."

Marie nodded and then followed Polly into the addition and watched as she knocked on the door to Sarah Heater's room. Evelyn opened the door and gave Polly a look of surprise and then a quick hug.

Polly waved to Marie and shut the door behind her.

"Polly Giller, are the rumors true about you?" Evelyn Morrow, Sarah's nurse whispered.

"Probably. And that's why I'm here. How's Sarah doing?"

"As well as can be expected. She drifts in and out. The drugs are keeping the pain at bay, but not all the time. She's either awake and hurting or asleep and quiet."

Polly took a deep breath. "When do you think I could speak with her?"

"Let's just see what we can do," Evelyn said and walked to the bed. They'd moved the large bed off to one side a couple of months ago and replaced it with a hospital bed so Sarah could find more positions to be comfortable. It was facing the south windows because she had fallen in love with the horses and donkeys in the pasture. Eliseo made sure to exercise them in the pen where she could see them and as it got warmer, they spent more and more time playing outside.

Polly smiled at their antics. This had been the perfect room for Sarah. The windows to the south were filled with gorgeous horses and the windows to the west looked out over Eliseo's garden to the sycamore tree-lined creek. Spring had brought a great deal of beauty to Polly's back yard and she was glad Sarah could enjoy it.

"Sarah?" Evelyn asked quietly. "Can you hear me? Polly is here. Are you able to talk to her?"

Sarah's eyes fluttered open and a tiny smile crossed her lips. Her eyes shut almost immediately, but she reached her hand out and Evelyn took it.

"When she's too tired to speak, she still communicates with us," Evelyn said. "Take her hand. She'll squeeze it when she has something to say."

Polly took Evelyn's place by Sarah's bedside and then took Sarah's hand in hers. All of a sudden she had no idea what to say to the woman. Everything that had been important up to this point suddenly seemed trivial. Even the fact that she'd been kidnapped yesterday meant nothing in the face of Sarah's last few days on earth.

There was no need to talk to her about what was happening here. Sarah trusted Polly and the people around her to care for Rebecca long into her daughter's future. That and making sure that Rebecca knew how much she was loved were the only things of any importance. This fact settled so deeply into Polly's soul that she was still and watched as the woman breathed in and out.

Evelyn smiled and gestured to the chair beside Sarah's bed. Polly sat down.

"We've said everything we need to say to each other," Polly finally said. "I can't tell you how grateful I am that you trust your daughter to me. I wish you could be here to watch everything she becomes, but I will always do my best to make sure she's happy."

Sarah smiled again and Polly felt her fingers gently squeeze. She wanted to hold this poor woman close - anything to generate enough energy so she could continue to live.

"You've taught me so much," Polly said. "Just now I learned a huge lesson about what's important."

Sarah lifted one eye as if asking a question.

"It's only love. That's all. Nothing else. None of the silly stresses we put on ourselves, no gossip or trying to be better than anyone else. Not competition or being a great business person. None of that. Just making sure we love each other. That's the only thing that matters right now. It's the only thing that should ever matter."

Sarah nodded her head and her eyes fluttered again. She opened her mouth and spoke so quietly that Polly couldn't hear.

"What?" Polly asked.

Sarah tried to speak again and Polly leaned in closely to hear her.

"I love you."

It was too much. Polly started to cry and leaned in to put her head next to Sarah's. She whispered, "Oh Sarah, I love you too. Thank you for what you've given me this last year."

"I love you," Sarah said again and squeezed Polly's hand.

Polly stayed for a few more moments until she felt Sarah's breathing even out. She stood up and then dropped back into the chair, her hand still in Sarah's. Evelyn crossed the room and put a box of tissues on the table beside them.

"Is this too much for Rebecca now?" Polly asked. "Are we asking too much of her to stay in this room with her mother?"

Evelyn stood at the head of Sarah's bed and stroked her patient's thin hair. "These two have been together for a lifetime. It isn't easy for either of them, but asking Rebecca to leave her mother at this point would be a terrible mistake. She might be young, but she understands what is happening."

"I feel like we're stripping away her childhood - making her grow up too fast. No one should have to experience death like this."

"How do you think Rebecca would respond if you asked her to walk away?" Evelyn asked.

"It would destroy her. I just wish she wasn't doing it alone."

"She's not, dear. I'm here and you're close by. Her friends, Andrew and Kayla, are sticking by her. And best of all, her mother is here. Rebecca dealt with much of her grief while her mother was still able to help."

Sarah squeezed Polly's hand and rubbed her thumb across Polly's finger. Then she pulled her hand away, patted Polly's and dropped it beside her.

"She just told me it's okay, I think." Polly said.

Evelyn smiled. "You're going to have the hardest job, you know."

"What do you mean?"

"After Sarah dies, Rebecca is going to feel lost. She spends every waking hour here, waiting on her mother. Those hours are going to be empty and she won't know what to do with them. Find things for her to do. Find ways for her to return to a normal life. Make it happen gradually, but help her make the transition."

"I can do that," Polly said. "Okay. I'll leave you two alone." She glanced at the recliner in the corner and noticed balls of yarn beside it. "Are you knitting, too?"

"I crochet," Evelyn said. "I'm teaching Rebecca. We're making granny squares for a blanket. I thought it might be fun for her to have to remember this time."

"You're an amazing woman."

"I've just been down this path a number of times. Each family makes it their own."

"Thank you for everything. I'll be back tomorrow."

Evelyn walked with her to the door of the room. "I'm just glad you were able to be with us today. You take care of yourself, okay?"

"I can't believe you heard about what's going on out there while being stuck in this room all the time."

"I have my sources," Evelyn said with a grin. "They keep me up to date on everything."

"Thank you again. For everything."

Polly left and went back into the main building. She ducked her head in the lounge and didn't see Marie, so went into the office.

"Have you seen Marie?" she asked Stephanie.

"She went back to the kitchen. Lydia and her friends came in. But you're supposed to stay here."

Polly rolled her eyes. "Surely I can walk back to the kitchen by myself."

"Please?" Stephanie begged.

"Fine." Polly sat down in a chair while Stephanie buzzed back to the kitchen.

In less than a minute, Marie, Lydia, Beryl and Andy joined them in the office.

"Are you ready for some excitement?" Beryl asked.

"Nope. Not on your life."

"Too bad. I'm here and it's time to get this party started. Let's go up to your apartment and see what we can stir up."

CHAPTER FOUR

"Henry, I just can't do this anymore," Polly said.

"What's that?"

"Don't give me that. I'm going out of my mind. I've been stuck inside for four days. They haven't found my truck, they've not seen hide nor hair of the men who kidnapped me and there haven't been any more threats. You can't keep me inside forever or I will lose it all over you." To emphasize her threat, Polly threw her arms up in the air and shook her head back and forth.

"But Polly."

"No. Your mother has been stuck here and my friends have run out of interesting things to do to keep me occupied. I've tried hard to be a good girl and not complain, but you have to release me."

"I can't let you go out there by yourself," he said. "I just can't."

"Would you let me go with someone else?"

He dropped his head into his hands. "There are two men who were so bent on kidnapping you that they drugged you, hid your truck and strapped you down. Do you think my Mom could protect you? How about Joss or Sal or any of your friends? Is it fair to ask them to be hurt because you want to go outside?"

"*That's* not fair," she said and began to cry. "I didn't ask for this to happen to me. And no, I don't want anyone to be hurt. You know that. That was a crappy thing to say to me."

"I'm terrified every day when I leave that something will happen and I'll get a call telling me you've been taken again."

"How long are you going to keep me captive?" she asked.

"I'll make you a deal. If you can wait until tomorrow, I'll take you out. We'll go to Des Moines or heck, I don't care, let's go over to Omaha."

"We don't need to go that far. I just want to be able to see my friends in their homes and I want to ride Demi again."

Henry scowled at her. "You haven't ridden him in the last three weeks and you want me to believe you're pining for a ride?"

"Well, if I had wanted to, I couldn't. You've made that impossible. Don't you think I'd be safe with Eliseo?"

He nodded. "You probably would. He's one of the few people I'd trust to take care of you in nearly any situation."

"Where are you working today?"

Henry opened his mouth to tell her and then stopped himself. "No. You can't come with me."

"Why not? You're going to be at the coffee shop, aren't you?"

He drew a breath in through his nose and shut his eyes as if to regain his equilibrium. "I can't keep an eye on you while I'm working." He opened his eyes and begged her, "And I can imagine all sorts of terrible things happening to you right under my eyes."

"Your nose," she said quietly.

"What?"

"The phrase is 'right under my nose' unless you want to say 'right in front of my eyes.'"

"Whatever. See, you have me so flustered that I can't even speak correctly. What if the kidnapper walked in off the street and took you out and no one noticed?"

"I just want to see how things are coming. I can't do anything!"

"One more day. I promise to take you out tomorrow. We'll go anywhere you want. If you want to see the progress at the coffee shop, we'll do that. If you want to have lunch or dinner at

Davey's, we'll do that. If you want to spend the evening at Secret Woods, we'll do that. Anything, I promise. Just please be patient today."

"Can we take the dogs for a walk somewhere? They haven't had a long walk in a week."

He sighed. "Sure. But can we leave Bellingwood to do that?"

"What do you mean?"

"I don't know. Can we go to Kansas City or Chicago for the weekend?"

"You know I won't go that far away from Sarah and Rebecca."

"I know," he said, dejectedly.

"What about tonight? Can we go somewhere tonight?"

"Where do you want to go?"

"I don't know. But somewhere. Maybe to Joss and Nate's house or out with Sal and Mark." She clutched at his arm. "Please. I'm begging you. If I have to get down on my knees, I will. Please."

"Why don't you invite them to come over here?"

Polly pushed him away. "It's not the same. Sal and Joss have been in and out all week long trying to keep me sane. I just want to leave these four walls!"

Han and Obiwan ran across the floor from Henry's office.

"See what you made me do?" she asked.

"What's that?"

"Doug and Billy heard me yell when they opened the door downstairs to let the dogs back in."

"So, I made you do that."

"Well, you did." Polly stuck her lower lip out.

Henry reached up and pinched it gently between his index finger and thumb. "Enough of that. You will live through this, I promise. I can't believe you are being so impatient."

"You get stuck inside for five days, not knowing when the next time you'll be able to leave. Tell me how easy it is then."

"Polly, think about our honeymoon."

She nodded. "Okay, yeah. It was a great week."

"How much of that week do you remember?"

"All of it."

"No. You remember highlights. It's all compressed in your mind. You look back on it now and it seems like we were gone such a short time. This week is no big deal in the overall scheme of our lives, but having you safe is a huge deal for everyone who loves you."

She jammed her lower lip out again and turned up her nose.

"That's pretty," he said.

"I hate it when you're right." Polly flopped down on a chair at the dining room table. "I'll be good."

"Thank you. I'm going to go knock on Sarah's door to see if Rebecca is ready for school." He turned to leave the dining room, then turned back. "We're going to have this conversation several more times before this is all over, aren't we."

"What do you think?"

"I think I need to hire two big, burly bodyguards."

"Just make sure they're hot."

"Got it."

~~~

Polly had promised to stay in the office so Marie could run errands and take care of things in her own life. She tried not to pout and be in a bad mood, but it was proving exceedingly difficult. Jeff had been in and out with different plans and ideas, but she knew he was just trying to give her something to think about. She'd finally kicked him out and shut her door.

A soft tap sounded. "Polly?" Stephanie asked.

"Yes." Polly gave herself a mental slap and told herself to quit taking her frustration out on people around her.

"The mail's here. Do you want it now or later?"

"Come on in. I promise not to bite," Polly said.

Stephanie opened the door, stepped in and put the mail on Polly's desk. "Can I get you anything? Sylvie and Rachel are practicing some sort of fancy pastry thing back in the kitchen. I thought I'd see if they needed a taste tester. Would you like a cup of the good coffee?"

Polly had picked up the stack of mail and was flipping through it, thinking to herself: bill, bill, junk, bill, bill, junk, junk. "Good coffee?" she asked.

"Do you want some?"

"Yes and I'd love one of the pastry things. Thank you, but I hate making you be my gofer."

"I don't mind," Stephanie said. "You've had a rough week."

"Not so much. I feel like the laziest thing on this earth."

"Like I said. Rough week."

Polly looked up and gave her a grin. "Thanks for understanding. I'm a little prickly today. I'll try to be better."

"You're fine. Do you need anything else?"

"No. I'm good. Thanks."

Polly pulled out a business envelope that was addressed to her personally. In fact, it said 'Personal' in the bottom left corner. As if anyone here would open her mail. She and Henry didn't get much personal mail, but sometimes cards and letters showed up. His business mail was sent to the office at his shop, but still. Marking this as personal mail felt like overkill.

She set it to the side and sorted the rest, tossing the junk into the recycling can under her desk.

"What do you think this is?" she asked out loud, picking up the envelope with her name on it.

"Excuse me?" Stephanie said, coming into the office.

Polly smiled. "Sorry. Just talking to myself."

"Here's coffee and a few funky little tarts. Sylvie said you'd like the raspberry."

"Five pounds."

"What?"

"I'm going to gain at least five pounds this week. I can't go out to walk my dogs and all Sylvie does is feed me good food."

"Oh. Okay."

Polly gave a quick shake of her head. "I'm sorry. More prickly Polly. This is wonderful. Thank you."

"It's okay. Do you need me to do anything with this?" Stephanie looked at the mail on Polly's desk.

"Thanks. This batch is for Jeff and here are the bills."

Stephanie made sure everything was entered and matched with purchase orders before handing it all back to Polly to approve. Polly wasn't sure why she got the mail in the first place. Stephanie knew everything that happened. They were probably just trying to give her something to do this week.

Once Stephanie was gone, Polly took a bite of the raspberry tart. Sylvie was having a great time experimenting with things for the bakery. So far, she hadn't had many failures.

"Now. What's up here?" Polly picked the envelope back up. She peeled back a corner and slipped her fingers underneath the flap and ripped it open to find a single piece of paper folded in thirds.

She flipped the top up and took a breath, then reached for her phone and dialed.

"Tell me you are still safe and sound in your little cocoon," Aaron said.

"Aaron, something awful has happened."

"What? Where are you?"

"I'm sorry. I'm in my office. I'm fine. Everyone here is fine."

"Oh. Okay. Don't do that to me. What happened?"

"I just got a piece of mail. I think it's from the kidnappers."

"What makes you think that? Where did it come from? And oh, by the way, quit touching it."

Polly dropped everything onto her desk. She remembered this.

"Stephanie?" she called out.

"Yes, Polly?"

"Could you do me a favor and run to the kitchen and get a pair of tongs. I'll tell you why in a minute."

"Polly?" Aaron asked.

"I'm getting tongs. I hope I haven't smudged anything with my fingers. I didn't even think about that when I opened it."

"Stop it. Don't worry. Now tell me why you think it's from the kidnappers?"

"The first line I read was *'Just because she looks a little like you doesn't mean that she was as good as you. I'll bet you don't know what we did next.'*"

"Anything else?"

"It's under the fold. Stephanie is getting tongs."

"You can probably touch the very corners of the thing."

Stephanie put the tongs down on the desk and turned to leave. Sylvie was standing right behind her in the doorway.

"What's up?" Sylvie mouthed.

Polly pointed down to the letter and Sylvie dropped into a chair across from her.

"I have tongs. Just a second," she said to Aaron. Polly held the top corner with her index finger and gently opened the second fold, then lay the tongs across it to hold it open. "There's a picture."

"Of what?" he asked.

"Of a young woman sitting in the front seat of my truck." Polly gulped. "I think she's dead. I can't tell for certain, but this doesn't look right."

"Does the letter say anything else?"

Polly took a deep breath and read. *"I didn't want to have to hurt her, but it just wasn't the same. Why did you leave? That changed everything. Until you come to me, I will have to find a replacement. I hope the next one is smarter than this one. Please don't make me wait too long. You know we belong together."*

"Aaron?" she asked quietly.

"Yes, Polly."

"Will you call Boston and make sure Joey is where he belongs?"

"I'll do that immediately and then I'm coming to see you. Please don't leave the safety of your office. Promise me that."

"I was making a big deal of it this morning with Henry. I think I'll back off now. I promise to stay right here."

"Thank you. Don't ever be alone. I'll be right up."

He hung up the phone and Polly wilted.

"Are you okay?" Sylvie asked.

"No. Not at all. He's psychotic. It has to be him."

"It sounds like he has someone else with him. That seems unlike the Joey you described. He wouldn't want to share you with anyone else."

Polly gripped her forehead with her left hand and massaged her temples. "I don't want to tell Henry."

"But you know you have to."

"The thing is, if it is Joey, Henry is probably in just as much danger as I am. Joey wants me to be his wife and Henry is a threat to that."

"He needs to know."

"Every man who steps into my line of sight is a threat to Joey. He beat Doug up and accused me of making a play for Aaron."

"What about that girl? Do you recognize her?"

Polly looked at the picture again and then sat back in her chair, feeling like she wanted to vomit. She swallowed a couple of times. There wasn't anything to make this better.

"Polly, what is it?"

"They put her in my shirt. Look at that."

Sylvie stood up and came around the desk. She leaned over to look at the photo, while wrapping an arm around Polly. She tapped a fingernail on the photograph. "I know where that is," she said.

"What do you mean?"

"See that water tower in the background? That's in Luther."

"Those blue water towers are all over."

"It's Luther. I'm sure of it."

Polly swiped her phone open and took several pictures of the photograph and the letter. Using the tongs, she flipped the envelope over. "Postmarked in Boone. They're not very far away, are they? I'm going to be stuck in this building for the rest of my life."

"Now stop that," Sylvie said, rubbing Polly's back. "You can't start feeling sorry for yourself."

"Start? I started this morning before I even got out of bed."

"It's time to stop now. You have other things to do."

"Like what?"

Sylvie gave her a gentle shove and sat back down across the desk from her. "Like I don't know what, but you aren't a pitiful, pathetic girl. Now's a lousy time to decide to take that up."

"I know. I know. I can tell you right now that I don't want to make this call."

"Suck it up and get it over with. I'll sit right here and give you moral support."

Polly chuckled. "Uh huh. I know what that looks like. You'll serve me my pitiful head on a platter if I get out of line."

"In a heartbeat. Now call him."

"Tyrant."

"Chicken."

Polly swiped the phone and made the call.

"Hey, sweetums. Are you calling to whine at me again?"

"Wow. I've got a bad reputation."

"I'll be nice. What's up?"

"A piece of mail showed up at Sycamore House today."

"I'm guessing it's a special piece of mail because otherwise, I'd be getting this call every day."

"Smart aleck. Yes. It's special. From the kidnappers."

There was a sharp intake of breath. "What did it say?"

"Threats and a picture of a girl wearing my shirt. Henry, I think they killed her."

"No." All of the life had gone out of his voice.

"She was posed in my truck. Sylvie thinks the picture was taken near Luther. And Henry, there's more."

"How could there be more?"

"I think it might be Joey."

"Joey. Your Joey?"

"He's not *my* Joey. But yes. Him."

"He's safely locked away in a mental ward someplace, isn't he? Tell me that he is."

"Aaron is checking on it."

"What makes you think it's Joey?"

"The last line said that we were meant to be together."

"We have to leave town."

"I can't have that argument again with you, Henry. You know why I can't. But I promise to be good about staying inside."

"Okay," he said, while inhaling a deep breath.

"But honey, you have to be careful. He gets crazed when he thinks another man is vying for my attention."

"I know. I'll keep an eye out. Can we stay in tonight?"

"I think that's a good idea. I'm sorry, Henry."

"What are you sorry for?"

"I guess for ever deciding to go out with him in the first place."

"Do we know for certain that it's him?"

"Well, no. But it makes sense. Who else would do this to me?"

"I want to hire burly bodyguards for sure, now."

"Aaron's coming over. Do you want me to ask him about this?"

"No, I'm probably kidding. What do you want for supper?"

"Ice cream sandwiches. Lots of ice cream sandwiches."

"I love you, Polly."

"I love you too. Just stay safe, okay?"

Polly put the phone down and looked across at Sylvie. "Okay. I told him. Now we're both scared. Know any bodyguard types?"

Sylvie scowled at her. "The only one I know that could pull that off is my ex-husband and not having him around is something we all want to encourage."

"Speaking of that, I thought he was going to get more involved with Andrew and Jason? Have you heard anything?"

"Not a peep. The lawyer threatened him and he backed off. I know he's still in Fort Dodge, but last I heard, he had a chickie up there who was young, cute and childless. Maybe she'll keep him busy for a while."

Sylvie pointed at the raspberry tart. "What did you think?"

"It's good! That's a really flaky crust. Are you adding that to your baked goods?"

"The bride wanted something different for her reception tomorrow night. We're doing these along with little cakes."

Polly took another bite. "It's good. And thanks for stepping in and making me be normal."

"It's what I do." Sylvie stood up to leave. "If you need any more butt-kicking, just send someone to get me."

CHAPTER FIVE

Polly felt Aaron's presence in her office before she saw him and looked up from her computer screen.

"It's over there," Polly said, pointing. Using the tongs, she had moved the letter and photograph to the farthest corner of her desk. "I can't look at it anymore."

Aaron took an evidence bag out of his pocket and put on a pair of gloves, then put everything into the bag before sitting down. He read through the letter while she watched him and then turned it over to look at the photograph, which he had slipped in behind the piece of paper.

"I'm so sorry, Polly."

"She's dead because of me, isn't she," Polly said flatly.

"No, honey. She's dead because these people are sick."

"But if I'd stayed instead of running away, she would still be alive."

"Given what you knew at the time, would you have changed your behavior?"

"No!" Polly exclaimed. "I had to get out of there."

"Yes, you did. Stop blaming yourself."

"I can't help it. I've been complaining because no one will let me leave Sycamore House and this poor girl died while I've been safe."

Aaron leaned forward in his chair and glared at her. "This is the last time you and I are going to have this conversation. You are not responsible for the sickness in someone else's mind. What happened to this girl is a horrible, terrible thing. It breaks my heart that we are going to have to find her family and tell them that she is dead. But this is not on you. Don't let yourself go down that path. Ever."

"I know what you're saying makes sense, but still."

He scowled at her. "Should *I* feel guilty because we haven't been able to find them yet?"

"Well, no."

"Since I'm the one whose job it is to take care of the citizens of Boone County, should I tear myself up because these men are still out there?"

"Of course not, but I know you do anyway." She felt her protests fading away.

"Then let me. It's my job."

Polly nodded at what he had in his hand. "Sylvie says that water tower is in Luther."

He looked at the photograph again. "She's right. They have to be somewhere to the southeast. There is plenty of wooded area down there. This will take some searching."

"They were smart enough to run from the house where they kept me, do you think they'll stay in one place very long?"

"I don't know what to think right now. I don't have enough information to build a pattern for their actions yet."

"That makes sense." Polly set her jaw. "I know I'm still complaining about this, but I'm going to be stuck in here forever, aren't I."

"We'll find them."

"I know. I hate being a baby."

"You aren't used to having to sit still while people take care of things for you."

"No I'm not. I'm thinking about hiring a burly bodyguard."

Aaron chuckled. "That's not the worst idea in the world, though I'd hate to see what you'd put him through."

"Be nice," she said.

"Would you really consider a bodyguard?" Aaron asked.

"If I'm stuck inside for too much longer, I might."

"I could ask questions. A few of my people wouldn't mind making extra money."

Polly's eyes lit up. "Really?"

"We'll see. It's not something I like to encourage, but I'd rest easier knowing the people who were in your life."

Jeff knocked on the door frame. "Polly?"

"What's up, Jeff?"

"I just got a strange request for room rentals here at Sycamore House."

Aaron shook his head and said, "No. You can't rent any rooms here right now. It's not safe."

"You might want to know about this one. They're going to be coming into town in about forty-five minutes."

"Who is it?" Polly asked.

Jeff pursed his lips and then broke into a grin. "He said that I was to tell you he packed an extra bib for you so that you could drink kool-aid."

"Ray!" she said. "He's coming here?"

"Him and his brother. Jon, was it?"

"Did he say why they were coming?"

"Something about you needing them. So do I give them the rooms upstairs in the addition?"

Polly looked at Aaron. "Ray and Jon Renaldi. Drea's brothers. You know, the two who helped me with Joey in Boston?"

He slowly nodded. "It sounds like your bodyguard situation just changed."

"Why would they come out here? And how do they know that I need them?"

Jeff shrugged and gave her a sly grin. "Do you want the number to call them back?"

"Of course I do." Polly held out her hand and Jeff stepped in to hand her a piece of paper.

"Do you mind?" she asked Aaron.

"Go ahead. I'd like to know how they knew to come out here, too."

Polly dialed the number and heard a familiar voice say, "Hello?"

"Jon Renaldi, what are you doing in my neck of the woods?" she asked.

"If it isn't my favorite little girl. Do you have room for two lonely men?"

"Of course I do, but why are you in Iowa?"

"We heard about your little escapade earlier this week."

"From who? I didn't tell anyone. I haven't talked to your sister in a few weeks."

"Your other friend. You know the tall, dark, drink of water that moved out there. She called Drea."

"Sal? She didn't say anything to me. But that still doesn't make any sense. Why are you in Iowa?"

"Would it make more sense if we told you that your little psycho boyfriend escaped the clutches of his gatekeepers?"

"I knew it," Polly gave a quick shudder and gritted her teeth. "Joey is here. But how did you find out?"

"As soon as Drea told me what happened, Ray drove up to that little sanitarium to see him. They hemmed and hawed and went round and round. Tried to tell him that he didn't have any permission. You know how well that went."

"Not very, I'm guessing."

"An investigation has been launched. It seems that your boyfriend walked out of there three weeks ago and nobody thought to let the authorities know."

"Three weeks?" She turned to Aaron and Jeff. "Joey escaped from the mental hospital three weeks ago and they didn't tell anyone."

"The lily white, pansy-assed doctor that Ray finally strong-armed..." Jon stopped for a moment and then said, "I'm sorry. The doctor that Ray spoke to said that he was certain of Joey's return. Apparently, he's gone off the reservation before and always come back."

"Are you kidding me? Their security is that bad?"

"Not now, it isn't. You'd be surprised at how much an attorney general hates hearing they have a problem like this."

"But..."

"Yes, you're right. That doesn't fix anything for you. Which is why Ray and I have come to offer our services."

Polly chuckled. "As what?"

"We know you. We knew you before you moved to Iowa and started getting into trouble. From what we've heard, you've gotten much, much worse."

"Now come on," she said in protest.

"Let's see. Ray, what has it been four days? Five days?" Jon listened for a moment. "We figure almost five days. Are you making everyone insane because they won't give you any freedom?"

"How did you know that?"

"Like I said, we know you. And Mama wasn't going to leave you out here alone without some family protection. That's what we're here for. We're family and we're protecting you."

"I don't know what to say."

"Now, *that* doesn't sound like you. You always have plenty to say."

"What about your jobs?"

"Not what you need to worry about. You have to feed us and maybe introduce us to some cutie pies. I've heard about those corn fed chicks."

"You aren't breaking hearts out here, Jon Renaldi."

"That's not fair. I've run through everyone I could find on the east coast. Come on, you have to have something for me."

"Not on your life. Do you know how to find me?"

"Ray made me program the GPS in the rental car. I think we can do this. I can't wait to see you, little sis."

"I can't wait to see the two of you, either. Thank you." Polly released a breath she hadn't realized she'd been holding and brushed a tear from her eye.

"Don't get all misty on me, little girl."

"How did you know?"

"Because it's what you do. Your reputation, remember?"

"I'll see you in a bit."

"Tell your little town to buckle up. The Renaldi brothers are about to be all up in their business."

Polly shook her head and smiled as she put the phone down. "I don't believe this," she said.

"I'd like to know how they were able to find out that Joey was gone and I still haven't received confirmation," Aaron said. He took out his own phone and swiped a call open. "Anita?" he asked. "Yes. Have you heard anything back from Boston yet?"

Polly watched him set his jaw. "Get me the number of that sergeant we talked to on Boston PD when Polly was kidnapped two years ago. I want answers and I want them now."

"They aren't talking. I'll find out what's going on, though." He took a deep, cleansing breath and looked at Polly calmly. "Do you have any idea who Joey might have hooked up with?"

"He didn't have friends," Polly said. "And I can't believe he's working with someone. He wouldn't share me. And he's not a killer. Especially a woman. It's so out of character for him."

"That's what I'm afraid of. This whole 'out of character' thing makes me nervous."

"What do you mean by that?"

"Nothing. It's just thoughts I've been having. And none of them are especially good." Aaron stood and took the evidence bag. "I'm going back down to Boone. I'm glad your friends are coming into town. I don't know how you do it, Polly."

"Do what?"

He nodded at her. "Actually, that's not true. I know exactly how you do it."

"Do what!" she demanded.

"How you manage to have people around to take care of you when you need them."

"It's weird, isn't it."

"No," he said with a warm smile. "It's not. You're willing to do whatever it takes to help others. When it comes time to do something for you, it's not even a consideration, it's a natural response."

"Yep. That sounds weird."

"We love you, Polly Giller. So you take care of yourself. Or at least let us take care of you." Aaron strode out and she turned in her chair to watch him walk to his car in the parking lot.

If the Renaldis were spending time at Sycamore House, she needed to set in supplies. The little bit of food she had in her refrigerator wasn't going to do at all. This stunk. She hated being trapped and having to ask others to run her errands. Especially when they had their own lives to lead and their own work to do.

She picked up her phone and swiped a call.

"Hey sweetums. Has your day gotten any better?" Henry asked.

"Aaron was here and he's gone."

"What did he say?"

"Not much. But I'm confident that it's Joey who is doing this. I just don't know who he's with."

"What raised your confidence level?"

"My two new bodyguards."

He chuckled and asked, "Where did you find bodyguards?"

"They found me. We're going to have guests for the weekend and I need you to go to the grocery store because these boys can eat."

"Guests? Boys?"

"Jon and Ray Renaldi are on their way here. They should be here in about twenty minutes or so. We're putting them in the addition."

"Drea's brothers?"

"Yep. They didn't tell me they were coming until it was too late to stop them. Henry, they knew that I'd be driving you all crazy, so they came in to take care of me. Isn't that great?"

"It's a little odd."

"That's what I thought. But they don't think so and Aaron says it's not weird."

"Did I miss something about you and them?"

"Stop it. No. They think of me as their little sister." She whispered, "And besides, I think Ray is gay and Jon's a horndog. Sweet little Polly never interested either of them that way."

"How in the world are they both able to take time off from work? What do they do?"

"Jon works front office for the Bruins and Ray owns a gym. He travels around the world running different athletic competitions. He organizes them and oh, I don't know. I'll ask when they get here."

"And they're just going to land in Bellingwood to take care of you."

"I know. But can you go to the grocery store and pick some things up? I'll send you a list."

"They eat regular food?"

"Their mama is Italian. She'd hit them over the head if they didn't. And trust me, when Mama Renaldi hits one of those boys upside the head, the entire block hears it happen."

"Send me a list. We're finishing up here soon anyway."

"How's it looking?"

"Good. I'll take pictures and show you later."

"I love you, Henry."

"Uh huh. I'll see you after a while."

"Henry?"

"Yeah."

"What's the 'uh huh' about?"

"What? Oh. Sorry. I need to go."

~~~

Polly was in the kitchen talking to Sylvie and Rachel when she heard a loud voice call her name. "Polly Giller!"

"It's them," she giggled. "You've gotta see this."

She ran out to the main foyer and Ray grabbed her up and

swung her around. "Polly Giller, you're still the prettiest thing I've ever seen," he said.

As soon as he put her back down on the floor, Jon put his hands on her cheeks and pulled her in for a long kiss.

"Whoa!" she heard Rachel say. "That's hot."

Jon let her go and then pulled her in close beside him. "It's good to see you, Polly. Boston's light dimmed the day you left."

"Stop it. You're incorrigible." Polly could barely speak, she was so flustered. She patted his chest and watched Sylvie roll her eyes. "Jon and Ray Renaldi, this is Sylvie Donovan and Rachel Devins. Girls, these are Drea's brothers."

Sylvie stepped forward to shake their hands while Rachel wiped hers on her apron before approaching them.

"Sylvie is our chef and Rachel is her assistant."

"No wonder we were able to find Bellingwood so easily. We told the GPS to find beauty and it sent us here," Jon said.

"Now you've gone too far," Ray said, pushing his brother's shoulder. "No one will ever believe you if all you do is exaggerate." He winked at Polly. "Even if he's correct about the beauty you have here. This place and its people are wonderful."

"Come on, boys," Polly said. "I want to show you my home. Let's start with your rooms."

When they got to the office, Jon stepped in front of Stephanie's desk and said to Polly, "Do you only hire beautiful women here?" He gave a slight bow and lifted Stephanie's hand up from the desktop to brush his lips across it. "I'm Jon Renaldi and you are?"

Stephanie's wide eyes darted back and forth from Polly to Jon. She finally drew her hand back and said hesitantly, "I'm Stephanie." She seemed to want to say more, but couldn't form the words.

"This has to be yours," Ray said, stepping into Polly's office. "I'd recognize your Star Wars addiction anywhere."

Jeff had come out of his office and Polly introduced them all to each other. "We're going to start with their rooms," she said. "And now that my bodyguards are here, I'm ready to experience the outdoors. We'll probably go down to the barn so they can meet

51

my menagerie. If Henry is looking for me, will you tell him where I am?"

"You go on," Jeff said. "It's good to see you like this again."

Polly smiled. "I had no idea how much I've been dragging. Just thinking about going outside has lifted a weight from my shoulders." She hugged Ray, who was closest to her. "Thank you so much for coming! I can't wait to show you everything."

"Tell me what's been going on with everyone," Polly said. "Where's the last place you traveled, Ray? Jon, what celebrity girls have you been dating? How's your mother and is Drea doing okay? I haven't heard from her in a while, but she said she had some big projects that she was working on. Do you think she'll ever get married? And ..."

"Stop right there," Ray said, putting his hand on her arm. "You've worked up a full head of steam. We have time to discuss everything. One of us will always be with you."

"All of the time?"

"Okay. We'll let you and that husband of yours ... what's his name, Hank?"

"Henry. And you know that. Be good."

He laughed. "Anyway, we'll let you and Hank have your time together, but during the day if you aren't locked in your apartment, one of us will be with you."

She linked each arm into one of theirs and led them down the hall to the addition, singing *"We're off to see the wizard, the wonderful wizard of Oz."*

The boys pushed the double doors open and when they arrived in front of the elevator to the second floor, they stopped and looked down at her. "Now what?" Jon asked.

"I stop being a happy goofball and take you up to your rooms. I've sent your room keys to your phones. You'll have access to those doors and the outside doors."

"Everyone has those? Even old guests?"

"No. We knock them off the system when they leave. It's easy to do."

"Okay. Just checking."

Polly opened the door to the front bedroom and then stepped back and opened the door to the back room. She looked down at the small black duffels they were carrying and said, "That's all you have? Even for you, that seems paltry."

Jon dropped his bag in the front room. "Another couple of bags in the car. We'll get those after we're settled. Now, don't you worry about us, little girl. We're here to take care of you, not the other way around."

"You're going to have to stop with this little girl thing," Polly said. "People see me as a business woman here in Bellingwood. It's all quite proper."

Ray walked into the back room. "I don't buy the proper thing. That's never been you. But this place certainly does fit you. It's peaceful and comforting." He ran his hand across the desk as he walked to the back window and looked out at the sycamore trees along the creek bed.

"Damn girl, but this is nearly perfect. I can see why you left Boston to come back here. What a wonderful place to breathe." He came back over to her and took her hand. "I'm very proud of you. I always knew you were special, but it warms my heart to see what you've done." He held her hand and she followed him to the windows looking to the south and the pasture where the horses were playing.

"These are yours too?"

"Those are my Percherons." She pointed at them. "That's Nat, Daisy, Demi and Nan. And those two donkeys? They're Tom and Huck." Polly leaned against him. "I never thought I'd be able to show you what I have here. I'm so glad you've come."

"You keep saying that. We should have come earlier. Life just keeps us moving, though."

"I know that. I'm so mad that Joey is messing in my life again, but at the same time, if it's what brought you two out here, then I can't hate him."

"Yes you can," Jon said. "You can hate him all you want and still be glad that we're here."

"So really, Jon," Polly teased. "Still no one special in your life?

53

There's no girl that's going to pine for you while you're out of town?"

He puffed out his chest and ran his fingers through the thick, black hair on his head. "You think one woman can handle this?"

She huffed out a laugh. "I guess not. What about you, Ray? No one?"

Ray sighed and gave her a small smile. "You were the only woman for me, Polly-girl."

"That's not what I mean. You know I would have dropped everything for you back in those days, but you didn't want me."

"No. You're right. And Drea would have killed us if we'd ever put the moves on you."

"Still not what I mean. You're avoiding this. Why?"

He shook his head. "Not now. In answer to your question. There's no one."

"I'm sorry. I always thought you'd find a way to make a family."

"So did I. Maybe someday."

Jon heaved a dramatic sigh. "Enough of this family hooey. You promised to show us around. I want to see those big ole horses."

Polly reached up to kiss his cheek. "I'm not going to stop saying it. I'm so glad you're here."

CHAPTER SIX

"Alrighty then, show us those horses of yours," Ray said.

Polly practically skipped out of the room in her excitement. She was finally going to be allowed freedom.

The two brothers followed her down the walk to the first pen, and through to the barn.

"Hello!" Polly called out as they walked into the main alley.

Eliseo came out of one of the back stalls, carrying driving tack with two dogs at his heels. They bounded over to greet Polly, but at a click of his teeth, they slowed and came to a stop. "Good boys," he said, bending down to rub the tops of their heads. "Good boys."

Polly glanced at him, he nodded and she knelt down in front of the dogs, Khan and Kirk. She'd named them when they were in Arizona, and Eliseo had decided the names fit them. "You boys are growing up to be as big as Han. What kind of dog do you think was the father?" she asked Eliseo.

"I don't know. They have some bull terrier in them, I think, but I'm guessing they're just big mutts." He set the tack on a bench and put his hand out toward Ray. "I'm Eliseo Aquila."

Ray took it to shake and Polly jumped back up. "I'm so sorry. Eliseo, this is Ray and Jon Renaldi. You remember my friend, Drea? Her brothers. They're here to keep an eye on me. Can you believe it?"

He shook Jon's hand and nodded his head, looking at them appraisingly. "You're here from Boston?" he asked.

Ray said, "We are. It's good to see where Polly ran off to. You have a nice place here."

Eliseo wasn't finished, though. "Why are two city boys coming to Iowa to watch over our Polly?"

Polly started to speak, but Jon stepped in front of her. "We aren't trying to get in anyone's way, but since the day Drea brought her home for dinner, she's been a member of our family. Mama told us to take care of her and that's what we're going to do."

"You should meet their mama," Polly said. "She's intimidating."

"So you're spending vacation time in the great state of Iowa?" Eliseo wasn't ready to accept this.

Ray bristled and said to Polly. "Are we going to have to explain ourselves to everyone we meet?"

She smirked. "Maybe. Imagine an entire town made up of the neighbors on your block."

Jon gave a dramatic shudder. "How do you do it?"

"It's wonderful most of the time. The rest of the time you learn to live with it." She put a hand on Eliseo's arm. "It's okay. They are like my brothers. I can't imagine anyone else I'd rather have show up out of the blue to keep an eye on me."

"We're protective of Polly," Eliseo said. "Especially now."

"You weren't here when Joey kidnapped me," Polly said to him. "It was Jon and Ray who were at the airport in Boston. They took me through that whole week at the police station and everything."

"I wish I would have stepped in and made him go away after that first date you had with him," Ray said. "I knew he was trouble. You could see it in his eyes."

"Who knew?" Polly asked. "The man was some kind of psychotic break about to happen."

"We should have known. I should have known." Ray's eyes lit up and he started chuckling.

"What?" Polly asked.

"Tom and Huck?"

She turned and saw the two donkeys coming in to investigate their visitors.

"Do you have carrot bits?" she asked Eliseo.

He didn't say anything, but turned and went back into the feed room. The donkeys were confused, trying to decide whether to follow him in hopes they'd get a treat or check out the new people. They went with the new people, sniffing and nosing at Jon and Ray.

"They're quite friendly," Polly said.

When Eliseo came back out with a bag of carrots, she smiled at him in thanks, took it, and pulled a few out, placing them in Jon's, then Ray's hands. "This will cement your friendship forever."

"Polly, can I show you something back here?" Eliseo asked, touching her elbow.

"Sure. I'll be back in a minute, guys." She handed Ray the bag of carrots. "Here, make 'em go slow, though."

"What's up?" she asked, once they were in the donkey's stall.

"Are you sure about them?" he asked. "They look awfully pretty to be much of a threat to anyone, especially someone intent on kidnapping you."

Eliseo had seen her through several bad situations and she recognized his over-protectiveness. She put her hand on his forearm. "You have no idea what's under those shirts. Those boys grew up as thugs. Most of their buddies are Boston PD and they handle themselves well in most any situation. They're also one of just a few people in this town who know Joey enough to recognize him no matter what. And ... they're pissed off that he made it to Iowa without them knowing he was gone. Yeah. I'm sure."

"I would do anything for you, Polly. I just think it's odd that they've come all this way just to be your bodyguards."

"I think it's weird, too," she said in agreement. "But you don't know what it's like to be part of that family. Their mother scared *me* and I didn't grow up with her. She loves me as much as one of her own and I'm not at all surprised that they're here because she sent them. Everything you've ever heard about Italian mamas is true about her. She rules the roost and has a strong sense of what is right and what is wrong. Mama Renaldi ran that neighborhood and when Jon or Ray got in trouble, they had to deal with her before they dealt with those whom they had offended. It didn't stop them all the time, but they turned out pretty well."

"Not a life I understand," Eliseo said.

"Me either, but it was fun to watch it happen. The first time I was there for a meal, Jon reached across the table for the bowl of potatoes. In the flash of an eye, his mama's spoon connected with his forearm and he dropped his hand back into his lap. Very respectfully, he apologized to her, then to me and then asked for the potatoes to be passed to him. I thought I was going to die right there, but he wasn't embarrassed, she wasn't embarrassed and everyone else just moved on like it hadn't happened."

Eliseo chuckled. "I guess they've been well-trained."

"Yes they have," Polly agreed. "So we're good?"

"For now. I'll withhold judgment until I get to know them better."

"Eliseo! Uhhhh"

Polly and Eliseo stepped into the alleyway to see Jason standing at the door with his mouth open.

"Hi Jason," she said.

"Uh, hi Polly."

"Jason, these are two friends of mine from Boston. Jon and Ray Renaldi. Remember the two brothers who met me and Joey at the airport a couple of years ago? This is them."

He nodded and with wide eyes, approached the two men, who held their hands out.

"This is Jason Donovan. His mom is Sylvie. You'll meet his brother later."

Polly studied Jason as he greeted the two men. He was as tall as Jon and much thicker. It was surprising to see him this way. She saw him with new eyes. The boy just continued to grow.

"What were you in such a rush about?" Eliseo asked.

Jason handed him a piece of paper. "Look."

Eliseo opened it and then handed it to Polly.

"They want you to try out for football?" she asked.

"Mom has to sign it. Can you believe it?"

"That's going to take up a lot of your time," Eliseo said. "Are you ready for that?"

"I know. We have to talk about things. I won't be able to ride the bus and a bunch of other stuff. But it's pretty cool, don't you think?"

"It is," Eliseo said, putting his hand on Jason's back. The two walked to the back of the barn and then out to the pasture.

"I think they forgot about us," Polly said. "Sorry."

"No, that's cool. Football is a big deal," Ray said. "We both played in high school. Maybe we'll meet the horses another day."

"We can go out and see them, if you like."

"It's okay. Your stable man doesn't think too much of us yet. We can wait."

"He's just protective. We've been through some stuff. He's shed blood for me more than once."

Ray put a protective arm around her shoulders. "It bothers me that you have so many opportunities out here for people to shed blood for you. Drea has stopped telling your tales at the dinner table because Mama gets so upset. More than once, she's demanded that we come get you and bring you home so she can keep you safe."

Polly laughed. "She's pretty wonderful."

"Yes she is," Jon said. "But don't you ever tell her I said that."

"She knows."

~~~

After dinner, Jon offered to take the dogs out for a walk. He'd spent the evening doing everything in his power to build a relationship with Obiwan. It had worked. Both dogs followed him, waiting for attention.

"This is what he does to women, too," Polly said to Henry. "It's pathetic to watch. Granted it took him longer with Han and Obiwan than it usually takes with a girl. I've seen him turn one of those into a fawning idiot in five minutes."

"Hey," Jon said. "That's not..."

Ray interrupted. "It's true. You can't deny it. You love 'em and you leave 'em."

"I'm just waiting for the day Jon falls in love," Polly said. "I'm pretty sure the earth will stop spinning."

"Come on dogs," Jon said. "I need to escape before they go any further." He started for the front door and Polly stopped him.

"Let me show you the back way out," she said. "Leashes are at the bottom of the steps. Don't let Han try to tell you where to go. Obiwan is much more responsible. Pay attention to him."

"Got it. We'll be fine."

The dogs obediently followed him down the steps and waited while he snapped their leashes on. Polly just shook her head. He had a great touch with them.

She went back into the media room. "Anybody for more wine or another beer?"

"It was a great dinner," Ray said. "Thank you."

"I will cook for you as often as you like, but there are great restaurants in town. Now that you're tagging along, maybe Henry will actually let me go out."

"The whole town knows to keep an eye on you now," Henry said. "You've probably never been safer. Let's plan on going to Davey's tomorrow night. Steak and all the fixin's."

Polly came back from the kitchen with a plate of cookies. "We should make it a party. I'll see who's available. I might as well introduce the two of you all at once."

"Fine with me," Ray said. "All the better to identify who the good guys are. I wish I knew who was stupid enough to hook up with Joey Delancy. It doesn't bode well that he's got a partner."

Obiwan and Han came racing into the room and Polly looked down at them. "You two are back early. What did you do to Jon?"

"Guys?" Jon called from the steps. "We might have a problem."

Ray was up before Polly and Henry had even registered Jon's words. "What do you mean, a problem?" he asked.

Jon came into the room holding a stick. On the end of it dangled a woman's blouse.

"Where did you find that?" Polly asked.

"Your dog was the one who sniffed it out. It was hanging on the handle of the main kitchen door. Someone wanted us to find it. I didn't want to touch it, so I found the stick. Are you calling the Sheriff or should I?"

Polly looked at the clock. It was only nine thirty, so Aaron was surely still awake. "I'll do it. He's used to hearing from me."

Luke had decided that the dangling shirt was quite interesting and made one half-hearted attempt to jump up and grab it. Henry managed to snag him out of the air before he made contact and Jon took the stick and shirt back into Henry's office and put them on his desk.

"Aaron?" Polly said when he answered.

"You're supposed to be safe in your house. I hear you have two bodyguards. Tell me no one is dead."

"I don't know about that last statement, but Jon just found a woman's blouse hanging from the kitchen door handle outside. I know they checked every door before we closed the place down. It just showed up."

She heard him take a deep breath. "I do that to you a lot, don't I?" Polly asked.

"What's that?"

"Make you breathe deeply."

He chuckled. "I guess you do. I'll be right over. I think Will is in town this evening. He'll meet me there. Do you want to pull video for me?"

"I never think about that," Polly said. "Sure. I'll see what we've got. That's the one door that doesn't have good coverage. Maybe they crossed in front of one of the other cameras, though."

"Stay safe and I'll be over." Aaron hung up and Polly walked into Henry's office. She poked at the shirt with the stick, wondering whose it might be.

"It's my size," she mused. "But not a brand I've ever had." It was a western style red plaid blouse, with snaps on the cuffs and down the front. As she poked at the shirt, she heard a rustle. She picked it up from the desk to make sure it wasn't on top of any papers and heard the rustle again.

"There's something inside the shirt," she said out loud. "Like maybe they pinned a note?"

Henry had come in the room to stand beside her. "Leave it for Aaron. He'll kill you if you mess with his evidence. You can be patient, even if it's just for a few more minutes."

She looked at him with a glint in her eyes. "Do you remember who you're married to?"

He took the stick out of her hand and set it on top of the blouse, then took her arm and steered her back into the media room. "Will one of you sit on her? She's a menace."

"You have changed, Polly," Jon said. "You were such a nice, sweet girl when we knew you back in Boston. You didn't get into trouble, you didn't find dead bodies, and you didn't have psycho freaks kidnapping you."

"I'm still nice."

Ray laughed. "Maybe it's the fact that the nice, sweet Polly Giller came home to the nice state of Iowa. All of that nice came crashing together into a cataclysmic eruption that she'll never be able to escape." He turned to Henry. "And you're the crazy man that waded into the middle of it, expecting to stay safe."

"I live in the eye of the storm," Henry said. "It's safer there than anywhere else."

"That would explain it all," Polly said. "See, Henry! I told you that things were normal when I lived in Boston. Nothing weird ever happened to me. I was as dull and boring as you could be. Am I right?"

Jon nodded agreeably. "She's right. When Drea told us about the skeletons falling out of your ceiling... Wait. Was that up here?"

"Yep," she said. "Those bathrooms out there."

He chuckled. "That's funny. It's kind of like realizing you're sitting in the middle of a movie set. All of these stories that we heard about happened right here. *Polly's Paranormal Party.* Yeah. That would make a great horror movie. Maybe you can get Stephen King to write the screenplay."

"Funny. Uh huh. You're a riot," she said, flinging a throw pillow at him.

Jon snatched it out of the air before it hit the lamp on her reading table. "You still can't throw worth a darn," he said. "You have to keep an eye on your target, not the item you're throwing."

"She can't catch either," Henry said, tossing a cookie to her.

Polly flung her hand out to catch it, only to have it sail past her and into Ray's outstretched hand.

"This is not nice," she said.

"How did your dad not teach you to throw a ball?" Ray asked.

"Or catch it?" Henry pressed.

"We had other things to do. Whatever." Polly stalked out of the media room and headed for the kitchen. "You guys are mean," she said loudly.

Ray trotted over to catch up with her. "You're right. We are. We're adults and should know better. You've done an amazing thing here and that's your strength. Right?"

Polly stuck her tongue out at her husband.

"What was that for?" he asked.

"Just because I feel like I'm back in elementary school and you deserved it."

Henry laughed. "Maybe one of these days I'll take you out back and teach you how to catch. That's when you have to keep an eye on the ball." He and Jon joined them in the kitchen and he asked, "Now what are you doing?"

"Putting water on for tea. We're about to have more people in the house and I'm being polite."

"It's Aaron. You know he won't have anything."

"I'm still going to offer. And I don't know Will Kellar yet. Who knows? Maybe he'll be one of those polite boys who has to accept tea when it's offered."

"You're kind of a mean one," Jon said, opening cupboard doors.

"What are you doing?" she asked.

"Looking for dog treats."

Polly pointed to the correct cabinet. "But they don't need any more reason to love you. You've already gotten them to adore you."

"Positive reinforcement. And besides, once this is all over, they're going to need to go back out. We didn't get very far before I had to bring them back inside."

Henry's phone rang. "It's Aaron," he said and answered it. "Hello?"

He listened and then said, "I'll be right down." He headed for the door. "I'm going to meet them downstairs. They want to walk the property and check the doors, just in case."

"I'll come with you," Ray said. "Jon, you stay here with Polly."

After they left, Jon said, "I can't believe you take this so well. Why aren't you freaking out?"

"I don't know," Polly said with a shrug. "I handle it like this when I'm in the middle of it. Poor Henry has to put up with me later when I turn into a blithering idiot. But I know that freaking out doesn't achieve anything, so I just wait until things get quiet."

He gave her a quick hug. "I'm proud of you. You're an amazing girl. I should have paid attention to Mama when she told me to grab you up and marry you."

Polly pushed away from him with a laugh. "You aren't ready to be married yet, Jon Renaldi, but when that day comes, you'll have found the perfect girl and no one will question whether or not it's the right thing for you two to do."

"I hope so. I really hope so. I kind of envy this happy life you have out here with ole Hank."

"Stop it, you brat."

"I like him, though. I don't think you could have found anyone better. He's your lobster."

CHAPTER SEVEN

Nodding hello to Aaron and Deputy Kellar when they came in the front door with Henry and Ray, Polly pointed to the other room. "It's on Henry's desk. I didn't touch it, but I wanted to. I think there's something pinned to the inside of the shirt."

Henry beckoned to Will Kellar to follow him and the two men went to retrieve the shirt.

"Was there anything else?" she asked Aaron.

He looked at Ray and slowly nodded. "A pair of jeans was hanging on a tree branch back by the creek, we found a bra tucked into a drainpipe, and a pair of panties dropped in Eliseo's garden."

Polly wilted. "This has to belong to that girl."

Aaron nodded. "That's our assumption."

"The shirt is my size," Polly said. "That's why my clothes fit her."

"You're handling this better than I expected," Aaron said, sitting down beside her.

"What else am I supposed to do? You know I don't do panic-screamy girl." She looked up and gave a sad smile to Henry. "Until you all leave and then Henry has to hold on while I cry."

Will came in holding a clear evidence bag, filled with the shirt.

"What was on the note?" Polly asked.

He handed Aaron another, smaller bag.

Aaron looked at it, shut his eyes, and turned it over, shielding the contents from Polly.

"What?" she asked. "You can't hide this from me. What is it?"

"We're calling Digger now," Aaron said. "I don't want to do this alone any longer. If he wants to call the FBI, I'm fine with that."

Will nodded. "Yes sir, boss."

"Why are you calling the FBI?" Polly asked quietly. "Please tell me what's going on."

Aaron handed her the bag, with the note facing up. She read it.

"Oh Polly, why are you hiding? You know I will stop at nothing to have you. Everything you've done up until this point can be forgiven.

I didn't want to do this, but we had no choice. She looks just like you, but in the end, she isn't you at all, is she. I'm so sorry that you don't understand how important this is.

My friend says that we should keep trying. Maybe we'll find someone who is even better than you. I know that can't possibly be true. Can it?"

She took a deep breath and turned the bag over to find a photograph of another girl, again dressed in Polly's shirt and jeans. This time the girl's eyes were open and terrified, her hands strapped to the steering wheel of the truck.

Polly dropped it in Aaron's lap and slumped back in the couch.

"They didn't waste any time," she said.

"No they didn't and we're going to work as fast as possible to find her. We had teams out this afternoon looking for your truck and the last girl."

"Do you know who this girl is yet?" Polly asked.

Aaron shook his head. "Not yet. We don't have any missing person reports."

"Boss?" Will said.

"What?"

"We do now."

Aaron stood up and walked over to Will, looking down at his tablet. "Show me."

Will said, "She's from Des Moines. Didn't come home last night. Her boyfriend didn't think much of it. She comes in late sometimes. When he woke up this morning she still wasn't there and then she didn't show up at work today either. Name's Angela Leffert. Age twenty-six."

Aaron looked at her and then the photograph. "That's her. We've got to move fast. Call everyone in. They're not sticking close to Bellingwood, so they have transportation."

"Can I help?" Polly asked.

"You can stay inside and safe," he responded. "And you," he said to Henry. "You need to stay safe, too. Delancy is ready to forgive Polly, but if he thinks that you're a threat to him getting her back, you're in danger."

Henry started to speak, but thought better of it and nodded.

"Are you two staying here?" Aaron asked Ray and Jon.

"We have rooms in the addition."

"Okay. That's close enough. They don't leave without you. I talked to your police sergeant buddy in Boston. You two are better than you let on."

"What does that mean?" Polly asked.

"I'll let them tell you," Aaron said. "But the only reason I'm not putting you into protective custody or shipping you out of the country is because these two are here. And I'm not going to tell you that you can't leave the house. If one of these two says that he can keep you safe outside these four walls, you can go. But, if they say stay, you stay. Got me?"

Polly nodded. A silly thought occurred to her and she gave a small hysterical giggle.

"What's funny?" Aaron asked.

"It's not funny at all," she said. "But there's a dead girl out there and I'm the only one that can find her."

"That's not the least bit funny," he said.

"I know, but do you think I'm wrong?"

"We aren't letting you go out looking for this girl. It's too dangerous."

"I never look for them," she said. "I just end up where they are."

"Go on," Aaron said to Will. "Get things started. I'll be down later. I'm going to make a few calls and then I have to explain to Lydia that her weekend plans have changed."

Deputy Kellar left and Aaron sat down across from Polly. "This is going to sound like a strange request, but I need to start somewhere. Tell me where you would have gone tonight if we hadn't curtailed your movement."

"Henry and I were talking about taking the dogs away from here. Somewhere so they could have a long walk, maybe even run." She turned to her husband. "Where's that place you take me sometimes on the Boone River? It's just a canoe put-in site, but it's pretty back in there. That's what I was thinking about."

"Tunnel Mill," he said.

Aaron nodded and entered it into his phone. "Where else."

"If we didn't do that, there's a place over north of Ogden that's nice."

"Don Williams Park," Henry said. "We've been there a couple of times, too."

"Is that it?"

"That's all I had in my head," Polly said. "I don't know if I would have come up with anything else. I kinda thought about going out to the winery tonight, too. But that's inside and they wouldn't have been able to hide a body there."

"Stu's heading up to Tunnel Mill tonight and we'll look at Don Williams Park tomorrow. I need to make some calls right now. My buddy in Hamilton County will want to know why we're in his territory. Digger is about to lose his weekend, too. Can I use your office, Henry?"

"Sure. There's pen and paper in the top drawers. Use whatever you need."

"Thanks. I'll be out of your hair soon."

Aaron headed for the office and then stopped. "You do know that Lydia will be over to see you bright and early tomorrow, don't you? It's going to be difficult for me to keep her away tonight."

Polly smiled. "That's fine. But she can call me any time."

"Thanks. That'll help."

"Well," Jon said, after Aaron left the room. "Anybody for a nice game of Parcheesi?"

Ray sat down across from Polly. "Do you want to explain what that was all about?"

"Only if you explain what Aaron meant when he said you were more than you let on."

Polly watched the two brothers glance at each other. Jon bit his lower lip and gave an almost imperceptible shake of the head. Ray looked at the floor.

"What?" she asked.

"You might as well talk to her," Henry said. "She's as tenacious as anyone I know. Now that she has hold of this, she'll find out."

"Mama doesn't know and Drea only does because she's so danged smart," Ray said.

Polly creased her brow and scowled at them. "What is it? What aren't you telling anyone?"

Jon, who had been pacing the room behind them, thrust his head between her and Henry and whispered, "We're vampires and have been assigned to protect Boston from all evil-doers."

Both Polly and Henry jumped.

"Show me your teeth," she said once her heart dropped back to where it belonged.

Jon grinned, showing a full set of normal pearly-whites. "We filed the canines down so that we can pass for normal humans. The government changed us. There are brothers in blood all over the country, on patrol day and night, protecting humanity."

Polly rolled her eyes at him. "Whatever."

"He's not kidding," Ray said.

She started to laugh. "You know, there are a lot of things you could have said to me and I would have believed any of them. But this, this is ridiculous. If you don't want to tell me the truth, I'll let it go tonight. But someone is going to tell me."

"Are you going to tell us why the Sheriff is calling his men to look in places you might have gone tonight?"

"It's stupid," she said. "But I'm not kidding when I tell you that if someone has died from suspicious causes, I find them. Aaron hates getting phone calls from me."

"I'm not too fond of it myself," Henry said.

Ray folded his hands in his lap. "So you think that if you had gone out to one of these places tonight, you would have tripped over the body of this poor girl?"

"I don't know," she retorted. "It's not like I expect to find bodies. It just sort of happens."

"They won't find anything tonight, even though they're going to places you recommend," Henry said. "It just doesn't work unless you're the one who's looking."

"I hope not," she said. "I'd like to not be responsible for this. As it is, I feel completely responsible. Joey's doing this because of me."

Ray shook his head. "But the other guy isn't. He's doing it for an entirely different purpose. It has nothing to do with you."

"How do you know that?"

"I just know that. He's using Joey. Your old boyfriend is only a tool for him."

"What aren't you telling me, Ray?" Polly asked.

"Nothing. We don't know anything yet. Until we find that girl's body, we can't be sure of anything."

"Then someone needs to let me out of this house so I can find her."

Aaron walked back into the room and everyone looked up at him expectantly.

"We don't have anything yet. I'm sorry. We're working all night, but until dawn comes, I'm not sure we'll find anything."

"I can't believe you don't know who the first girl is," Polly said. "There aren't any other missing person reports that we can look at? If they went down to Des Moines for this last girl, maybe they went further away to find her. I could look through reports, try to help. I need to be doing something."

"Polly," Aaron warned.

"No, it isn't because I feel responsible. I feel helpless. I can't do anything. I'm barely working here. I can't help Henry at the coffee shop, I can't work at Sycamore Inn, and I can't help in the barn with the horses. I can't even walk my own dogs. Someone has to give me something to do or I'm going to go berserk."

"I tell you what," Ray said. "If they haven't found the girl's body by tomorrow morning when you get up, Jon and I will take you out and let you show us Bellingwood. You'll be perfectly safe with us." He looked at Henry. "I promise."

"Really?"

"Sure," he shrugged. "It might be best if you introduce us to your friends. We want to meet the people who know you and get a sense for the community."

"I need to go down to Boone," Aaron said. "I'll have Lydia call you in the morning before she comes over, just in case you're out and about."

Ray walked to the front door with him and said," Let us know if you find anything. We have resources."

"I'll do that." Aaron pulled the door shut and Ray stood there for a moment before returning to his seat on the couch.

"You have resources?" Polly asked. "Don't make this any more difficult than it is. Just tell me who you are."

Ray took a deep breath and sat forward on the couch, his elbows on his knees. "I run the North American division of an international security firm. We work with governments and private corporations worldwide. We don't talk about it. We don't advertise."

"Like spies?"

"Sometimes. Most of the time we guard people in the public eye. We're involved in training, provide secure communications technology for governments, and gather intelligence when necessary. Our company provides security for many of the high-profile sporting events around the world..."

"That's my area of expertise," Jon interrupted.

"I thought you worked front office for the Bruins," Polly said.

"I have an office there. It's a good cover. We don't need people looking at us too closely. We can move easier that way," he responded.

"I don't know what to think," she said and turned to Henry.

He shrugged. "I don't know these guys. They're *your* friends."

Polly looked at the two men she'd known for so long. "I feel like the world just got smaller and I have no idea who you are."

"I'm worried that the next thing they're going to tell us is that they have to kill us now that we know about them," Henry said.

"It's not like it's a state secret," Jon said. "It's just easier if people don't associate us with that life. It's easier on them. Think about it. Now that you know about me, you'll watch Wimbledon and wonder if I'm doing security and if anything happens, you're going to worry about me. Or at the Olympics or international soccer events. If there is any bad news, you'll wonder if I'm in the middle of it."

"You're right," Polly said, nodding. "I will." She looked up. "You guys were at the Boston Marathon bombing, weren't you?"

They both nodded. Ray said, "You knew that. Drea told you."

"She said you were helping. I just assumed you were there to cheer her on and got drafted."

"We *were* there to cheer her on, and it wasn't my company who ran security that day, but we had people there. It was a big miss, though we learned a great deal from it."

"I didn't even think about those people."

"What people?" Henry asked.

"The ones like Jon and Ray... in charge of security. How awful for them. They'd feel like failures and it was something no one could have predicted. Two brothers decided to do an abhorrent act and then followed through."

"It was an awful day," Jon said. "But we can't focus on those days. If you only knew the number of lives we've saved over the years, the good things we've done. You see the big, awful things and we will never be able to talk about the little things that make it possible for us to live good lives."

Polly chuckled. "I'd probably be a paranoid nut if I knew any of them. I can scent a conspiracy from a mile away. I don't understand how you live, knowing about the bad things and awful people that are out there."

"Because I know so many good people like you," Jon said. "We can't get too caught up in the intrigue of our world. It would take us over. For every one instance of conspiracy or fraud, there are thousands of normal people who live normal lives. If we focus on the one over the other it gets to be too much."

Ray had picked Leia up and put her in his lap, stroking her from head to tail. She purred like a freight train and her eyes closed as she absorbed the attention. "Maybe I should get a cat," he said. "She likes me."

"I'm going to take the dogs back outside," Jon said. "Then we should let these two get some sleep. Do you want to walk with me, Ray?"

"No, I like it here. Have you ever had a cat purr like this, little brother?"

"You have to be kidding me."

"I'm not. This is relaxing."

Jon shook his head. "Come on dogs. Let's try this again. No more random clothing finds, okay?"

After he left, Ray said, "If we don't find Joey over the weekend, I have another team on the way."

"Have you talked to Aaron?" Polly asked.

"They're coming in to protect you two. They aren't here to investigate or deal with Joey or his buddy. Their only purpose is to make sure that he stays away from you. I'm bothered by the fact that he got so close tonight."

Polly shuddered. "At least he didn't get inside."

"I don't think that was his purpose. He wanted you to know that he could get close when you didn't expect it."

Henry took a deep breath and stood up. "I want to just leave town with her. We won't tell anyone where we're going. We'll just go."

"But she won't let you, will she?" Ray said quietly. "There's a little girl downstairs that holds Polly here."

Henry shook his head and stalked into the kitchen.

"He doesn't like being helpless," Polly said. "For that matter, neither do I. This sucks."

"I know it does. I wish we were here as your friends. I wish you didn't have to know what we did. I wish none of this were real, but it is and everyone is trying to make it as easy as possible for you. For both of you."

"Henry knows that. He's just frustrated. I tend to walk into too many situations that he can't control."

Ray smiled at her. "He's a good man. You couldn't have married anyone better." He put the cat back down on the floor.

Leia shook her head and gave him a look, almost as if she were offended that he'd stopped petting her.

"I'll be back another time, little girl," he said. "Jon's had plenty of time with the dogs. We're going to check the property tonight. Make sure doors are locked and everything is as it should be. We'll look in on the animals down at the barn. Anything else we should know?"

Polly shook her head. "The creek is a good place for people to hide, but it's high right now from spring rains. It wouldn't be a comfortable hiding place."

"Good to know. You two sleep and we'll start fresh tomorrow. If you need anything, just call and I'll be right here."

Polly stood up with him and he crossed to her and pulled her into a hug. "It's going to be okay, Polly," he said.

"I know. But thanks for being here."

Ray left by the front door and Henry came back out into the living room. "I'm sorry," he said.

"For what?"

"For walking out. I'm tired of not being able to take care of you, but things get so out of control that it's more than I can handle."

"Good night, all!" came Jon's voice from the bottom of the steps as the two dogs raced into the room.

Polly started to respond, but heard the door shut instead.

"It's just us now," she said. "What do you want to do?"

"Honestly, I just want to sit on the couch and watch stupid television until I'm too tired to do anything but sleep."

"Great. I'll make popcorn."

CHAPTER EIGHT

"I'm glad you're going to get out for a while today," Henry said. "You've had enough."

Polly had just come back upstairs from checking on Rebecca and Sarah. She remembered from experience with her own mother that it was nearly impossible to find your way through the waiting period before a death. You went back and forth between pleading for it to be over and hoping that you would have one more day.

Rebecca tried to draw, but was so attuned to her mother's breathing that any hesitation had her running back to Sarah's bedside for a soothing touch. Sarah drifted in and out of consciousness, but her presence in those few fleeting moments was enough to keep Rebecca motivated.

This morning, Sarah woke up for a few minutes while Polly was there - long enough to give Polly a smile and then pat the side of her bed, asking Rebecca to sit beside her. When Polly left, Rebecca had placed her head on the pillow beside her mother and wrapped an arm around the woman, tucking in as tightly as she could.

These were the moments Rebecca would remember, the closeness she felt to her mom as they faced this together. Polly didn't want to intrude. These moments were theirs and would take Rebecca through difficult lonely nights down the road.

Polly remembered her own mother's touch. A gentle caress on her cheek, a weak smile, whispered words of love. She hadn't been allowed to spend a great deal of time with her mother. Mary had taken her to the hospital in Ames often enough, but there was only so much time in an evening and everyone felt it was important to get Polly home and into bed so she could go to school the next day. If only they would have realized how important those last days were going to be.

"You're a million miles away," Henry said.

"Sorry. I was just thinking about Rebecca and Sarah and then about my own mother. I'm glad Rebecca gets to have this time with her mom."

"You constantly amaze me."

"Why?"

"No jealousy at all."

"What do I have to be jealous of?" She looked at him in astonishment.

"You know that you're going to raise that girl as your own, but you aren't pushing to do that until it's absolutely necessary."

"It's no big deal. Sarah is her mother. I'll never be able to take her place. All I can be is Polly. Rebecca's relationship with me will be completely different."

"Like I said. You amaze me. You are pragmatic about so many things and yet you have this infinite depth of passion."

Polly reached over and kissed him on the cheek. "I love you too."

"What are you planning to do today?" he asked.

"I thought we'd have lunch at the diner. I'll take them to the library to meet Joss. See what Lydia is doing this afternoon. Maybe we can all do supper at Davey's tonight. Then, we'll just take it as it goes."

"Tell me you aren't going to be out looking for that girl."

She shook her head. "It's not on my agenda. I think I'd prefer it if Aaron or one of his guys actually took care of that this time."

"I'm not counting on that. Not around here, anyway."

"You haven't heard from Aaron this morning, have you?" Polly asked.

"No. Do you think he'd call me before you?"

She shrugged. "I thought maybe while I was downstairs with Sarah and Rebecca."

"Nope. Nothing yet."

Polly sat down at the dining room table. "Do you think they'll find my truck?"

"I suppose so. At some point."

"I'm not going to be able to drive it ever again, you know."

"Because it's been defiled?"

"I'm not kidding. I can't drive it after all that's happened. Could you?"

Henry looked down at her while he refilled her coffee mug. "No. That would be creepy."

"And who knows how long they'll keep it for evidence gathering, even after they find it."

"Could we just report it as stolen?"

"It *has* been stolen," she said. "I didn't think about it, but we need to have somebody down there fill out a report on it."

"Why don't I take care of that while I'm home today? I'll call Anita down at the Sheriff's office and get it started."

"Thanks. I didn't expect you to do my busy work."

He sat down beside her. "Do you want a truck again?"

"Yes. Is that strange?"

"Not for you, honey."

"I haven't used it like a truck, though. I don't haul anything except people. Maybe I should get an SUV."

"I'll ask you again," he said. "It's up to you. Do you want another truck?"

"Well..."

"If that's what you want, get it. Don't do this to yourself. You wouldn't catch me driving an SUV."

"But you haul things in the back all the time."

"You're making this too difficult. We'll look for something once this is over."

"Just don't let them make me take back that horrible thing. Do you promise?"

"Of course. I promise."

"And you're hanging out here at the house today?"

Henry reached down to pat Han's head. "I haven't had much down time lately. Until you're able to help us make decisions at the coffee shop, we're at a standstill. So I'm taking time off today, maybe actually get work done in my office, rearrange schedules to keep people working next week and take a nap."

"I'm sorry this is screwing up your schedule." Henry worked hard to make sure that his people had solid hours. There was nothing he hated more than laying them off and re-hiring them. It had to be done sometimes, but it stressed the poor man out.

"Don't worry. We're on time and we have plenty of other things going on. All I need to do is shift people around."

Polly put her hand out. "Can I have the key to the coffee shop? I'd like to go in and see what you've been doing. I can't believe it's been a whole week since I was there."

"Sal would never forgive you, y'know."

"For what?" Polly looked at him and then realized that he was teasing her about finding bodies. "Wipe that smirk off your face. You have to quit saying these things. You act like I do it on purpose or even worse, like it's something that happens every day. I am not in control of this."

Henry gave her a pouty face. "You're right. I'm sorry. I shouldn't be mean to my beautiful, wonderful wife."

"And don't you forget it. Now do you need anything before I leave for the day?"

"Only your promise that you won't fall in love with the two hunks who will be escorting you."

She laughed. "That just isn't going to ever happen. It would be like me telling you not to fall in love with your sister, Lonnie. It's just so ridiculous."

"Then if nothing else, I want to hear all about people's reactions when they see you riding with two young Italians in their black Rubicon."

"They're driving a Rubicon?"

"I assume so, since that's the vehicle sitting outside in the parking lot."

"Do you think I'll need a step ladder to get up into it?"

"I suspect Jon would have a wonderful time lifting you up and putting you in the seat. Yes," Henry said. "I want to hear the stories. Pay attention to people today. Please?"

"You're horrible." She swatted his arm. "And I love you."

"I love you too. You have to promise to be safe out there. The last time you left, you ended up in a very bad place."

Polly shut her eyes and felt a catch in her throat. "I didn't even think about that."

"Oh, honey. I'm sorry. I didn't mean to remind you."

"But you're right. This is the first time I've really left the house. I know that I've been complaining about it all week, but at some point I got used to my cocoon."

Henry scooted his chair closer to her and gathered her into his arms. "I'm sorry. I didn't mean to make you go there. I'm glad Ray and Jon are here to make you feel safe today. You need to get out of here and see that the rest of the world is continuing on its path around the sun. People are living their lives and doing their jobs."

"I'm going to miss hanging out with my animals. They've gotten used to having me here."

"They're going to have to get used to having me here today and tomorrow. Now, are you ready to go?"

"I think so."

"Call your escorts and get yourself out of here. And text me, okay?"

Polly pushed back and stood up, then bent over to kiss him. "I love you and thank you for trusting that things will be good today."

"You'll be fine and I love you too."

A knock at their front door made both of them jump.

"I've got it," Henry said. "You stay here." He walked out into the living room and called, "Who's there?"

"It's me. Jon. Can I steal your wife?"

"Come on in, Jon. I think she's ready to be taken away."

"You're holding down the fort today?" Jon followed Henry into the dining room.

"There's plenty of work to be done and I can do it here. You two just make sure she gets home safe."

"We've got this, bud. No worries." Jon stopped and looked at Polly. "Ray is driving around to your garage. Can we go down the back way?"

"This feels strange," Polly said. "Like I'm a prisoner under escort. Do you two have ear wigs and can I have one if you do?"

Jon chuckled and tapped his left ear. "Nothing in here except my own Eustachian tube today."

"I feel a little cheated," she said, poking him in the side.

He took out his phone and made a call. "We're on our way down."

Henry walked with them through the media room and into his office, the dogs running along beside and the cats trying to cut them off.

"It's a real process trying to get out of here, isn't it?" Jon said with a laugh.

Polly picked Luke up and put him on Henry's desk. "It isn't usually this bad, but I haven't left all week. They don't know what to do." She hung back and gave Henry a hug. "Seriously. I feel like either a prisoner or a celebrity."

He kissed her lips and then whispered in her ear. "I'll make you feel like a celebrity when you come home tonight."

She felt her face turn bright red and stepped back, stumbling on Obiwan. "I'll see you later."

Jon was at the bottom of the steps waiting for her and held the door while she walked through. She would usually wander into the kitchen and say hello to everyone, but felt like she needed to stay on task since her bodyguards were staying so close. He opened the door into the garage and then the door going outside.

She let him look around, then when he beckoned, she left and walked to the Jeep.

"You take the front seat," he said.

"It doesn't look too comfortable back there."

"I'll be fine." He opened the door for her and waited for her to get in, then closed it and stepped to the back door.

"Wait!" she said.

"What?" Ray asked. "Did you forget something?"

"No. It's what I saw."

Both men went on alert.

"I'm sorry. No, I remember seeing something in the side mirror that morning I was kidnapped, just like I saw Jon now."

Ray took a deep breath. "Don't do that to me, I have a weak heart."

"Do you remember what it was you saw?" Jon asked.

"It's intangible. Like a dream."

"Was your window rolled down that morning? Do you remember?" Jon asked.

"Aaron asked me that same question. I don't remember." She pulled her seatbelt on and buckled in, then turned to him in the back seat. "I wonder if Rebecca would remember." Polly shook her head. "Probably not. She's only thinking about her mom. I ride with my window down even if it's raining sometimes, so, like I told Aaron, it's a good possibility. Why are you asking?"

"Because if he came up from behind and plunged a needle in your neck, you might have seen him in the mirror, even if it was only for a split second."

Polly unconsciously rubbed her fingers along her neck. "It would work that fast? So fast that I don't remember anything?"

"Sure," Ray said. "Anything is possible. So, where to first?"

"Do you mind just driving for a while? I want to go out past the hotel and then drive into the parking lot of the winery. I want to wander around town and just be out. Maybe we can drive down to Boone or go over to Ames. Can I roll down the window?"

Ray smiled and patted her hand. "Not while we're in town, okay? Maybe later."

Polly pulled her hand back and slumped toward the door. This was all hard enough to face, but that had just made her feel like a naughty little girl. She knew he didn't mean to be patronizing, it was her own issue. But darn it, she was trying to be obedient. Every single one of her friends got to do their regular daily activities without thinking about it, but she was stuck between two bodyguards because an insane boyfriend managed to escape from his asylum.

"Polly?" Ray asked.

"What?" It came out snotty and she immediately regretted it.

He gave her a look of confusion and she returned a weak smile. "I'm sorry," she said. "Did I miss something?"

"Which way?" He was at the end of their lane.

"Oh. Turn right. The hotel is down this way." All of a sudden, none of it was important. She didn't care whether or not they went anywhere in town. It was her own bad attitude, but the excitement of being out and about had drained away. Bellingwood hadn't changed in the last week and it didn't make any difference whether she was stuck in her apartment or outside. She couldn't fix what Joey was doing. Henry was right. They should have just left town. If only Sarah weren't in her last weeks. But it wasn't her fault either. None of this was anyone's fault except Joey's. He was the one she wanted to yell at.

"Polly," Ray said quietly. "Are you okay?"

She looked up. He had pulled into the parking lot of Sycamore Inn and was looking at her with concern.

"We might as well just go home. This is ridiculous. I'm putting you in danger and nothing is going to change just because I'm finally outside. I'm sorry." Tears sprang to her eyes and she quickly turned to look out the window so Ray wouldn't see.

Jon leaned forward and put his hand on her shoulder. "Polly, this is why we're here. You aren't putting us in danger and we're here to give you more normalcy in your life. You shouldn't be stuck in your house."

"And I appreciate it. But I'm feeling sorry for myself. I've dealt with weird things since I came back to Iowa, but I can always do it face to face. I don't like to hide. But I don't want to put anyone else in danger." She smacked the dashboard. "I'm so damned mad at him. Why is he doing this to me?"

Polly glanced at the side mirror and shut her eyes. When Ray tried to speak, she put her hand up to stop him. He went silent.

"I saw him," she whispered. She opened her eyes and turned to face Ray. "I saw him! I know what he looks like!"

"The guy that's with Joey?"

"Yes! I know what he looks like. At least I think I do. I need to tell someone. Do you think Aaron has an artist? Or we could go to Beryl's house. She'd sketch what I tell her."

"Shut your eyes again," Ray said, motioning to Jon. "Keep trying to picture him. We're going to call Aaron and see if he can help us."

Jon leaned forward after a quick phone call. "They don't have anyone there right now. Do you think your friend can do this? She doesn't have any training."

"But she's amazing. She can probably get close. Let me call her," Polly said.

She swiped her phone to make the call.

"Hello sweet tooth, how are you?" Beryl said.

"I need you," Polly replied. "Do you think you could draw someone's face based on my description?"

The woman laughed out loud. "Like a police sketch artist? That's a new one for me."

"I'm serious. Do you think you can help?"

"Who do you want me to sketch?"

"I saw the man who kidnapped me in my side view mirror. My brain was so foggy that I forgot about it until just now. Can you?"

"Well, uhhh."

"Beryl, please. I'm so afraid I'll lose the image again."

"Fine. Come on over. I don't make any guarantees, but I'll see what I can do."

My bodyguards are with me."

"Those hot Italian boys? Everybody is talking about them. Do you mean I get to meet them before any of your other girlfriends?"

"Other than Sylvie, yes."

"She doesn't count. She gets to see everything that happens at Sycamore House. Bring 'em along. I might even have to make a quick sketch of their chests. Just for my own personal viewing."

"You're a sick woman."

"Come on over. I won't make any guarantees, but we'll give it a shot. I'll see you in a jiffy."

"She'll try," Polly said and gave Ray the address. "Now she's a little wild and will probably flirt with you shamelessly. No one in town quite knows what to do with her, except for the few people she calls friends."

"I think we'll be fine."

"Beryl," Jon said, musing. "Beryl Watson?"

"Yeah. Do you know her?"

He slapped Ray on the shoulder. "Didn't we get hired to do security at one of her shows? There were a whole bunch of Boston Brahmins and Hollywood elite there. Wasn't that the night that you thought Halle Berry was flirting with you?"

"She wasn't flirting with me." Ray shook his head in disgust. "We were having a conversation. No big deal."

"You guys did security for a show of Beryl's?"

"I think so. It was a few years ago. Before you moved out here."

Polly shook her head. "Little, tiny world we live in."

CHAPTER NINE

Curious as to how this was going to work out, Polly directed Ray to Beryl's house. When he pulled in, Beryl's front door opened and an index finger emerged, curling to beckon them in.

"I told you," Polly said. "She's a wild woman."

"What is she doing?" Ray asked.

"Who knows? She probably has some crazy reason for it. We should find out. I'm sure it will make you laugh."

Polly reached for her car door and Ray put his hand on her arm. "Let Jon. Please."

"I'm trying not to argue with you about it, I really am..." Polly started.

"Thank you," he said and got out.

Jon was standing beside her door, grinning. He opened the door and put his hand out as she stepped on to the running board.

"I know, I know," she said. "Chivalry and all that."

"Exactly, ma'am." Jon bent at the waist and backed up to let her go first.

She led them to the front door and reached up to ring the doorbell, but before she could, the door swung open and Beryl grabbed her by the arm, pulling her inside. Then, Beryl looked at the two men with Polly and stepped back, put her hand on her chest and said, "Be still, my heart. Where have you been hiding these two gorgeous hunks of flesh?"

Ray shut the door and smiled.

"These are my friend Drea's brothers from Boston. Ray," Polly touched his arm. "And Jon."

"Polly told me about you, but I never dreamed that two such fine young specimens of manhood would ever be in my home. I might swoon." She winked at Polly and said in a stage whisper. "Would they catch me if I did? Because I'll do it, just to see."

"Go ahead," Polly said with a laugh. "I warned them about you."

"What did she say?" Beryl asked, hooking her arm through Jon's to lead him into the living room. Did she tell you that I'm the most exciting person she's ever met in her life? Did she tell you that I'm a honey pot for the Russians? Maybe she told you that I've been involved with every president since Eisenhower."

"All of that and more," he said, putting his hand over hers. "And we believe everything she's told us."

"Oh, Polly," Beryl said, turning to look over her shoulder. "He's perfect. Can I keep him?"

Polly looked up at Ray. "I have no words."

He just chuckled.

Beryl had brought her pencils and a sketch pad into the front room. She stroked Jon's bicep twice and made a sound much like a purr before letting go. "You're a very, very pretty boy. You and I could make beautiful ... ummm ... artwork together."

"Beryl Watson," Polly said. "Do I need to call Lydia?"

"Don't worry. I already have. She'll be here in a half hour or so. I wanted her to wait until you and I had a chance to start on the sketch. This makes me nervous. I've never done anything like it."

"I've seen your portraits," Polly said. "You're amazing."

"But that's when I know what I'm looking at. I've never done a sketch based on a description."

Polly pursed her lips. "And I don't even know how great my

description will be. I only saw him in a side mirror and even then, it was just before I got a happy drug that knocked me out."

Beryl picked up a pencil and sketch pad and sat down, motioning for Polly to sit across from her. "Start with a basic description, but I don't want you to watch what I'm doing. After you've seen it all in your mind's eye, we'll let you see my sketch and go from there. This could go very well or very badly."

"Where should I start?" Polly asked.

"Let's start with his face. Was he lean or overweight? Was it a long face or squat and wide?"

Polly shut her eyes and began to speak. "He had a wide face. It made me think of a wrestler. He also had a thick neck. His hair was short and kind of spikey. No. Wait. Yes, it was short. But not like a crew cut or anything. Okay. Spikey."

"What about his ears. Were they close to the head or sticking out? Did his hair cover the ears?"

"No, it didn't cover them. They weren't very big, I guess." Polly reached up to touch her own ear. "Close to the head." She opened her eyes. "And he had a little stud in the left ear. That's weird. I can't believe I remembered that."

"Go on," Beryl said. "What about his chin. Did it have a cleft or a divot? Was he freshly shaved? What about a mustache?"

"He had stubble, like a Van Dyke." Polly touched her upper lip and chin. "Just around his mouth. I don't know what that's called. It wasn't very thick. His hair was sandy brown. There wasn't any kind of divot in his chin. It was just round like a normal chin."

Beryl's pencil was flying across the pad as she listened. "Think about his cheekbones. Were they pronounced?"

"No," Polly said. "Kind of round. In fact, make his jowls thicker. Like he has an extra twenty pounds on him. He wasn't lean at all."

"What about his nose. Describe what you see there."

"I could see his nostrils, so it was turned up in front. Not very big. But, oh," she said, opening her eyes again. "I'll bet it was broken sometime. It had a turn to the..." she shut her eyes and ran her index finger down her own nose, angling to each side. "Turn to the left. Not very much, but I'll bet that's why."

"Okay," Beryl said. "Before we get to the eyes, I want you to look at his forehead. Was it long or short? Did his spikey hair go up from the top or was there any that came down below the hair line?"

"Do you know the pastor over at the Christian church?" Polly asked.

"Sure, I've seen him."

"That's kind of like his hair. But not quite as neat and tidy."

"Got it." Beryl erased and then the sound of her pencil scratching on the pad resumed.

Polly kept her eyes closed, waiting for Beryl to tell her to go on. She didn't want to lose this image.

"I'm ready," Beryl said. "Let's talk about the brow ridge. Was it thick and heavy or delicate?"

"Wow," Polly said. "I hadn't thought about that." She drew her hand across her eyebrows. "It was thick and pronounced. And he had bushy eyebrows too. They weren't really dark, but there was a lot of hair on them and it was darker than the hair on his head. Not quite a unibrow, but thick."

"Now we have to talk about his eyes. Tell me what you can."

"They were normal spaced. Not little or beady or anything. They were just normal eyes."

"Okay, a couple of other things just occurred to me," Beryl said. "What about his skin. Was it smooth or pockmarked like with acne. Did he have any scars or anything?"

Polly touched her right cheek. "There was a scar here, but yeah. It was like an acne scar, not like he'd been cut or hit or anything." Then she touched the corner of her left eye. "And another one here. I can't believe I noticed that." She looked up. "I hope it wasn't because there was a raindrop on my mirror."

"You're doing well," Ray said.

Polly nodded and tilted her head, while still keeping her eyes closed. "He had a chain around his neck, but I didn't see if there was anything on it. That was under his t-shirt."

She opened her eyes. "Is that enough?"

"Give me a few more minutes," Beryl said. "Why don't you

show these young men around the place. There's tea in the refrigerator. Give me peace and quiet while I flesh this out. I'll let you know when I'm ready."

"Are you sure?"

"Go away. This is on me now."

Polly stood up and beckoned for Jon and Ray to follow her into the front room of the house. It fascinated her every time she was here and she finally had time to sit down in a chair and take in the entirety of the room.

"She's quite the woman," Ray said quietly.

Polly nodded. "Beryl puts on this crazy mask for the world, but she is truly amazing." She pointed at the paintings on the wall. "I mean, look at this. She sees things and then turns them into beauty. I'm always amazed by her."

"Did she do that painting at Sycamore House?"

"The one with the tree? Yeah. That's hers."

Jon dropped into one of the chairs and picked up a book sitting next to it. "She *is* the woman whose show we covered. I remember her now."

"She didn't act like she remembered you."

"That was because she was busy and we were in the background. But you know, she's a pretty big deal in Boston. Her art hangs in places you can't imagine."

Polly smiled and shook her head. "Of course it does. No one but Lydia, Aaron Merritt's wife, even knows that about her. I mean, look at this place. She lives in Bellingwood in relative obscurity. She annoys her neighbors and torments shop owners in town. We have no idea."

"This would be a great place to live if you didn't want to deal with the insanity of big city life. If you were an artist like her, maybe it's the best place to live."

"She gets to be eccentric and people accept it," Polly said. "But in Boston or Chicago or even Kansas City, she'd be like so many others."

"Drea told me that it was quiet here in Bellingwood," Ray said. "I don't think I realized what that meant. This is so different than living in the city. I haven't heard a single siren since I've been in town and since we've been here this morning, I haven't even heard a car drive by. You can hear dogs barking and birds chirping, but not much else."

"That's why I love it," Polly said. "I'll never move back to a city again. I like being close to Boone and Ames and even Des Moines so I can get fast food every once in a while, but I think my entire system took a breath and slowed down when I moved to Bellingwood."

"Polly? Come here and help me make changes," Beryl called.

"Here we go," Polly said. "Let's see if she and I made any sense." She pulled herself up out of the comfortable chair and walked back into the living room.

"Sit here beside me," Beryl said, patting the couch. The pad was turned upside down on her lap.

"I'm going to turn this over and I want you to take a quick look at it. Tell me yes or absolutely no. If it is yes with caveats, we'll work those out."

"Okay. I'm ready."

Beryl turned the pad over and Polly gasped. "That's close. You understood what I said."

"I did?"

Polly looked into Beryl's face. The woman was nervous! "You really did."

"But I need to make changes, right?"

The two worked on the sketch, reducing the brow ridge and opening the space between the eyes and the bridge of the man's nose. Polly had Beryl add length to his hair and smooth out his jowls.

Then Polly pulled herself back to get distance from the sketch. "That's him," she said and turned to Ray. "What do you think?"

He shrugged. "If you're happy with it, it's perfect. You should call your sheriff friend. He'll want to get this out."

Ray took out his phone and snapped a few pictures of the sketch Beryl had made. "Just for insurance purposes," he said. "Call the Sheriff."

"Okay," Polly said. "I can't believe this worked."

Beryl gave her a wry grin. "I can't either."

"Whatever," Polly said, swatting at Beryl's leg. "Apparently, you're a hot commodity on the east coast. Some kind of star out there."

"Honey, I'm a star everywhere I go. Puhleeze. I'm Beryl Watson." Beryl stood up. "I'm going to the kitchen to make lemonade. Because I'm such a star. Who wants some?"

The doorbell caught everyone's attention, making Polly jump.

"It's Lydia," Beryl said. "I can't believe she didn't just walk in."

Ray strode toward the door. "I locked it. Habit."

"Oh," Beryl said, her mouth very round. "You're being all protective and shit. I get it. And just when I think you brought me a present, Miss Polly. Now I find out that they're your bodyguards."

The doorbell rang again. It sounded insistent.

"I'm calling Aaron," Polly said. "Someone needs to let Lydia in or she'll think there's a problem."

"Go ahead," Jon said, gesturing to the hallway. "I'm right behind you."

Beryl winked at Polly. "I could get used to this."

Polly shook her head and swiped her phone to call Aaron.

"What's up?" he asked.

"I'm not sure whether I'm happy or sad that you hear from me so often nowadays that you know it's not a dead body."

"I'd hate to disappoint you. I'll work on that."

"Beryl did a sketch of the guy. It's very good. What do you want us to do with it?"

He chuckled. "She did? It worked?"

"She's pretty amazing."

"I know that, but I didn't know what to expect. Can you send a photograph of it from your phone? Tell her I'll stop by to pick up the original later on."

"Sure, I can do that."

"How's my..." Lydia stopped talking when she saw that Polly was on the phone.

Polly mouthed, "It's your husband."

"Is that my wife there?" Aaron asked.

"She just got here."

"Send the sketch with her." He paused and then said. "No, on second thought, I'll pick it up. I do *not* need her anywhere near this investigation. Don't even let her see it. I have this terrible image of her recognizing the man, making a scene and getting herself and everyone around her in trouble."

"I thought it was just me who did crazy things like that." Polly attempted to nonchalantly flip the cover closed on the sketch pad. Fortunately Lydia was handing off a basket and a bulging paper bag to Jon and Ray.

"You are a terrible influence on her."

"That's what I hear. Ray already took a picture of it. I'll have him send it to you."

"Thank you. How does it feel to be out and about?"

"It's okay. Not as great as I'd hoped, but I'm just feeling sorry for myself. You guys haven't found anything? Not my truck, not the girl, not anything?"

"I'm sorry, Polly."

"No. I get it. It's nobody's fault. I just hate this."

"I do too. Stay safe today, okay?"

"I'm working on it."

Lydia, Jon and Beryl had gone into the kitchen.

Ray watched Polly put her phone down. "Are you okay?"

"I'm not very good about letting people take care of me. The last time Joey was in town, I discovered just how bad at it I really am and I haven't gotten better. All of those years living on my own and taking care of things by myself were just stripped away because some idiot thinks he should control me. Now all of a sudden, my life is worthless."

"That isn't true."

"Yes it is. Nobody would think to just kidnap *you* because of an obsession. You'd deal with them. You'd hit them over the head or knock 'em out or whatever. But because I'm a girl, everyone wants me to hide in my house."

"It's not just because you're a girl. It's because you're Polly and people love you. They can't imagine something awful happening to you. We don't just protect girls, you know. We protect big, brawny men too. Especially when they're being threatened by psychos."

She wrinkled her nose and looked away, then said, "Could you send a picture of the sketch to Aaron? He gave you his contact information last night, didn't he?"

"He did." Ray swiped his phone several times and said, "Done."

"Are you telling people what you do for a living?" Polly asked. "Do we tell Beryl that you guys met her before? I didn't want to say anything just in case."

"It's okay. I have a feeling that she isn't one to gossip."

"No," Polly said with a sad smile. "She isn't. She is amazing and very few people here know her at all. If she weren't friends with Lydia, I would never have gotten to know this incredible woman. I don't know how Lydia does it."

"Does what, dear?" Lydia said, coming into the room.

"Puts people together. I was just telling Ray that I wouldn't know Beryl if it weren't for you."

"But we've been friends for years. Okay, she and Andy were friends back in high school. I was a few years younger than the two of them. It's Andy you should be thanking."

Polly hugged her friend. "How about I start with you?" She looked back toward the kitchen. "Is it safe to leave the two of them alone in there?"

"I'm here to ask what you'd like for sandwiches. I stopped at Sycamore House to pick up a loaf of bread from Sylvie. She needs to open that bakery. I'll never have to bake again."

"Let's see what you have," Ray said. "I'm pretty hungry."

Jon was slicing bread when they got into the kitchen.

"They've got you working," Polly said.

He brandished the knife at her. "I'm always working."

"You're always working something," his brother responded.

Beryl stood and stared at the two brothers, then finally said, "I'd like to paint the two of you before you leave."

Ray shook his head vigorously. "It's not a good idea."

"What do you mean? It's a great idea. You two are gorgeous. Heck, maybe I could make a million dollars selling my painting of you as cover art for a hot romance novel."

Jon tossed his head to the side, as if flinging long hair, and struck a pose. "Like this?"

Polly laughed and rushed over to him, putting her hand on his chest and leaning into him. "Here. Am I helping?"

"That's it," Beryl laughed.

Ray grinned, took out his phone and snapped a picture. "Yeah. Mama will want to see that."

"You won't let me paint you?" Beryl asked, opening the refrigerator. She took out bottles of mayonnaise and mustard and put them on the table.

"We can't," Jon said. He looked at his brother, who gave a slight nod. The two were on the same page

"That's too bad. Why not?"

"Because we're undercover spies," Jon said.

Beryl looked at them in confusion.

"You're what?"

"Okay. We do security. And we don't need to have our visages..." he encircled his face with his hand, "out there for the world to see. We like to stay in the background."

Beryl nodded.

"Kind of like we did when we ran security for a show you did several years ago in Boston."

"You what?" Her face contorted in shock.

Lydia stopped what she was doing and watched them.

"Ray and I met you at a show you did. There were a bunch of Hollywood stars there and quite a few politicos and money people from Boston."

"I remember that show," Beryl said. "I can't believe I don't remember you, though." She peered at Ray. "Wait a minute. Were you the one who was flirting with Halle Berry that night?"

CHAPTER TEN

"And where to now?" Ray asked, once they were back in the Jeep.

They had finished lunch, been highly entertained by Beryl and Lydia, and by the time Polly made noises to leave, the boys were more than ready to escape.

"What would you like to see?" Polly asked.

"Show us the highlights. We saw your lovely little hotel. Anything else? Didn't you say you had a winery here?" Jon pressed. "Mama would love it if we shipped her red wine from Bellingwood."

Polly shrugged. "Okay. We can go out there. They're open on the weekends now. It's more fun in the evenings, though. Local musicians play and they have wine tastings."

"We can go downtown," Ray said. "You told us you wanted to go to the library."

"Joy. A library," Jon huffed from the back seat.

"We don't have to go. My friend, Joss, is the librarian, but she's been to Sycamore House a couple of times this week. It's fine."

Ray stopped at the stop sign and said, "What's this way?" He pointed north.

"Just the ball park and then you head out of town. Eliseo lives up that way, not far from Henry's aunt and uncle."

"Eliseo. That's your grounds keeper?" Jon asked.

"Yeah. I guess that's what you call him. He kind of does everything. The animals, the grounds, the gardens, the building. He has a couple of older guys who like to come over and help out." Polly smiled as she thought about it. "Old Mr. Bedford loves to work with the horses and Mr. Gardner likes helping out with the vegetable garden. Both of them are helping Eliseo work up more land behind the creek."

Ray drove up to the ball fields and pulled into the parking lot. "It really is just this quaint."

"What do you mean?" Polly asked.

"Look at this. There are nice bleachers and lights for when it gets dark. Not too many people, but just enough that they have fun when they get together."

"Yeah? So?"

"It's like something out of a movie. Good family fun."

"Don't you be getting soft on me, brother," Jon said.

"No. I don't think I could stand living like this, but it's kind of nice to know that it exists. The world makes so much more sense with this here."

Jon leaned forward and tapped Polly's shoulder. "He's getting thoughtful. We need something to do. Where to next?"

"Let's go downtown. There's ice cream in the general store. Henry gave me keys so we can look in on the coffee shop that Sal owns. Do you remember her? Sal Kahane?"

Ray nodded. "If she can make the move, anyone can."

"She wasn't too happy without having a coffee shop on every corner, so she's building one, but otherwise, I think she likes it here," Polly said. "She hasn't made many friends yet, but that will come."

He pulled back out onto the street and said, "This way?"

"Yeah. You'll run right into it.

He turned onto the main street and drove west. People turned and stared at the big, black Jeep.

"Are they looking at the car or wondering who we are?" Jon mused.

"Probably both," Polly said. "And don't forget. Everyone knows what happened to me last week, so they're probably trying to figure out if you guys are the kidnappers and if I'm willingly riding with you."

Ray drove through town and turned in next to the library. "Do you want to go in and say hello? We have plenty of time."

"It's okay. There's nothing I need from there."

"Polly. You're out of the house. What would you normally do on a Saturday?"

"I don't know. I just take it as it comes. Something is always happening. I might go to Ames with Sal or take the kids to Boone to the bookstore. Maybe go out with Henry. If there's nothing else, I'd go down to the barn and play with the donkeys."

"You play with them?"

"Sure," she said with a laugh. "They're playful. They have a couple of big balls that they like to play with."

"Balls," Jon said. "And donkeys."

"It's a riot when Eliseo and Jason are playing with the donkeys and horses out in the pasture."

They watched kids go in and out of the library, some with parents, others with their friends.

"There's nothing in town that you want to do?" Ray asked.

"No, but I don't want to go back yet," Polly said. "Head west out of town. Let's just drive for a while. Do you mind?"

"Not at all. In fact, that sounds great."

"In a mile or so, you're going to come to the road to Boone. Go north instead. I'll show you where that Tunnel Mill place is," she said. "The Boone River is pretty. People canoe on it in the summer unless it's too low."

"You canoe, too?" Jon asked. "You are not the same person we knew in Boston."

"Yeah. I am. These are just parts of me that I didn't take the time to show everyone. I've always just been a simple girl from central Iowa."

"Simple girl, my ass," Jon said. "There ain't nuttin' simple 'bout you, lil' miss."

"You'd be surprised. Here, turn here."

They drove north and Jon made them stop in front of an old-fashioned windmill. "Drea has to see this," he said, taking a picture with his phone.

There wasn't much in the way of traffic on the road. Ray slowed down as he drove up behind a large tractor taking up both lanes of the highway. The farmer pulled over to the right and they passed him with a wave.

"It's just so much slower out here. No one gets too excited about things, do they?" he commented.

Polly laughed. "Sure they do. We drive over the speed limit and tailgate and honk our horns and scream at slow drivers, but there aren't quite as many people, so you do it once in a while rather than all the time."

She pointed out directions to Ray as he drove along. He saw the sign for Tunnel Mill and turned on his signal.

"No," she said. "Go on. I want you to see the river valley here. It's just so pretty. The road winds in and out and there are trees everywhere. This is why I love this area."

Ray drove on past the entrance and crossed the bridge over the Boone River, slowing so that they could look up and down the river. He came to a stop on the bridge since there was no traffic coming from either side.

"It is beautiful," he said. He pointed up the river. "Look. Canoeists."

"They might have put in at Webster City," Polly said. "They'll either come out here or down at Bells Mill."

"Tunnel Mill. Bells Mill. Are they mills? Like saw mills?" Jon asked.

"No. More like grist and corn mills. But they don't exist any longer. They did a hundred years ago, but not now."

"Think about it, Jon," Ray said. "People were heading out west and decided to stay here in Iowa. Even back then they were trying to be free of the cities."

A car coming from the north spurred Ray into action and he took his foot off the brake and drove on across the bridge. At the next field entrance, he pulled in, backed up and turned around.

"Did you want to drive into that Tunnel Mill place?" he asked.

"Nah. There's not much there."

"I wouldn't mind getting out and walking," Jon said. "The river is beautiful and Mama would love to have pictures of the places you love."

Ray turned into the drive and found a place to park. They watched and waved as three canoes passed them and went under the bridge.

"She's going to hurt," Polly said.

"The chick in the middle of the second canoe?" Ray asked.

"Yep. She's not wearing enough clothes and that's gonna burn."

"You can tell the deputies were here last night," Ray said, picking up a broken branch. "This whole area was scoured. Everything has been turned upside down." He chuckled. "You certainly sent them on a wild goose chase."

"I didn't mean to. Aaron didn't have to listen to me."

"Yes he did." Ray's phone buzzed. "Just a second. I need to take this." He walked away past the Jeep and up toward the road.

Jon sat down on a stump beside where Polly was standing and they looked out over the river. "Sometimes I think he's ready to quit and settle down into a normal life. I don't know if that would be good for him or not. He's such a natural at this job. We'd be lost without him running the place."

"Has he ever found anyone that he wants to make a life with?"

"Nah. I don't think he's even tried. He poured everything he had into the job. He goes out every once in a while, but he's never met anyone he trusts enough to tell them what he does."

"Neither have you," she said quietly.

"Yeah. But I'm young. I'm the baby of the family. Everyone expects me to be a player. Ray is the oldest. The responsible one."

"Is your mother comfortable with who he is?"

"You mean single?"

"No. You know what I mean."

He gave a quick shrug. "She knows. Everyone knows. But I don't think that even Ray is comfortable with it. So I think it's just easier for him to ignore that part of himself."

He looked up at the sound of Ray's boots on the gravel. "What's up, bro?"

Ray's face was white. "We're going to Boone. I need to talk to the Sheriff and his buddy at the DCI. There's a problem."

"What's the problem?" Polly asked. "You look like you've seen a ghost."

"Give me a minute to process on this." He looked at her, then strode up, took her in his arms and held on tight.

"What?" she sputtered when he let her go.

"In a minute. Everybody in the Jeep. Let's go."

Polly realized he wasn't going to say anything more and followed Jon to the passenger side of the Jeep, then waited for him to open her door. She looked at Jon, hoping he'd ask for more information and he just shrugged.

"Not yet," he mouthed at her.

Silence filled the car as Ray drove, no one wanting to break it.

When they got to the north side of Boone, Ray finally said, "Point me to the Sheriff's office, will you?"

"Are you going to tell me what's going on?" Polly asked.

"Later. Will you call and make sure he's there?"

She nodded, took her phone out and made the call.

"Hi Polly," Aaron said. "What now?"

"Are you at your office? Ray needs to see you."

"Sure. What's going on?"

"He won't say. He just insists on speaking with you and Digger too, if he's available."

"He isn't here right now, but we can get him on a conference call. You don't know what this is about?"

"Nope."

"Come on down, then."

Polly pointed the way for Ray and he drove through town, then turned to head for the Sheriff's office.

"If things weren't so tense," she said. "I'd point out the beautiful homes in town and the fact that the county courthouse is nowhere near the business district. But I guess you don't care about that right now."

Ray just breathed. "How much further," he asked.

"It's like a different part of town. You don't even know it's there, then you're on top of it."

She looked up and saw the courthouse and pointed to the north side of the street. "Right there."

He found a parking spot and pulled in. By the time they reached Aaron's office, Polly was nervous. Ray had turned into someone she didn't recognize. He was no longer her friend or even Drea's brother. He'd become all business, on full alert. Nothing could penetrate his defenses.

She braced herself for what he had to tell them, but couldn't imagine that it was as awful as he seemed to believe it was.

They performed their greetings and Ray said, "Have you had any luck with that sketch that Polly's friend made?"

"Not yet," Aaron said, shaking his head. "Why do you ask?"

Ray opened his phone, swiped it a few times and then said, "Check your email. My company has access to many databases. I had them run facial recognition on it."

Aaron took a breath, clicked his computer a couple of times and then took another, deeper breath. "Oh my god," he said.

"What?" Polly asked. "What's going on? Who is he?"

She wasn't prepared for the look that Aaron gave her. It was filled with grief and fear, pity and terror. He rubbed his forehead and then propped his elbow on his desk, his head resting in his hand, rubbing his temples. "I need to call Digger. We aren't prepared to handle this."

Polly gritted her teeth. "Damn it. All of you. Just damn it. If someone doesn't tell me what's going on, I'm going to turn into a wild-eyed, screaming banshee. Talk to me."

Aaron turned the monitor so she and Jon could read what he had brought up. Jon took one look and let out a frightened sigh.

"What am I looking at?" she asked. And then she saw it. "Oh god."

The name on the file was Marcus David Allendar. He was wanted in several states for a series of murders. All young women. He always worked with a partner and when he was finished, he killed the partner and moved on.

"This is the man who had me?"

"You're the one who identified him," Ray said.

Aaron had turned the screen back and was scanning through the information. "They believe that the partner keeps him in line for a while, because he's training them. But as time progresses, he grows more and more out of control. I don't know why he stops. But he shuts down for a year or so before starting up again."

"How did he find Joey?" Polly asked.

Ray practically snarled. "That's a good question. Delancy wasn't supposed to have access to visitors that weren't on an approved list."

Aaron continued to read. "He's been difficult to keep track of because his victims change so much from series to series. One of the observations here is that he allows his new partner to establish the pattern. They don't know for sure which is more important to him, the kill or the training."

Polly felt her stomach twist into knots. "So why is he letting Joey play games with me? Has anyone ever gotten away from him before?" She thought for a moment. "Joey may be obsessed with me, but he's not a killer. This is just really out there for him."

"You don't know what's happened to him in the last two years," Jon said, reaching out to touch her arm. "We don't know how long this Marcus guy has been talking to him, enticing him. Until we speak with someone at the hospital where Joey was held, we don't know much of anything about what's been going on since he was admitted."

"But this doesn't sound like him at all. He's brilliant and thoughtful. He loves history and beautiful artwork. He's just not a murderer." Polly knew her protests were weak, but this was nearly impossible to accept.

"Sheriff?" Will Kellar stood in the doorway. "I hate to bother you, but Investigator Douglas is here with someone to see you."

"Okay. Send 'em in."

Aaron stood to greet his friend, Darrell "Digger" Douglas, and introduced him to Jon and Ray. In turn, Digger introduced the woman with him. She was medium height with short brown hair. Dressed in a blue pant suit with a tailored white blouse, Polly thought she looked like the epitome of an FBI officer.

"This is Marla Lane of the FBI," he said. "She's been in the Omaha office and drove over after we sent the sketch you had made."

"Who's this?" Lane asked, pointing at Polly.

Polly stood and said, "I'm Polly Giller. It's nice to meet you."

"I see," she said dismissively. "You're the victim. We should take this into another room."

Polly looked at Aaron, her eyes creased in concern. "Don't. Please. This guy is after me. They have my truck and are putting girls into my clothes. He's with *my* old boyfriend who is obsessed with *me*. You have to tell me what's happening and let me try to help."

"I'm sorry," the woman said. "This is unacceptable." She turned to walk out, stopped in the doorway and said, "I'm sorry for what you've been through, but this needs to be contained to law enforcement."

Digger gave a quick look of apology to Aaron and followed Marla Lane out of the office.

"Aaron," Polly pleaded. "I've done everything you've told me to do and now I can't know what's going on?"

"I've just lost all jurisdiction," he said. "I'm fine with that as long as they keep you safe. But think about it, Polly. If you hadn't been sitting in my office when she walked in the door, you wouldn't have even known anything was happening."

"But I *am* sitting here and I know that you all know who this guy is. You know what he's done in the past and..." Polly knew that it was useless. Aaron was right. Marla Lane was all business and she had all the power she needed. Slumping back into her chair, Polly shook her head, completely defeated. For the first time this week, she'd felt like she'd actually done something to help find Joey and Marcus Allendar. And now, it was all washed away.

"Jon," Ray said. "Take Polly home. Sheriff, can you find a way for me to get back to Bellingwood this evening?"

"Of course." Aaron looked up from his desk. "What are you thinking?"

"All it will take is one phone call and I'll be on the task force looking for Marcus Allendar. Ms. Lane can run it, but she won't shut us all out."

"I'll take you back to Sycamore House myself," Aaron said, a grin creasing his lips. "Is that okay with you, Polly?"

She jumped up and hugged her friend. "Thank you."

"There are going to be things we don't tell you, Polly," Ray warned her.

"I know, but at least I won't feel like it's all happening over my head. That's all that matters."

Ray beckoned to his brother and the two left the office. They were in the hallway for just a minute before Jon came back in and said, "Looks like we're out of here, Polly. Ready to roll?"

"Go straight home," Aaron said. "And text me when you're there, okay?"

Polly desperately wanted to hug him, but he was standing behind his desk all stiff and stern. "Aye Aye, Captain," she said.

"Go away, crazy girl and be careful."

She winked at him and walked with Jon to the Jeep.

CHAPTER ELEVEN

"Shall I take your dogs out for you?" Jon asked, opening the door at the bottom of the steps.

"Just a second," Polly said, and then called up the steps. "Henry? Are you up there?"

The two dogs came running to the top of the stairs, wagging their whole bodies with joy. Polly trudged up to meet them and sat down on the top landing, burying her face in Obiwan's neck. "I guess it's you and me again this week," she said. "I'm never leaving Sycamore House again. I can tell."

"You're home early," Henry said, stopping to stand over her.

"Yeah. I am. And you can bet that no one is letting me go outside again."

"What's up?" he asked, looking down.

"I'll let her tell you. Should I walk the dogs?"

Henry shrugged. "They haven't been out since you left this morning. We were about to go, but here you are."

Obiwan gave Polly a sloppy lick on her face and then ran down to meet Jon, who had patted his leg and rattled the leashes together. Han was close on his heels.

After Jon and the dogs left, Polly held her hand out and Henry pulled her up to stand beside him.

"What happened?"

"They know who's with Joey. It's some horrible serial killer and now there's a woman from the FBI involved and she won't tell me anything. She called me a victim. I'm not a victim, damn it."

"Andrew and Kayla are in the media room," he said quietly.

She looked at him and mouthed the word, "Shit." Out loud, she asked. "Have you seen Rebecca today?"

"The kids went down to see her in her mother's room, but she hasn't been up here."

"Okay." Polly took a deep breath and said, "I just want to lie down and take a nap. I don't want to see anyone or be nice to anyone or do anything. I'm trapped again."

He squeezed her again and then took her hand as they walked into the media room.

"Hi Polly," Andrew said, jumping up with a notepad. "Look what we've been doing."

"What's that?" she asked. Polly knew that she should put more energy into her voice, but she didn't care.

Andrew caught the inflection immediately and withdrew, stepping back toward the sofa. "It's nothing."

Henry squeezed her hand and she looked up at him. He didn't scold her or even pity her, all she saw was love.

She dropped down onto the sofa beside Andrew and said, "I'm sorry. It's been a bad day, but that's not your fault. I want to see. Show me what you've been doing."

"We're turning Sycamore House into a castle. I'm not as good a draw-er as Rebecca, but Kayla and I have been looking at pictures and we've drawn a big wall around the whole town. It would have been called a village back then. Nobody could get in unless King Henry's guards let them. That way the Queen would always be safe."

Tears sprang to her eyes. When would she ever get over being emotional at every sweet thing this kid did? Polly put her arms around him and smiled over at Kayla. "You two are fabulous.

Wouldn't this be great?" She took up the notebook and trailed her fingers across the drawing, noting the turrets and covered walkway to the stables.

"Who took Obiwan and Han outside?" Kayla asked.

Polly realized they hadn't met Jon and Ray yet. "You could call him one of the king's guards. His name is Jon Renaldi and he's an old friend of mine from Boston. He and his brother, Ray, came to Bellingwood yesterday to help keep me safe."

Andrew's eyes lit up. "Are they bodyguards?"

"You could say that," she replied. "Do you remember my friend, Drea? She was here at my wedding last summer."

The boy nodded slowly, trying to remember. "I think so."

"They're her brothers and are very good at making sure people are safe."

"Jason's worried about you," Andrew said. "I told him that Henry wouldn't let anything happen, but he said that sometimes you get yourself into danger. He asked Mom if he could skip school so he could be here to keep an eye on things."

Polly smiled. "That's sweet. Hopefully he'll feel comfortable knowing Jon and Ray will keep an eye on me."

"He still talks about your old boyfriend. Is that who kidnapped you? That's what he said. But I told him there were two people. That's what everybody in town is talking about."

Polly realized that even though he and Kayla had been here nearly every day, she hadn't spent time explaining things to them. "There were two people and yes, we think one of them is Joey. He escaped from the hospital in Massachusetts."

"Are you scared?" Kayla asked.

"A little. But I know that everybody is working hard to catch them and keep me safe."

Andrew reached over and touched Polly's wrist. The redness was still there, though it didn't hurt any longer. "Did they do anything bad to you?"

"No. I managed to get out of there before anything bad happened."

"Mom said she couldn't believe you escaped."

"They weren't very smart," Polly said. "They only had my wrists and ankles bound. I was able to scooch around and unbuckle them."

Kayla was wide-eyed. "I wouldn't have been able to do that. I'd've been too scared."

"That's the thing, Kayla," Polly said. "You can't ever let fear control you." She stopped and thought about what she was saying. "No, I take that back. Sometimes you get scared and there's nothing you can do about it. But, you can't let it take over. You have to think and see what else you can do. And if you can do it, no matter how hard it might be, you have to try."

"Stephanie said that's why we came to Bellingwood." Kayla nodded her head in understanding. "We had to stop being scared all the time. It was hard, too. I miss my mom."

"Of course you do, honey. You two faced some hard times, but you were both pretty brave. Starting over in a new town is very scary."

Kayla didn't talk about her family very often. Jeff had taken Stephanie back to Ohio to press charges against her father for rape after he killed their mother, but Kayla hadn't needed to face that. Her older sister was doing her best to keep her away from the ugliness and give her a good start in life.

The two dogs dashed into the media room and headed straight for Polly. Obiwan threw himself at her feet, rolling over to expose his belly while Han stood in front of her, his tongue hanging out and his bottom wiggling with joy.

"You two are pretty wonderful," Polly said, putting a hand on each of them. "I'm glad you're here."

Jon strode in and grinned at the scene in front of him. "Who do we have here?" he asked.

Polly stood. "Jon Renaldi, I'd like you to meet Andrew Donovan and Kayla Armstrong."

He reached across the table to shake Andrew's hand and then Kayla's. "Nice to meet you both. Donovan," he mused. "Did I meet your brother at the barn yesterday?"

"Yes, that's Jason," Andrew said.

"And was that your sister I met in the office? I think her name was Stephanie," he said to Kayla."

"Yes," she said and ducked her head shyly.

"Are you Polly's bodyguard?" Andrew asked. He put the notebook down on the table and glanced at an empty chair.

Jon took the hint and sat down. "I'm here to help make sure that she's safe."

"Is it really Joey Delancy?" Andrew asked.

"We believe so."

Andrew was not finished with his questions. "Who's the other guy? Does he know Polly, too?"

Jon looked at her as if asking how much to tell.

"We don't know much about the other guy," Polly said. "At least not yet."

Polly hated not being honest with Andrew, but she was more worried about Kayla. She had discovered that the kids made good decisions when they were given the right information, but Kayla didn't have a great foundation and was easily frightened. Andrew, on the other hand, was fascinated with everything and didn't understand fear.

Andrew picked the notebook back up and thrust it at Jon. "Wouldn't it be cool if we built a wall around Bellingwood so no one bad could get in?"

Jon looked down and pointed. "Is this Sycamore House?"

"It's the castle where King Henry and Queen Polly live," Andrew said. "We're writing a story about it. There are dragons and everything."

"Queen Polly, huh." Jon looked up at her and grinned. "Is she a good queen?"

"She's the best. She takes care of everybody in town. Even this old guy who lost a leg because he fought in a war for her."

"Interesting," Jon said. "It sounds like you're quite a story teller."

"I almost won a contest one year," Andrew said. Polly watched him, waiting to see him puff up with pride, but he didn't have it in him. He was simply stating a fact. "Someday I'll write enough stories that we can make a book. Polly and Mrs. Mikkels help me with spelling and stuff. Polly likes words. She's always telling me about cool words."

"That makes sense." Jon handed back the notebook and stood up, looking at the bookshelves. "You know she used to work in a library." He pulled a book off a shelf, thumbed through it and put it back. "I think she has enough books here to have her own library. Do you two read any of these?"

Kayla nodded and Andrew walked over to the bookshelves on the other side of the room. "I have this set at home," he said, pulling out a book from a TimeLife series on ancient civilizations. "Polly gave it to me when we cleaned out a dead guy's house. She takes us to the bookstore in Boone all the time. There are good used books down there. I buy those, but sometimes I like to buy a new book when it comes out." He walked into Henry's office and turned around. "Come on. I want to show you my office under the steps. Henry made it for me when he rebuilt the stairs for Polly."

Jon looked at Polly helplessly and she just smiled, so he followed Andrew back downstairs.

"You can go too, Kayla," Polly said.

"That's okay. I've seen it lots of times." Kayla looked down at the floor again.

Polly sat down beside her. "Are you okay? I know it's strange being here with just Andrew. Do you miss Rebecca?"

"I'm fine. I know Rebecca needs to be with her mom."

"Yes she does. And you're a good friend to understand that. Especially with all you've been through this last year. Do you miss your mom?"

Kayla shrugged, "I guess. She wasn't very happy, though. It's probably better this way."

"Oh honey, I don't know that it's better. We can't change it, but it's okay to feel bad about what she went through."

"At least Rebecca knows her mother loves her."

"Your mother loved you."

"Stephanie says that, too, but why did she just let us leave and why didn't she make Dad stop hurting Stephanie?"

Polly desperately wanted to reach out and pull Kayla close, but knew from past experience that the girl would react poorly. "Sometimes people make choices we don't understand because we don't have all the information. Your mom let you leave so that you would be safe from your dad. She stayed so that he wouldn't come find you and hurt you even more."

"Why didn't she stop him?"

"I don't have those answers, sweetie. But sometimes it's just too hard. He probably scared her. And when you're scared, you make decisions based on fear, rather than on what makes sense to other people who aren't involved."

"She was scared all the time." Kayla had yet to look up at Polly, but instinctively leaned in toward her.

Polly moved in, allowing Kayla to make the final move if she wanted physical contact.

"I'm sorry you had to go through that," Polly said. "Do you talk to Stephanie about this?"

"Sometimes. But she had it worse and sometimes I hear her crying in her room at night."

"You can always talk to me." Polly held her breath as Kayla's hand brushed her thigh. "Can I give you a hug?" she asked quietly.

Henry quietly walked into his office and she heard him go down the back steps. If there was one thing in her life she could count on, it was that he would take care of the world around her.

Kayla didn't move any closer and didn't say anything, so Polly waited.

"Is Rebecca going to get to live with you when her mom dies?" Kayla asked, looking at Polly for the first time.

"She sure is." Polly sat back, startled at the unexpected turn of conversation. "She'll live in her room across the hall full-time."

"Stephanie bought me a real bookshelf. We went to a store in Ames where they have a lot of cheap things. We bought some clothes and we're going to see if they have a table for the dining room. But we don't have a truck to bring it back."

"Maybe Henry could help you with that when you're ready."

"That's what I told Steph, but she said that you already do too much for us, so we can't ask for anything more."

Polly put her arm up on the back of the sofa. "Kayla, you are part of our family now. There's no such thing as too much. When you find the table you want, we'll be glad to help bring it back."

"I told her that, but she said no."

"Your sister is doing her best to take care of you. She'll figure it out. Don't worry."

"Can I tell you something else she's worried about?" Kayla scooted closer to Polly as her voice dropped to a whisper.

"What's that?"

"She's worried about when school is over. I don't want to stay in the trailer alone all day. There aren't any nice kids my age there. Steph said I could sleep late in the morning and then she'd come for lunch. She said she'd find things for me to do in the afternoon until she came home after work, but that sounds boring."

Kayla came to Sycamore House every day after school and when Stephanie helped with a weekend wedding reception, she came to spend time with Rebecca. Polly was proud of her young charge when she discovered that Rebecca had just made it happen. There hadn't been any question of where Kayla would be. She would be with her friend and Stephanie hadn't protested.

"Do you want me to talk to your sister about spending days here with Andrew and Rebecca? There are things the three of you can do. In fact, I wouldn't be surprised if Eliseo, Sylvie and I might find jobs so you can earn money."

"Really?" Kayla scooted the last few inches in and tucked herself under Polly's arm. "What kinds of things? Can I work in the barn and help with the donkeys and horses?"

"Yes you can. And Obiwan and Han will need to be walked several times during the day. Eliseo would like more help in the garden out back and Sylvie will need help while she's putting the bakery together."

"You'll ask Steph if it's okay?"

Polly lightly dropped her arm around Kayla's shoulders and gave her a squeeze. "I will. There's no reason for you to stay home by yourself when there's so much to be done here. Besides, last fall when Andrew and Rebecca went back to school, I got lonely. I like having kids here." She leaned in and said, "You know that Rebecca is going to be sad when her mother dies, so it will be even more important for you to be here. She's going to need a friend."

"She has Andrew."

"You're right. She does." Polly let out a chuckle. "But sometimes girlfriends understand things that boys just don't get. Am I right?"

"Maybe."

"Like how cute is that bodyguard of mine?" Polly asked.

Kayla looked up at her in surprise. "You're married."

"And Henry is the love of my life, but sometimes a girl just has to appreciate a fine lookin' fella, doesn't she?"

Kayla giggled and scooted back on the sofa. "He is cute. Is he married?"

"Nope, he's not ready to settle down yet. And honey, you should see his older brother." Polly fanned herself.

"He's cute too?"

"He's gorgeous."

"Is he married?"

Polly shook her head. "No, he's not ready to settle down either. They travel around the world taking care of people like me and don't want to leave families at home wondering if they're okay."

"Do you think they'll ever get married?"

Polly lifted her shoulders and her eyebrows, "I don't know. Neither of them has found the right person yet. Maybe someday."

"Maybe one of them would take Steph out on a date."

She'd walked right into that one. Rats. "I suspect that they'll be too busy making sure Joey doesn't find me. And I don't think Stephanie would appreciate you trying to set her up, do you?"

Kayla frowned. "No, she'd be mad at me. She tells me that I get up in her business too much."

"I never had a sister, so I don't know what 'too much' is, but I'll bet that Stephanie loves you even when you do that."

"Yeah," Kayla said. "I know. She worries all the time about stupid things. If she would let people help her, it would all work out. I keep telling her that she should talk to Jeff, but she tells me to keep my nose out of it."

"For now that's probably the right thing to do." It was killing Polly not to press Kayla. There were so many things that would be easy to fix, but she knew enough to realize that wouldn't help Stephanie establish her own independence. People made life so hard for themselves sometimes.

Andrew stuck his head in the door. "Can we come back in now? Henry said we should wait, but I wanted to get my notebook."

"Is he back there?" Polly asked.

"No. He and Jon are still downstairs talking. They didn't know I came up."

Polly laughed. Henry had no idea he'd lost the boy. "Go tell them that we're done talking and Kayla made me feel much better." She looked at Kayla. "What do you think about helping me make brownies? I have everything we need in the kitchen."

"Yes!" Kayla said, jumping up. "I love your brownies."

Andrew went to the back steps and shouted down. "It's okay. You can come up now. Polly says the girly stuff is over." He ran back to the couch and picked up his notebook, then carried it across the room to the dining room table.

When Polly looked at him with her eyebrows raised, he said, "It's easier to draw here."

"You just want to be close to the batter bowl, you don't fool me," Polly said.

He winked at her and flipped the notebook open to the page he'd been working on. Henry and Jon came into the room and Polly grinned up at them.

"I'm much better now," she said. "We're making brownies. You can do whatever you want. Andrew is waiting to scrape the bowl."

"I am not," Andrew protested.

Polly cracked an egg into the bowl and smiled at her crazy little family. She never knew who was going to be in her house from day to day, but it was never boring and it was never without love.

CHAPTER TWELVE

"I'll let Ray in," Jon said, responding to a buzz on his phone. " You guys go on."

They were playing a rather raucous game of "Pit" at the dining room table, the kids picking up on the trading game quite quickly.

When the two brothers came back into the dining room, Ray looked grave and Jon went on in to the kitchen to pour another cup of coffee.

Polly felt ill. Whatever Ray had to tell her, it was going to be bad. She wasn't sure what to do with Andrew and Kayla, but desperately wanted to know what he knew.

"So," Jon said to Andrew. "Has Polly made you watch Star Wars yet?"

"It's my favorite movie!" Andrew exclaimed. "But Kayla's only seen it a couple of times."

"I've seen all of them," she said, rolling her eyes. "All of them a couple of times. I've even watched the Clone Wars shows. You're addicted."

Andrew shrugged and laughed. "I'm addicted. Do you watch Star Wars?"

"I'm more of a Trekkie," Jon said, "but I could be convinced to see it again."

"Polly has the Star Trek shows and movies too. It's been forever since I watched the movies." Andrew ran over to the cupboard where the DVDs were stored and pulled one out. "Let's watch this one. Come on, Kayla."

She gave a dramatic eye roll and dragged herself off the chair, slowly walking to the media room. "Someday you have to watch something other than space stuff, Andrew," she said.

"I got this," Jon said to Polly. "You three go somewhere so Ray can tell you what's going on. I know enough and we'll talk later."

"Thank you," she breathed and stood up. She was nervous about what was to come and felt her stomach roil. Her knees trembled and she stopped to take a deep breath.

They sat in a small grouping in the living room. The wedding reception on the main level of Sycamore House had kicked off and the noise filtered up the steps. Polly didn't want to have to go downstairs, face people and answer questions.

"How long will this reception last?" Ray asked.

"I don't know. People are usually out of here by one or one thirty. They dance and party late into the night."

"I don't like it. Anybody can come in that front door. If I'd put this together, I would have had my team here today."

She looked at him. His face was drawn and worried. "I don't know what to tell you."

"And Joey knows that you live on the second floor, right?"

Henry nodded. "Sure, but when he was here, Polly was living only on one side. This was all open. He doesn't know we've closed it off."

"Jon and I are staying with you until the reception is over. We'll clear the entire building before leaving you alone."

"Do you think they'd try to come in with you two here?"

"We don't know what they know or what they'll do."

Polly needed to be finished with small talk. "Just spit it out. What did you learn today?"

"Marla Lane is a smart woman. She's been part of the task force looking for Marcus Allendar for the last three years. They tracked him to the Midwest, which was what took her to Omaha. As soon as she saw your sketch, she drove over to Boone. This guy is scary, mostly because he uses someone else's obsession to drive him. That means that his patterns don't always establish themselves until later in the process. He allows his partner to choose the victims."

"How does he find these partners?" Polly asked. She couldn't help that she sounded breathless. Everything had been sucked out of her. "How did he find Joey?"

Ray looked down and slowly turned his face back up to look at her. "He posed as a psychiatrist. Actually, he *is* a psychiatrist. But he hasn't been able to practice legally in the last seven years. He forges documents, gets a job in a facility such as the one which housed Joey and then takes on patients. Once he finds one that is obsessive in a manner that will satisfy Allendar's needs, he helps the patient escape and they spend the next few months on a hideous spree."

Henry reached over and took Polly's hand. His warmth engulfed her and a sense of calm settled over her. "I guess they know his alias and how he got Joey out," she said.

Ray nodded.

"But that isn't important, is it?"

He shook his head.

"How bad is this going to get?"

"It could get bad unless we catch a break. Joey jumped the gun by wanting you at the beginning. Allendar usually has his partner practice until they take the person's true obsession. Then, Allendar waits until his partner kills the victim and ends that person's life."

"Joey is too crazy to be controlled by anyone," Polly said. She sat back on the sofa and put her hand on Henry's shoulder, not wanting to lose contact with him. "But since I escaped, does that mean this Allendar guy is going ahead with his normal plan?"

"We think so."

"Do I dare ask if he uses the same method of killing?"

"That's where it gets difficult. Because they kill using what the partner knows, it's never the same. We need to find the first girl's body in order to determine how she died."

"What does Allendar get out of this?" Henry asked.

"It is assumed that he likes having power and control over the two characters in his little scenario."

Henry shuddered, "Is it sexual?"

Ray shrugged. "It could be. That wouldn't surprise anyone, but it's more about controlling the partner. If it's sexual for that man, then Allendar encourages it. If it's different, Allendar encourages that."

"I just can't believe he's in the middle of Iowa," Polly said. "I mean, there's an entire country out there. What are the odds? There can't be that many serial killers, can there?"

"Actually, Polly," Ray said. "There are believed to be between thirty-five and fifty serial killers operating in the country at any given time. And that number is on the low side."

"That means anyone could be a target."

"It's not that frightening. You're right in the middle of this one, but do the math. There are three hundred million people in the United States and fifty of those are serial killers."

"But there are only fifty states. If there were one in every state..." she let out a shuddering breath. "There's one in Iowa right now and he's after me."

"I have a team flying in tomorrow night. We're going to do everything we can to protect you."

She shook her head. "What about girls who look like me?" Polly stopped. "See, that's what doesn't make sense. How is he talking Joey into accepting these other girls as substitutes? Joey knows better. He's obsessed with me, not someone who looks like me or has hair like mine."

Henry interjected, "Is this FBI agent okay with having you on the team?"

"I bring a lot to the table," Ray said with a slight smile. "We'll just leave it at that."

Polly sat forward again. "You won't let me go outside ever again until you catch these two, will you."

"Maybe," Ray said with a wan smile. "Knowing who the man is helps. It makes him less frightening to me. Now I know who I'm dealing with and he's not an amorphous scary person who could do something crazy out of the blue. We can be better prepared to protect you." He looked at her and smiled. "But I'd feel better if you never set foot outside until this was over."

"Are my friends safe?" she asked. "Has he ever focused on extended family or anything?"

"Never," Ray said, shaking his head. "Not once."

Polly let out a breath she didn't realize she'd been holding. "That makes me feel better."

"I want to make sure you do get outside once in a while, though," Ray said.

"What?" Henry demanded. "I thought you said..."

"I know what I said, but the truth is, these two aren't going to go away. We can protect Polly, but they'll keep killing and wait for us to get tired and let our guard down. Jon and I can't stay forever and Allendar has all the time in the world."

"You're going to use my wife as bait?" Henry moved forward on the sofa, his fists clenched.

Ray leaned in and said, "You have to trust that I will never let anything happen to Polly. I am more committed to her safety than anyone I've ever protected. But this siege can't continue. If they see that Polly is trying to live a normal life, they will make attempts and those attempts will expose them."

Polly slowly rubbed the palm of her hand up and down Henry's back, waiting for him to process this. She needed him to come to grips with it all so she could fall apart later.

"I don't like it," Henry said.

"I don't like any of this," Ray said agreeably. "This is the worst possible thing I could ever imagine having happen. But here we are. The best thing we can do is stay calm, think intelligently, and not lose focus."

They all jumped at a knock on the front door. Ray was up and moving before Polly and Henry registered the sound. Jon came running in from the other room.

"Ask who it is," Ray said under his breath.

Polly swallowed, stood up and walked over to the door. "Who is it?" she asked.

"Sam and Jean Gardner," came a familiar voice. "We heard you have some trouble and figured you might be stuck inside. Jean made pie."

Polly grinned. The universe just laughed at her some days.

"Can I open it? They're friends from down the street."

Ray nodded slowly. He took a position on one side of the door and Jon stood behind Polly as she unlocked and opened the door.

"Come on in," she said. "Thank you. You're wonderful."

Sam came in the door and turned to look at Ray who was doing his best to not look menacing. He glanced at Jon and then at Henry, still on the sofa. "Did we interrupt something?"

Jean pushed her husband on in and after putting a basket on the floor, wrapped her arms around Polly. "We would have been here earlier, but Sam thought you might be nervous about having people just show up. I told him he was being preposterous, but I didn't want to wait any longer than today to tell you how worried we've been. Sam's been working with Eliseo in the garden, so we know a little of the story."

She let Polly go, picked up the basket and pushed her husband forward another step. "Let's take this into the kitchen. We brought enough food for everyone for tonight. I know how much you like my barbecue pork, so I made up a big pot of that. Sam bought what he always buys, which means you have plenty of ice cream to go with these pies. I made a strawberry rhubarb and everybody's favorite." She looked at Jon. "Your favorite is apple, isn't it? I can always tell an apple pie lover when I see him."

Ray's eyes had grown big once she started. He checked the area outside the front door, then closed and locked the door.

Polly helplessly followed the Gardners into the kitchen, watching as Jean unpacked the basket and two bags that Sam carried.

"Hi there, kids," she said to Andrew and Kayla. "I knew there would be at least a few of you here today, so I made something special for you, too." She took a plastic container out of the basket and put it into the freezer. "Those are homemade strawberry popsicles whenever Polly tells you that you can have one."

She looked around the room. "Where's your Rebecca? I know she loves strawberries. That's okay. She can have one later. Sam, where's that ice cream? We need to put it into the freezer right away. Polly has plenty of room in there." She winked at Polly. "I guess Henry hasn't been out buying ice cream sandwiches for you lately. If I'd known that, Sam could have picked some up."

Sam Gardner handed her two containers of ice cream and she caught sight of the brownies on the counter. "Ice cream and brownies will work just as well as ice cream sandwiches. You're all set."

"Jean," Polly interrupted. "You didn't have to do this."

"Yes she did," Sam said. "She's been a wreck all week, thinking about you and not feeling like she could just bust in to take care of you. It was easier for me to let her take a walk today. We knew the place would be unlocked with that wedding happening downstairs."

He handed his wife the bag the ice cream had come in and turned to walk out of the room. "She wears me out," he said before leaving.

Henry, Ray and Jon had all been standing in the doorway to the living room and when Sam walked toward them, they split apart to let him through.

"Do you need anything?" Henry asked Polly.

"No, we're fine here," she responded. "Go ahead."

He nodded and left the room.

"Okay," Jean whispered. "Who are those gorgeous young men? Are they your bodyguards? I'm sorry I was so wild when I walked in, but they surprised me."

"They're actually old friends from Boston. Their sister is one of my best friends. They're Italian and I'm part of the family, I guess. At least that's what their mama believes."

"But they're here to keep an eye on you, right? Because that old boyfriend of yours has lost his mind?"

Polly knew that whatever was said from this point forward would quickly make it into Bellingwood's gossip mill. "Yes, they are. When Drea, that's their sister, found out what had happened, she told them to get on a plane and come take care of me."

Jean nudged Polly. "It doesn't hurt that they're so pretty. Did you ever date either of them?"

Polly laughed. "Nope. Drea wouldn't let me. They're like brothers to me."

"Not that Henry Sturtz isn't a catch, but zowie." Jean put her hand on her heart.

"I know!" Polly said. "I've often said something just like that about those two boys. Will you stay for a while?"

"We won't take up too much of your time. Sam wanted to talk to Henry about redoing our kitchen cabinets. After thirty years it's time to update that room. And I wanted to make sure you weren't stuck inside with nobody to talk to but your husband and kids." She turned back to the basket and pulled more containers out. "These are cheap containers, so don't try to get them back to me. And if you run out of anything and want more, all you have to do is call."

She put the first into the refrigerator and said, "You know, if you need us to do anything, you should call me. We can make a trip to the grocery store or drive down to Boone and pick things up for you. Please let us know how we can help."

"Thank you so much, Jean," Polly said. "It's hard to know what to ask for, especially when I'm so used to doing things without thinking about it."

"There are people in town who want you to know that they're worried. I heard talk of some of the men who said they'd be glad to set up surveillance around Sycamore House so you felt safe. Nobody's done anything about it yet, but if this horrible mess keeps up much longer, they're going to take it into their own hands."

Polly felt tears threaten. "You're kidding me, right?"

"I'm not kidding you at all. Do you know how many families have had weddings here or have come to your parties or for meetings and groups? Nobody messes with us or our family and you're part of the family. And the Sturtzes have been in town a long time. Henry and his dad have worked on a lot of homes and businesses in town. You two have touched people."

"I don't even know what to say to that. I'm a little blown away."

"We'd do it for anyone, you know. But you're important to this town." Jean Gardner finished emptying the basket and folded up the grocery tote bags and stuffed them inside. "We should get out of your hair."

"Won't you have pie with us?"

Jean pointed to the brownies on the counter. "It looks like you just had dessert."

"That's been hours ago. If the kids don't want pie, they can have a popsicle or another brownie. Please stay?"

"Well..."

"The knives are in that drawer," Polly pointed, "and the pie server is in the drawer right next to it. I'll get the men and we can eat here in the dining room. I'm sure Jon and Ray would love to have pie with us."

Jon had walked in as she said the last and turned back to speak to the men in the living room. "It's okay. You're staying and we get to eat now."

The other three men came in to the dining room. Henry went into the kitchen and took down plates while Polly went into the media room to talk to Andrew and Kayla.

"You two can join us if you like," she said. "It looks like we're going to have a party."

Andrew jumped up and ran to the dining room, slipping in to sit between Ray and Jon.

"He's really nice," Kayla said.

"Who is?" Polly asked.

"Your friend, Jon. He doesn't talk to me like I'm a little girl."

"He's a good guy."

"I'm glad he's here to take care of you."

"Me too."

CHAPTER THIRTEEN

"Doing okay?" Jeff asked when Polly walked into his office on Monday morning.

"I'm fine," she said flatly.

"You don't sound fine."

She dropped into a chair in front of his desk. "No, I'm fine. Anything else and it just makes me sound like a whiner."

He tapped his computer screen. "I see we have new guests out at the Inn. You checked them in last night?"

"Yeah. More bodyguards for me. Aren't I lucky?"

"More?"

With all that had been going on, Polly realized he hadn't been around for the revelations that had occurred over the weekend, so she explained about Joey and the serial killer and that Jon and Ray were here to protect her. He took most of it in without reacting. Even the fact that she had a serial killer stalking her.

Finally, she had to ask. "Why are you so calm about this?"

He gave a shrug. "What am I supposed to do?"

"Gasp? Clutch your chest? Threaten to leave or run away? I don't know. Something."

"I can't fix it," he said. "I'm helpless to help you. And all of this information you're telling me is a couple of days old. I figure you and Henry are probably panicked enough for all of us. If you tell me what I can do to help, I'll drop everything and do it."

She stuck her lower lip out. "You're getting used to my shenanigans, aren't you?"

"No, I wouldn't say that. But I have to assume that everyone is doing all that they can to take care of this. If you tell me that we need to shut this place down to keep you safe, I'll do that right now. Do I need to be worried about any of our employees or guests?"

"They tell me no," she said, shaking her head. "Joey and his partner are focused on me or girls who look like me. There isn't any history of attacking family or friends."

"Then we're safe, right?"

"I think so."

Lisa Bradford, the mail carrier, poked her head in. "Hello, Polly," she said. "Are you doing okay this morning?"

Polly turned. "Hi Lisa, I'm good."

"We want you to know that if there's anything we can do, we will. Folks up town are talking about what they can do for you until this crazy man is caught. If you need anything, just let us know. Even if it's having some of our good old boys drive around in their trucks looking tough."

"That's so nice."

"It's no big thing. You live in a small town. Everybody's paying attention to everything."

"I think for now, just keep an eye out. Has Aaron handed out pictures yet? He was going to do that."

"I saw one at the post office before I left this morning."

Polly smiled. "That's all I know to do now."

Lisa put her hand on Polly's shoulder. "You do a lot for us. Even for my daughter. Melissa isn't too happy that today is her last day here."

"That's right," Polly said. "This is the last week of school. Isn't she having a party for the kids?"

"She sure is. I'll be back to help out." She patted Polly and said, "So I'd better get going if I'm going to be finished in time. Remember, let us know. That's not an empty offer. Okay?"

"Thank you," Polly said.

"They're good people," Jeff said after Lisa had left.

"I don't know if that guy and Joey know what they've gotten themselves into. They thrive on secrecy and fear, but get a bunch of Iowa small town boys involved? They don't have a chance."

He grinned. "Especially if their pictures are out there. These boys ... and girls ... will be on the lookout."

"I hope they find something soon. There's a girl out there who is being held by them and another one who has been killed. No one is able to find them. Or my truck." Polly knew she sounded frustrated. She was frustrated. "You'd think it would be hard to hide a truck, but Aaron doesn't even know where to look. It's like they've disappeared. And they aren't sticking to one area. One of the pictures sent to me was taken down by Luther, one of the girls was kidnapped from Des Moines, and the postmark on the letter was from Boone. Who knows where they're hiding."

Jeff nodded. "There are plenty of places they can hide, that's for sure. We have everything from river valleys to abandoned farmsteads to city anonymity."

"They just need these guys to make one mistake."

"At least they made their first mistake by not tying you down," Jeff said.

"You're right," she agreed. "One more mistake."

Jeff looked around and said, "So, where are your bodyguards this morning?"

"Who knows," Polly said with a snarl, then she took a breath. "I'm sorry. I'm just in a bad mood. I'm tired of having people in my space who aren't my family. I love Jon and Ray, but they're only here because I'm in trouble. And I don't know how long they'll be able to stay. They brought in two more people that I don't know and now they'll be all up in my face. I can't just go hang out with my friends when I want to. I haven't seen Joss's babies for a week. I can't drop in at Henry's work to see Jessie and

Molly." She frowned at him. "And I didn't get to have pizza with the girls last night. That just sucks."

He laughed. "That's what this is all about, isn't it? You do that every Sunday night."

"Yes we do and they went without me last night."

"Those horrible girls," he said mockingly. "They didn't!"

"They didn't want to, but I told them they should anyway. Sal offered to bring me pizza, but it's not about the food. I like getting out of the house. But what? I was going to take two bodyguards along with me to girl's night?"

"I'm guessing the girls wouldn't mind so much," Jeff said with a chuckle.

Polly draped herself over the front of his desk. "I'm so tired of this. I'm up again and down again. My emotions are all over the place. Sometimes I'm totally fine with being safe here and the next minute I'm all depressed because I'm cooped up. You should probably just send me back up to the apartment so I'll quit complaining on you."

"It is tedious," he said.

Polly looked at his face, trying to decide whether he was serious or not. When she couldn't get a read on him, she said, "I'm sorry! I'm pathetic."

He laughed. "I was kidding. Stop worrying. Just do what you do and quit beating yourself up. This will end, Polly."

"I don't know," she said, slumping back in her chair.

"It's been one week. One..." He held up his index finger. "Week. How many weeks have passed since the beginning of the year?"

"I don't know," she grumped. She knew where he was going with this.

"How many weeks did it take to finish Sycamore House?"

"I don't know."

"How many weeks..."

"Yeah, yeah, yeah. I get it. Time passes, I'm being ridiculous." She stood up and brushed a stack of papers he had on the corner of his desk toward him. "There. I feel better. I'm going to my office to sulk by myself."

Jeff stood up and grabbed his coffee mug. "I'm going to the kitchen for Sylvie's good stuff. You want I should bring you some?"

"Yes," she said with a pout, ignoring his awful grammar. "Caffeine will help."

He gave her a push into her office and asked Stephanie if she wanted anything from the kitchen. The girl pushed her chair back and followed him out.

Polly sat down and looked at the stack of mail that Stephanie had put in the middle of her desk. She didn't want to look through it, just in case there was another letter from Joey. Steeling herself, Polly did a quick flip through the stack and when nothing jumped out at her, breathed a sigh of relief and finished sorting.

Jeff put a cup of coffee down on her desk. "Everything okay?"

"I think so." Polly reached over and pulled the coffee close, breathing in its scent. "I have to get out of here today. I'm becoming paranoid. All of my sensibilities have lost their mind."

"That would probably make them happy, you know," Jeff said. "I mean, I'm no expert in psychology, but if this is all about power, you can't give it to them."

Polly glowered at him. "Stop being so smart."

"Hey," he said. "This place should be hopping this afternoon. The kids are coming over and I think Melissa has a big afternoon planned. She's done great this semester."

Melissa Bradford had been successful with the Monday afterschool program they'd started at Sycamore House for kids to wait for their working parents. It had taken a while for it to catch on, but thirty-five elementary age kids showed up every week.

Joss had assured Polly and Jeff that the library had never had that many kids on Mondays, but the allure of horses and donkeys and Sylvie's snacks had been too much. As far as Polly was concerned, every single child attending elementary school in Bellingwood was welcome. If she could figure out a way to open the place up every afternoon, she'd do it.

Jeff didn't think that was a good idea. He wasn't prepared to be responsible for the problems that came with daily interaction with kids. She knew he was right, but it didn't stop her from dreaming.

A large truck pulled up outside the front door and Jeff jumped up. "I've got this," he said.

"What's going on?" Polly followed him out of the office.

"Don't you dare give me any trouble." He wagged a finger at her.

"Why would I..." When Jeff opened the door, she read the company name on the side of the truck.

"You're having a carnival," she said, accusingly. "You *like* hosting these kids."

"It's just a couple of bounce houses and games. Melissa did all the work and got donations to cover prizes and eighty-five percent of the activities. She's the one who rounded up volunteers and talked parents into being here this afternoon to help set up."

Polly was surprised. "She really dug in for this."

"Yes she did," Jeff said. "Now go back into your office so I can deal with these young men."

She sighed and turned, then wondered where her trusty bodyguards were. It wasn't like them to leave her alone this long. It had felt like she'd had someone in her face every hour she wasn't asleep this weekend. Whenever she came out of her bedroom, either Jon or Ray was watching television or reading.

Last night they'd introduced her to the new team members before getting them settled at Sycamore Inn. The two women were as different as they could be. Tonya was black, tall and slender, while Gerry - short for Geraldine, she said - was a stocky redhead.

Since most of Bellingwood knew Polly needed protection, they hadn't bothered coming up with a cover story for the newcomers. They would drop into Polly's life and stay until this was finished.

Last night after the new team had been safely ensconced in their rooms at the hotel, Polly finally pulled Ray off to the side to talk to him about the cost of this protection. She knew it had to be expensive. It was one thing to lean on a couple of old friends, but bringing in a specialized team was entirely different.

Ray had been offended. Polly had been insistent. Ray tried to blow her off. Polly wasn't going anywhere until he talked to her.

He finally told her that having his team come in wasn't cheap, but she wasn't to worry about it. The company made more than enough money, that when a friend needed help, no one would even flinch.

When Ray told Polly he believed this would be over within the week, she realized that didn't surprise her. One way or another, this was going to come to a head. Joey didn't have the wherewithal to do anything long term. She knew deep down that killing wasn't part of his personality and if Marcus Allendar was forcing Joey to do the actual dirty work, the man she knew would break.

"Miss Giller?" Polly turned to see Tonya standing in her doorway.

"Hi," she said. "Anything I can do for you?"

"I was just wondering what was good in town for lunch," Tonya asked. "Or do you usually eat here?"

"Joe's Diner is great," Polly said. "Or Davey's if you want to stay in town. There's a new Mexican place. Comida Mexicana, if you like that. I can find something here."

"No," said Tanya. "Let's go. You and me and Gerry. Ray says you've been stuck inside and that's ridiculous."

"Really?" Polly jumped up and pushed her chair in under the desk. "I'd love to go out."

"Do you want to walk your dogs first? As long as you don't leave the property, I'm all for that."

"Are you teasing me?" Polly wasn't sure whether to laugh or cry.

Tanya chuckled. "There are four of us here to protect you now. I think we can give you a little freedom. As long as one of us is with you and you don't run off on your own, this will be easy."

"I want to hug you," Polly said. "All of you. I'll be good. I won't run away. I'll stick close. I'll do whatever you tell me to do, as long as you let me live a normal life."

"Normal it is," Tanya said. "What do you want to do first?"

"I want to take my dogs for a walk." Polly looked at the time. "This is perfect. Then I want to call my friend Sal and ask her to meet us at the diner for lunch. And then I want to go over to where my husband is working and see what they're doing."

"Gerry will meet us at the diner in, say, twenty minutes?" Tonya said. "Will that be enough time?"

"Seriously. Hugging you," Polly said and grinned when Tanya backed up. "Okay, hugging you from afar. You made my day!"

She stopped at Stephanie's desk and the girl looked up at her with a big smile. "You're leaving us for a while?"

"It's the best thing ever!" Polly said. "I don't know when I'll be back."

"Have fun."

"Come on," Polly said to Tanya. "I'll introduce you to my animals."

While she stood outside in her back yard watching Han and Obiwan chase each other and play, Polly drew in a huge, deep breath, savoring the smell of freshly cut grass. Then she took out her phone and swiped a call to Sal.

"How're ya doing?" Sal asked. "Are those gorgeous boys still hanging out in your space?"

"They are and they brought in reinforcements. But Sal, they're letting me escape today. Can you meet me for lunch in fifteen minutes at the diner? I get to go out!"

"Well..." Sal hesitated.

"No," Polly said. "I don't care if you've already eaten. I don't care if you're in the middle of the best paragraph you've ever written. I don't even care if you haven't taken a shower. You have to come have lunch with me. Please!"

"I can do a shower in five minutes," Sal said. "How did you know?"

"Because I know you. Please?"

"Fine. I might be a few minutes late. Order an iced tea for me and I just want a cheeseburger with fries. I need to put the dogs outside and then I'll be on my way."

"I'm outside with my dogs right now," Polly said. "It's the best day ever. I can't wait to see you."

"Honey, it hasn't been that long."

"Stop talking to me and go take your shower. I will not be denied!"

"You are bossy."

Polly ended the call and looked up, wondering where the rest of the team was hiding. She assumed they had to be close. She still wondered where Jon and Ray had gone. Maybe they were tired of her, too. She'd been awfully whiny lately. Anybody could be tired of that.

"Come on, boys," she called out to Obiwan and Han. "Do your thing and let's go in."

Obiwan trotted over to stand beside her and she whistled for Han. He looked up from the tree he'd been sniffing, gave it a quick soaking and ran to join them.

Tanya was driving a silver Taurus and she pulled around to the garage to pick Polly up. Even though it was just a few blocks to the diner, she insisted they take the car. She parked and they walked across the street to the diner. Polly nearly fainted with joy at the familiar scents and sounds when she opened the door. It had only been a week, but she was beginning to wonder if she would ever get out of Sycamore House again.

Lucy smiled and bumped her as she walked past with a large tray filled with plates. She nodded her head toward the side where Gerry was already seated at a table. She and Tanya joined the young woman.

"This is great," Gerry said. "I love small-town diners." She turned to her teammate. "We need to take more jobs in small towns. I could get used to this."

"There's no gym. You'd beef up and be no good to us."

Gerry gave her friend a look. "You're a horrid person, saying that to me."

"Hey. You're the one who's always complaining about every little ounce."

"I do not."

Polly watched the two of them banter as they looked over the menu. She already knew what she was ordering. It was her favorite thing and she was having it.

Lucy stopped in front of their table and said, "Water? Pop? Coffee?"

"Sal's joining us. I have her order, too," Polly said. "Dew for me. Tea for her."

They both looked at Gerry and Tanya. "Water's good here," Tanya said and Gerry nodded in agreement. Tanya continued, "But we're going to need a few more minutes. She's trying to decide whether to enjoy herself or be good."

"Oh girls," Lucy said. "I wave out all the calories as I walk the food out to you. Don't worry about that."

Gerry finally gave in and ordered a patty melt and Lucy left after taking the rest of the orders.

"This is what I'm talking about," Gerry said, sitting back in her seat and stretching her legs out to the side. "Things are just nicer in small towns. People move slower and nothing much gets to them."

Polly thought about it. It had been nearly three years since she'd left Boston. She'd forgotten how insane the pace of life could get in the city. There was no time to ever stop and just be at peace. She hoped she never took this for granted again.

CHAPTER FOURTEEN

"Eventually they'll have to stop peering over at us," Gerry said.

Since Polly had her back to the rest of the diner, she couldn't turn and look, but she knew what was happening. "They're trying to figure out how you're related to me. Are you my bodyguards? Maybe friends they haven't met yet. Or maybe I'm entertaining business guests."

"You should put on your best 'I'm a Marine' look," Tonya said. "That'll scare 'em."

"I don't think so," Gerry said, glancing around. "Some of these boys, hell, some of the women don't look like they'd scare too easily."

Lucy came back and Sal dropped into the fourth chair as she set the last drink on the table.

"The place is checking you girls out," Sal said. "No one paid any attention when I walked in."

"That's different," Lucy said with a laugh.

"You might as well tell them that these are my bodyguards," Polly said with a smile. "At least then everyone can relax and eat."

Lucy put her hand on Polly's shoulders. "I'm so sorry about

what happened to you. I should have called to see if you needed anything, but I figured you had plenty of folks taking care of you." She looked at Gerry. "You're really bodyguards?"

"We are this week," Gerry replied. She put her hand out to Sal, "Gerry Moberly and this is Tonya Adkins."

"Sal Kahane."

"We're glad you girls are here, then," Lucy said. "Folks have been wondering what we can do. They're scared about a serial killer in the area, but Chief Wallers says his focus is on Polly and the rest of us are safe. Is that true?"

Tonya looked up and winked, "It's true. No worries. And as long as we keep an eye on Miss Giller, hopefully that will give law enforcement time to find these fellows and lock them up."

"You girls come on in any time. We'll fix you up," Lucy said. "My name is Lucy. Let me know if you need anything. We're glad you're here taking care of this one. She's some of our biggest entertainment." With a laugh, she walked away and stopped at another table.

"Entertainment?" Tonya asked Polly.

Sal interrupted. "She finds dead bodies. It's kind of her thing. What's your count now, girlfriend?"

"Shut up," Polly said, deadpan. "Not talking about it."

"Are you serious?" Gerry asked, leaning in toward Sal.

"Yes I am. The local police haven't found a single dead body since she moved in. Polly's done it all. From what I understand there used to be a pool down at the Elevator about who she'd find next. Your husband won it once, didn't he?"

"Seriously," Polly said. "Shut up." She chuckled. "You're a brat."

"Do Ray and Jon know about this?" Gerry asked.

Polly shook her head in mock disgust. "Yes. But they've known me for a long time. Their sister is one of my friends."

"That makes sense," Tonya said. "You're *that* friend of Drea's."

"I'm what friend?"

"This guy with the serial killer - he's the one you kicked in the balls after Ray dropped him at the airport." Tonya chuckled. "That was awesome. Ray was so proud of you."

"He talked about it?"

"Yeah. You're kind of a hero to him. You didn't panic, you didn't lose your head, you just did what you had to do and then let them take care of things. When it was over, you unleashed hell on the poor guy. You'd be great in law enforcement."

"Don't let Sheriff Merritt or Chief Wallers hear you say anything like that," Polly said with a laugh. "I stress them out."

"From what I heard, you handled yourself well last week, too," Gerry said.

She was going to say something else, but Lucy came up behind Polly and began putting plates on the table.

Lucy pulled a ketchup bottle out of her apron pocket and looked around the table, "Anything else?" she asked.

Everyone shook their head in the negative and she said, "Your check's been paid for today. Don't worry about it."

Polly looked up at her. "Who did that?"

"I can't say, but I wasn't joking when I said that you should stop in any time while you girls are in town. It's been covered. Come in for pie or coffee, breakfast or lunch. We've got your backs, okay?"

Polly nodded and turned back to her plate. She looked down quickly so no one could see that she had tears in her eyes. It took a few moments for her to choke back a sob.

Sal saw what was happening, though and said, "Thank you, Lucy. And tell whoever has done this, thanks. It means a lot."

"That's pretty cool," Gerry said quietly. "Who *does* this?"

"Small town Iowa, that's who," Sal responded. "I haven't been able to get used to it yet."

Tonya shook her head. "It just can't be real."

"They're as normal as everyone else," Sal said. "There are mean, nasty people here and some are selfish and stingy. Mark and I've talked about this. He's from Minneapolis and I'm from Boston." She chuckled. "We believe that because people here actually have room to breathe, it's easier to be nice."

"Are you okay over there?" Gerry asked Polly, taking a bite of her patty melt. "I hope so, because I need to concentrate on this sandwich. This is a taste of heaven. I can't eat here every day. It will kill me."

Polly looked up and smiled. "You know, probably one person said he'd get our meal today and then someone else chimed in and then someone else. I think for me it's all about seeing the best in people and letting that be what you know about them. The rest doesn't have to be the most important thing."

"But a whole town of that?" Gerry asked.

"The whole town isn't like that all of the time. Just Polly," Sal said. "She doesn't let them get to her."

"Yeah I do," Polly said. "Henry has to hear me complain when we're alone at night. But, for the most part, it's a good place to live. And I know that people want to do the right thing. If you give them the opportunity, they will."

"And she's always giving them the opportunity," Sal said.

Polly picked her tenderloin up and bit part of the breaded loin that was hanging over the side of the bun. She chewed it until she could speak and said, "I'm not supposed to talk with my mouth full, so I'm going to eat. You shut up."

~~~

Gerry left the restaurant before Polly and Tonya, who were heading to the coffee shop with Sal. She wanted to see what Polly thought of the work that had been completed.

Henry and his crew had gutted the entire main level and started from scratch. Cabinets and bookcases were in place, the floor was finished and the interior was really shaping up. It felt like they could be ready to go any time.

Sal was quite proud and even though she complained about not having time to write, she spent day after day in the shop, watching the guys work and talking to people from Bellingwood as they came by to check things out.

It had given her a new outlook on the community and Polly wasn't at all surprised to find that she was beginning to do more and more of her shopping in town. People recognized Sal and she knew their names. It was surprising when Sal introduced the owner of the new Mexican restaurant to Polly a few weeks ago.

Polly, Sal, and Tonya walked in the front door. A man Polly didn't recognize, who was working on framing the window into the kitchen, gave a wolf whistle.

Henry snapped, "Dale, that's my wife."

"You can't have all three of them," the man said.

"I'm not kidding, Dale. Be respectful." Henry walked over to them and hugged Polly, then shook hands with Tonya and Sal. "What are you three doing?" he asked.

Polly was brimming with excitement. "I'm free," she said. "I just ate at the diner and now I'm here."

He chuckled. "You look happier. I'm glad you're out. Do you want to see what we've got going on this week?"

"You have no idea how much," she said.

"We've been working on the counters and cabinets in the kitchen. Come on back."

They followed him through the main room and into the kitchen. The cabinets weren't much more than boxes hanging on the walls, but the room was beginning to take shape.

"This is great," Polly said. "I'm beginning to see it finally come alive. When do you think the bar will be done for the coffee shop?"

"Dad and Len are working on that right now. Len said they might be able to install it this week."

Polly tugged on Sal's sleeve. "We're going to have to start buying those tables now. We still have room in the storage unit where we're holding the bakery equipment."

"I saw two tables that I want over at the antique store," Sal said. "He told me that he'd let me have them for a steal since they're coming here. He also said that he'd keep an eye out for chairs."

"He's a good guy," Polly said. "That's a great connection."

"What else are you doing today?" Henry asked.

Sal shook her head. "I have to work this afternoon." She looked at her phone. "And the dogs are probably wondering why I'm not home yet. I should go."

Polly hugged her. "Thank you for meeting me for lunch."

"I wouldn't have missed your debut outing! Welcome back to the world," Sal said with a laugh. She shook Tonya's hand. "It was nice meeting you. Take care of our girl."

Tonya nodded and smiled.

"Well?" Henry asked.

"I don't know," Polly said. "I thought we could drive around. I'd like to see what's going on with the old school in Luther. I still have trouble believing they tore it down."

Henry nodded. "You did a good thing with Sycamore House."

"You know Steve talked to me about that school building, too," Polly said. "It was cheap to buy, but would have been a bear to bring back to code."

"And you never would have met me." Henry leaned in and kissed her cheek. "You go enjoy your freedom and I'll see you tonight."

Tonya and Polly stepped back out into the main room and Tonya stopped. "Let me make a quick call before we leave," she said. She stepped away from Polly and spoke into her phone for a moment and then came back.

"We're good to go."

"Am I screwing things up by leaving town?" Polly asked.

"Nope. That's okay. I just needed to let Ray know what we're doing. You're fine."

"What made you want to go to Luther?" Tonya asked, once they were in the car. "Is this what you do all the time?" She tapped through the GPS system and programmed it for their destination.

Polly shook her head, "No, I watched the old building come down earlier this year and from what I hear, new construction is supposed to be starting now."

"What's going in there?"

"You won't even believe it," Polly said with a laugh.

"Why?"

"It's called Portable Pro Iowa."

"What's so funny about that?"

"Porta potties."

"I guess someone has to do it," Tonya said and laughed. "But you never think about that." She gave a quick shudder. "I'm glad I'm not in that business. Can you even imagine what they deal with?"

"Not thinking about it," Polly said, waving her hands in front of her face. "I'm not thinking about it at all."

Even though the GPS was leading them, Polly pointed Tonya through a couple of shortcuts around Boone and soon they were driving into the tiny town of Luther. The lot where the school had once stood was cleared and flattened.

"What are the Ledges?" Tonya asked, pointing to a sign.

"A state park. It's difficult getting in and out when things are flooded, but it's pretty cool. There are some Native American mounds there." Polly pulled up information on her phone and said, "Yeah. Like 4,000 year old archeology. Oh!" she said. "It was the first state park in Iowa. I guess I didn't know that."

The road they'd used through Luther wound round and round as they wove their way back toward Boone and Tonya turned into the park.

"It would make sense for Joey and Allendar to have found their way in here," Polly said quietly.

"But didn't the Sheriff and his men go through this place?"

Polly swept her arm in front of her. "Look around," she said. "They aren't stupid enough to have stayed out in the open. They could have tucked away."

"I certainly hope not. That's the last thing we need to find. Maybe I should turn around." Tonya pulled into a parking space and put the car into reverse and Polly stopped her.

"What?" Tonya asked.

Polly pointed ahead of them in the trees.

"What am I looking at?" Tonya asked again.

Polly took a deep breath, shut her eyes and reached for the car door. Tonya grabbed her arm and said, "What in the hell are you doing?"

"It's the girl who was killed. I'm almost sure of it. Why else am I freaking here today!" Polly's voice rose as she spoke.

Tonya peered in the direction Polly had pointed "Are you sure?"

"Of course I am," Polly said with disgust. "It's what I do." She sighed and dropped her head. "I have to call Aaron. He just won't believe this."

"I don't want to let you go look," Tonya said.

"I don't want to go look." Polly turned to the girl. "And besides, Aaron would pulverize us both if we messed up the scene and Ray would be furious if I got too close."

Tonya snapped the lock down on the car door again and said, "Make your call. Can you tell them how to get in here?"

"Sure," Polly said, nodding. She swiped her phone open and made the call to Aaron Merritt's cell phone.

"Good afternoon, Polly," he said brightly. "How are you this fine Monday afternoon?"

"Well..." she said.

"Nope. You can't be calling me about a body because you're safe at Sycamore House with bodyguards everywhere."

"Well."

"Polly Giller, you have got to be kidding me." He sounded angry. "How in the hell did you get out and about?"

"I'm with Tonya. I'm safe."

Tonya chuckled and pointed at the back window. Polly turned and saw Gerry pull in beside them.

"Apparently I'm safe. The rest of the crew has found me, too."

"So why are you calling me?"

"Because I found her."

He let out a strained chuckle. "Of course you did. Are you sure?"

"No. I'm not absolutely sure, but why the hell else do you think I'm here at the Ledges showing Tonya the sights? For my health?"

"Stu and I will be right there. Don't get out of your car. Don't approach the body. Don't mess things up."

"I know, I know. We'll be good."

Gerry got out of her vehicle and tapped on Polly's window. "What's up?" she mouthed.

Polly pointed to the phone in her ear and rolled down the window while she described their location to Aaron. He was less than ten minutes away, and she had no place else to go. When she put the phone in her lap, Tonya leaned across her and said, "She found the body."

"What?"

Polly pointed to where she could just see the body of the young girl tied to a tree. It was far enough off in the distance and at such an angle that someone would have to be looking for it, but she was certain.

"Just a second," Gerry said and went back to her car. She returned with two pairs of binoculars and handed one set to Polly.

Polly brought them to her eyes and focused, then handed them to Tonya. "Damn it," she said. "What is up with me?"

"I don't understand," Tonya said.

"This is what Sal was talking about at lunch," Polly said with disgust.

"I heard her say the words," Gerry said, "but I guess I didn't understand."

"I find dead bodies. Since I've moved into Bellingwood, it's been my thing. If someone has died a suspicious death or something strange happened around a death, I find the body," Polly said, rolling her eyes.

Gerry leaned on the window sill of the door. "You're not kidding?"

Polly shook her head in disgust. "Why does this have to be my super power?"

"I've never heard of anything like this," Tonya said, looking through the binoculars again.

Polly raised her eyebrows. "Just ask the Sheriff. He won't be at all surprised to find her here. In fact, he'll probably be relieved. Even if he is going to be mad that I walked into it."

"You haven't walked anywhere," Tonya said. "Remember?"

"I almost did. It just seemed like the right thing to do. I can't believe we have to leave her there until everyone arrives. The poor girl needs some dignity," Polly said.

Gerry nodded and reached in to pat Polly's shoulder. "Honey, I think you just gave it to her. If this is all true and you had to be the one to find her, at least it finally happened and her family can be at peace."

"I suppose." Polly reached for the car door as Gerry looked up. "Do you mind if I get out of the car now? I should be safe enough, don't you think?"

Gerry stepped back and Polly climbed out, then they followed her as she approached Aaron Merritt's SUV.

"Where is she?" he asked, stepping out and to Polly's side.

Tonya handed him the binoculars and he followed Polly's finger. He brought his other hand up and rubbed it across his forehead, dropping the hand with the binoculars back down at his side. "That's her."

Stu Decker joined them and Aaron handed the field glasses across and pointed. "I don't want our people to go anywhere on this land until DCI gets here," Aaron said. "We don't need to make a mess of this for them. She can wait a little longer so we make sure everything is done right."

Nodding, Stu handed the glasses back to Aaron, who passed them to Tonya. Stu gave Polly a weak grin and went back to his vehicle.

"I should have known," Aaron said.

"You should have known what?" Polly asked.

"I needed you out and about. I don't know why I even thought I could do this without you. The universe has spoken."

"Do you actually believe that?" Gerry asked the Sheriff.

"I've been around long enough to recognize when things are beyond my control," Aaron said. "Our Polly is so far beyond my control that I just hope for the best and pray she lives through it. I don't know why the good Lord decided to plant her in Bellingwood. Whether it was to make my life easier or more difficult ... I don't know, but I've given up trying to second guess it. It is what it is and I answer the phone when she calls."

Gerry grinned at Polly and asked, "What does your husband think about this?"

"He's as pragmatic as anyone," Polly said. "He worries, but at least he hasn't started drinking."

Aaron smiled at her. "Why don't you three get out of here. You don't want to be caught up in the traffic that's about to arrive. Tell me that none of you left the parking lot."

Tonya shook her head. "No sir. Just our cars and now here."

"Okay. Take off. Polly, you should drive them through Dairy Queen and get ice cream. Isn't that your usual fix for stress?"

"You're a rat," she said. "But I'm not stressed. I guess I'm relieved that she's been found. That was breaking my heart. I feel sad and guilty that she was killed, though. No one should have had to go through that. I feel like it's my fault."

Aaron started to speak and she held up her hand. "I know. In my head I know that it's Joey and this Allendar guy, but my heart aches knowing that it's Joey's obsession with me that caused this."

He pulled her into a hug. "This is why we love you, Polly. Now go treat your friends to ice cream and we'll take care of this."

She nodded. "Thanks for trusting me, Aaron."

"Always, honey."

CHAPTER FIFTEEN

Polly was certain that she'd pushed Tonya over the edge. The ride back to Bellingwood was silent. Every once in a while, the girl would sneak a quick glance at her, but Polly figured Tonya was just checking to make sure there wasn't a third eye coming out of Polly's forehead or maybe wings sprouting from her shoulders.

What she wanted to do was yell, "Boo," but the fear that Tonya would drive into a ditch stopped her. Just as they turned east on the Bellingwood road, Polly finally gave up.

"I really am normal," she said.

"What?" Tonya asked, surprised.

"I'm normal. Everything else about me is as normal as can be."

"Except that you find dead bodies. Doesn't that creep you out?"

Polly shrugged. "It should, but they need to be found and if anyone has to, it might as well be me. Keep the scary, icky stuff all contained to one small package."

"You're really pragmatic about it," Tonya said. She still wasn't smiling, but at least she was engaged again.

"What else am I supposed to do?" Polly asked and pointed to the driveway leading to her garage.

Tonya turned in and pulled into a parking space. "I think I'd be more freaked out every time it happened."

"But each time, it's just what has happened. Until today, I didn't go looking for someone."

Tonya turned the car off and then looked straight at Polly. "Did you set me up? Did you know you were going to find her?"

"No, that's not it," Polly said, pursing her lips in thought. "It's not that I knew I'd find her, but that I had to find her. There wasn't any plan. I promise."

Tonya didn't look convinced.

Polly put her hand on Tonya's arm. "I promise. I did want to see where the old school in Luther had been. It's been a while since I've driven past there and I know they've been working on that space. Remember, though, you're the one who asked about The Ledges."

"I guess I did." Tonya shook her head. "Now I'm confused."

"You know, I've lived in Bellingwood for nearly three years now and all this time everyone is surprised when I find another body. I don't much like it, but I was never surprised by the whole thing. And maybe now, I've just come to accept that this is part of the deal."

"The deal?"

"You know. The tradeoff for me living in paradise. If I'm going to be this crazy happy, I need to pay my dues. They aren't bad dues ... it's just what I need to do." She giggled. "Do, do, do, do, do. Whatever."

"The middle of Iowa. Paradise. Who'd have thought it," Tonya said. She pointed to Polly's window. "Heads up."

Polly looked and saw Gerry standing there. "She snuck up on me."

"She's just checking to make sure it's safe for you to get out of the car."

"This is crazy. I feel like the President with his Secret Service agents."

"We're better," Tonya said with a smile. "They'd like to be as good as we are."

Gerry opened the door for Polly. "We're polite too," she said.

"You heard all that?"

She tapped her ear.

"You *are* like the Secret Service," Polly said. She walked toward the back door. "Now, here comes the dicey part."

"What's that?" Gerry asked, opening the door.

"Telling Henry what I just did. He tries hard to understand that this is part of me, but it still bothers him."

She opened the door to the stairway and saw both dogs standing there. "Henry?" she called out.

"What!" he yelled back from the depths of the apartment.

"Have you taken the dogs out?"

"Not yet." His voice grew closer as he came to the top of the stairs. "I just got home."

"Do you guys mind?" Polly asked, turning to Gerry.

Tonya stepped in. "That's fine. It's what we're here for. So you can be as normal as possible."

Polly couldn't help herself and giggled. "Yeah. Normal. You don't know how to handle the fact that I find bodies and yet, you call bodyguards with ear wigs in the middle of Iowa - normal."

She looked up at the two dogs and said, "Come on, boys. Let's go outside." The dogs' trigger word was 'outside' and they came bounding down the steps.

"Wait a minute," Henry said, following them down. "Body? Don't tell me."

"See?" she said, speaking to Tonya. Polly turned back to her husband. "I'll be back in a few minutes and tell you all about it. First, I'm going to enjoy being outside with my furry boys."

"But..." he started.

"No buts," she said with a laugh. "I'll be back. I promise. I have protection." Polly shut the door and laughed, then followed the dogs out through the garage and into the back yard.

"You're hard on him," Tonya said.

"I know. I drive him crazy on purpose sometimes. I never want him to think that it's going to be easy with me. He'd get complacent. And we don't want that."

The dogs took off for the tree line, a favorite spot for them, and wandered in and out, smelling and sniffing. Obiwan looked up at her as he started walking south toward the horse pasture and she nodded and pointed.

"Where did Gerry go?" Polly asked.

"Here and there. I'm not going to point her out, but she's close."

"Wow, you are good. Do you care if we go down to the barn? Do you like horses?"

"I haven't ridden in years. I think Gerry's family raised horses. Ray said yours are pretty big, though."

"They're Percherons. Big just about describes them. I'd never ridden a horse before I had these four in my life, so I didn't know any better. But you'll know you've ridden after you climb off the back of one of them."

Han barked as he approached the pasture and soon, his two siblings came running out of the barn. It had taken time, but the dogs were finally used to being around the horses, due in no small part to Eliseo's training. When he asked Polly to let him train Han, she acquiesced. Obiwan had taken to the four Percherons instinctively. Sometimes Polly wondered if he'd done that for her because she'd been so overwhelmed when the horses arrived at Sycamore House.

He bumped against her leg as she reached to open the gate. "You're my best friend," she said to him, reaching down to scratch his neck. "I don't know what I would have done without you."

Eliseo was standing at the inside gate and opened it for them.

"Eliseo," Polly said. "This is Tonya. She and a couple of others are keeping an eye on me so I have freedom."

"Nice to meet you," he said. "You are welcome to come down and ride any time, if you've an interest. I think the young woman with you is showing definite signs of interest in these horses."

Tonya glanced around. "What do you mean?"

"I'm not going to give anything away," Eliseo said, "but she can't keep her eyes off those four beauties. She should probably be paying better attention to Polly, don't you think?" He said it all with a grin, and Polly laughed.

"He doesn't miss much," she said.

Tonya shook her head. "Gerry says to tell you she doesn't see why we're necessary if you have people like this around you."

"It's nothing, ma'am," Eliseo said. "I just know my land and those woods behind the pasture are as familiar to me as the back of my hand." He turned his hand over and traced a finger across the scar.

"Middle East?" Tonya asked. "Gerry says Desert Storm."

He huffed a laugh. "I'm surprised you don't have dossiers on all of us. But tell your friend that she's right."

Tom and Huck, the two donkeys, came trotting into the barn through Demi's open stall door. Tom nudged Tonya's hip while Huck sniffed Polly's hand.

"They're terrible beggars," Eliseo said.

"Then I wish I had something," Tonya replied. "And as for your dossiers, I'm certain Ray has everything he needs. He cleared everyone here. That's all we needed to know."

"He what?" Polly exclaimed. "He investigated my staff?"

Eliseo laughed out loud. "She's a little over protective of us."

"Ray should have spoken to me before doing anything like that," Polly said. "This is ridiculous. No one here is involved with Joey. He had no right."

"He wanted to know who we'd be dealing with," Tonya said.

"No!" Polly knew her voice was strident, but she was incensed. The people who worked with her had a right to their privacy. Just because some idiot was threatening her life didn't mean they should be subject to investigation.

She strode out of the barn and whistled for her dogs. Obiwan and Han came running and followed her up to Sycamore House. Polly knew Tonya was behind her, but didn't want to speak to anyone right now. Once inside, she turned into the addition, hit the elevator button for the second floor and caught herself breathing heavily. She tried to calm down, but found that she couldn't.

"Polly," Tonya said quietly.

"No," she responded. "He's going to answer to me. I've had it with everybody treating me like I'm some type of damned victim. He can get all patronizing with someone else."

The elevator door opened and she stepped in, waiting for the dogs to join her. When Tonya attempted to enter, Polly put her hand up. "This is between me and Ray."

Tonya shook her head and stepped back.

Polly stepped off the elevator and held the door for her dogs. They'd never done that before. She smiled down at Obiwan. He would follow her anywhere and fortunately, Han would follow him just as far. When she arrived at Ray's door, it opened and he stood there with a grim look on his face.

"Come on in," he said, holding the door.

"I'm mad as hell, Ray," she said.

"So I hear. Tonya let me know."

"You should have told me." She ground her teeth. "It shouldn't have even happened. My people don't deserve to have their privacy invaded. They've been through enough in their lives and this is not how I treat them."

He opened his mouth and she put her hand in his face. "No. You don't get to speak. This is unconscionable. I know that you live your life not trusting people, but you do not get to come into my world and treat me or my family like that. If you've created files that can be tracked or traced or exposed or found by anyone, I want them destroyed. And I mean fully destroyed. I want them off every server you own and all paper copies shredded. I want them gone."

"Can I speak now?" he asked when she took a breath.

"I don't think so. I am so disappointed in you and I'm angry and I'm..." she took a breath and put her hand on the doorknob. "I'm disappointed. I can't tell you to get out of here because what you're doing for me is an incredible gift, but I don't think I've ever been this angry at you. You crossed a line and just because you are doing something nice for me did not give you the right."

Polly slammed the door open and waited for Obiwan and Han to follow her out into the hallway. Ray put his hand on her shoulder. She shrugged it off.

"Don't talk to me," she said. "No explanation will placate me right now. You don't understand who I am or what I've created here. You came in here, treated me like a child and took it upon yourself to do things I would never have asked."

She left and rather than wait for the elevator, took the back stairway down to the main level. Walking past Sarah Heater's room, she stopped to take a breath. What was happening in there right now was so much greater than anything in her own life. She knew she needed perspective. But then it occurred to her that he'd probably investigated Sarah and she spun up again. Damn him. He had no right.

"Come on, boys. Let's go home." Tears spurted from her eyes as she crossed the main floor of Sycamore House to the stairway leading up to her apartment. She didn't see any of her bodyguards, which was probably a good thing. Polly took another breath before opening the door and then walked in.

Henry met her with treats in his hand for the dogs. He sent them on their way and gathered her into his arms where she sobbed in anger. He pushed the door shut and tripped the lock.

"I don't want to see anyone tonight," Polly said.

"I get that," he replied.

Then she looked at him. "How did you know?"

He held his phone out to show her a text from Ray. *"I pissed Polly off. She's mad as hell and hurting. Sorry."*

Henry led her to the sofa and asked, "What did he do to you?"

"That son of a bitch has a file on every single person that works for me. He dug into their past. I'm sure he's looked at their finances and checked out their friends and family. He took away their privacy with no thought."

He nodded. "That makes sense."

"Makes sense?" she said. "Like hell. He had no right."

"Honey," Henry said. "He did what he knows how to do."

"Exactly! He treated my family like criminals. Did he even consider talking to me about this before it happened? Hell no. He just waded in like he knows better than anyone and made decisions. I'm so damned tired of everything."

Henry pulled away from her and scooted back on the couch so he could look her in the face. "Tell me what you're tired of."

"Everything," she said, throwing her arms up in the air. "I'm tired of every damned thing. I can't go out of town without a bodyguard. I can't even walk my damned dogs. And when I do leave town, I find a body. Then I find out that Eliseo's life has been exposed to someone he doesn't even know ... because of me! I can't see my friends without strangers sitting at the freakin' lunch table and I feel like this is the first time in forever I've been home alone with you." She took a breath. "And to top it off, I'm terrified that if I don't have those damned bodyguards around, Joey and that Allendar guy will kidnap me again and do something horrible to me."

She felt her face screw up as she tried to fight tears, but finally gave in and melted down. Henry moved back in and held her as she cried.

"I'm so scared, Henry. Why is this happening to me? Why is this happening to everyone around me?"

Obiwan sat up and put his face in her lap, nudging her hand until she rubbed the top of his head. When she continued to cry, he eased himself up between her and the arm of the sofa. She smiled at him and moved closer to Henry so the dog could have room. As soon as Obiwan was high enough, he reached out and licked her cheek.

Henry chuckled. "I won't clean up your tears that way," he said, reaching out for the box of tissues.

Polly put her arm around Obiwan and hugged him, letting her angry tears flow into his fur. She finally took a deep, hitching breath and then picked a handful of tissues out of the box. She blew her nose and smiled at Henry. "Sexy. I know."

"I should probably tell you that everything you do is sexy, but you'd know I was lying. Do you want to talk?"

"Not really," she said. "I'm so mad at him."

"Do you understand at all why he did it?"

Polly glared at him. "I understand why he thought he needed to do it, but I will not accept the fact that he did something so invasive without talking to me. I had to hear about it from one of his employees. He would never have said anything and that's so offensive. I'm tired of being treated like a silly delicate flower that might wilt at the first sign of stress."

"No one believes that about you."

"Really?" she asked. "As much as I appreciate what Jon and Ray are doing here, did they ask if I needed help? No. They assumed and flew out. I had no warning. They were just here. Sure, it's sweet and wonderful, but don't you see? If I were a man, they would have talked to me first." She huffed. "Oh, I don't know. It's hard to explain. I get of tired having a 'Fragile' sign painted on my forehead."

Henry smiled and sat back. "I know *that*!" he exclaimed. "That was one of the first lessons you taught me."

"You still have trouble applying it," she said quietly.

He nodded. "You're right. I should know better, too. It's not like that wasn't a painful lesson the first time."

That made Polly laugh. "What am I going to do?" she asked.

"About Ray?"

"Yeah."

"What do you want to do?"

"I told him that he had to get rid of the files, both paper and digital. I don't want anyone here thinking that they could ever be compromised because he got over protective."

Henry shook his head. "Polly, they've got files on thousands and thousands of people. Nothing's going to happen."

"Not to my people, it won't. I don't care. I want this gone. There are too many things that can happen."

"You're my paranoid conspiracist," he said with a laugh.

Polly swatted at him and said, "Don't you laugh at me. And I'm not going to apologize for coming unglued on him."

"Okay," he said with a shrug. "You said what you had to say."

"I probably came off sounding ungrateful."

"Maybe."

"Really?" Polly was surprised. She didn't expect him to agree. "You think I might have?"

"I wasn't there. It doesn't sound like you, but who knows."

"I am all over the place today," she said. "First I'm giddy that I can get out and about because he brought in female bodyguards and now I'm a furious loon."

"How anyone could expect your emotions to be on an even keel with everything that is going on is beyond me," Henry said.

"I have to be driving you crazy." Polly leaned against her dog. "I'm up. I'm down, I'm driving *myself* crazy."

"Why don't you give yourself a break? This won't go on forever."

"Do you promise?"

"I promise. Now were you serious about wanting to be home alone with me tonight?"

Polly looked at him curiously. "Why?"

"Because Nate called. He and Joss were going to come over with the kids and bring supper."

"That's awesome," she said and jumped off the couch. "I need to clean myself up. When will they get here?"

"In about fifteen minutes."

Polly started to laugh. "What were you going to do?"

"I'll admit I was in a bit of a panic. I wanted to tell you earlier, but you took off out of here so fast, I couldn't get it out."

She leaned over and kissed him. "I don't know how you put up with me and my insanity, but I love you."

"That's how I put up with it. I love you in spite of it, because of it and well ... I love you."

Polly practically skipped her way to their bedroom. "Do I need to do anything to get ready for them?"

"It's supposed to be a stress free evening. Nothing to worry about."

She danced back to him and kissed him again. "Thank you for everything. You are my rock."

"Uh huh," he said. "Remember that the next time I infuriate you, okay?"

CHAPTER SIXTEEN

Realizing she was feeling lonely, Polly walked into the kitchen. Henry was at the peninsula drinking a cup of coffee and scrolling through his phone.

"What's up?" she asked.

"Not much. But you didn't stir when we were moving around, so I fed the dogs and took them out."

"Okay," she said. "I'm going back to bed, then."

He looked up at her. "Are you okay?"

Polly shrugged. "I'm fine. No reason to get out of bed, though. I'm not going anywhere. I've found the body. I don't want to look at Ray and if I just live in the apartment and quit trying to have a normal life, he can send his extra bodyguards home and not spend any money." She started walking away.

"Hey," Henry said, catching up to her. He grabbed her arm. "Where did this come from?"

They'd had a great evening. Joss found a babysitter at the last minute and they'd come alone. After dinner, the four of them had played games and laughed until after eleven, when both Nate and Henry announced they had work the next day.

"It's useless," Polly said. "And I've decided to feel sorry for myself again today."

"I don't like you like this."

"But you get to walk away from me and go to work, where you'll play with your friends and do things and ... just leave me alone. I'm going back to bed."

Henry followed her into the bedroom and sat down beside her after she crawled back under the blankets. "I don't know what to do for you. You're never like this."

"Like what," she said with a pout.

"Like this. Feeling sorry for yourself, not out there trying to figure out what's going on."

"You and I both know that if I go out there, something awful could happen and it's been made very clear to me that if I put myself in danger, I put other people in danger. So. I'll just stay here and everybody stays safe."

"Polly," he said. "I'm at a loss. Do you want me to take the day off?"

If she was honest, she did. She wanted him to stick around and take care of her all day. But she knew she was acting like a baby and what she needed was someone to jolt her out of this.

"No. You don't have time for that." Polly pulled the blanket up over her shoulder and tucked it under her chin. "Would you mind telling Jeff and Sylvie that I won't be down today? And if you see Ray, just tell him that he and his people have the day off. I'm not going anywhere."

Obiwan jumped up on the bed beside her and she pulled her arm out of the blanket to scratch his head. "Since I can't take the dogs out, would you mind coming home for lunch?"

"Sure," he said tentatively. "I guess I'll see you later."

"Are you taking Rebecca to school?"

"Yeah. I've got it."

Polly heard the front door open and shut, then waited for the rest of the animals to join her on the bed. She turned over and let her mind wander, hoping to fall back to sleep.

The next thing she knew, Obiwan barked and Han yipped

when her front door opened and shut again. Polly grabbed her phone and swiped it open. She'd only been asleep for a half hour.

"Hello?" she called out.

Henry stormed into the bedroom and said, "No. This is unacceptable. You don't get to play this game any longer. You've played it too long as it is. You're up and you're down. I'm sorry that you have to go through this, but this is it."

He yanked the blankets back, scattering the animals. "Get up."

"What?" she asked.

"I said, 'get up,'" he repeated.

"You're being mean and yelling at me," she whimpered.

"This is about all the mean I've got in me, but I'll find more if I need to. Now sit up. I mean it."

Polly sat up.

Henry pointed at the bathroom door. "Go take a shower and get ready for your day."

"Why should I bother?" she asked.

"Because you're Polly Giller, you're my wife and you don't give up. You've let fear and anger stop you in your tracks. You might be mad at Ray Renaldi, but you can't deny that his people are giving you freedom. Use it. Take it. Be a human being. What you're doing right now is just plain ridiculous. Now move!"

He barked the last two words and Polly giggled as she jumped out of bed.

"You're scaring me," she said.

"Good. Now why are you still here? Move it. Move it move it!"

"I had no idea I married a drill sergeant." Polly went into the bathroom and turned the shower on.

When she came out, Henry was sitting at the desk in the bedroom holding out a cup of coffee. "You get to drink this when you're fully dressed," he said.

She sashayed over to him. "I can make it worth your time if you let me stay naked."

He broke character and laughed at her. "That's better. But we don't have time. I have to go to work and you're taking a ride with Eliseo and Tonya this morning."

"I'm taking a ride? On Demi?"

"Yep. They've checked out the route and are waiting for you at the barn."

Polly bent over and kissed his forehead. "You're kind of sexy when you get bossy," she said.

"I still don't have time for this," he said. But he put the coffee cup on the desk and pulled her onto his lap, then kissed her again.

"Not even just a few minutes?"

"Woman, you are enough to send me over the edge. No, I don't have time." He trailed his finger down her breast bone. "But dang it, you tempt me."

"Come on," she said.

"There are people waiting in the barn for you. They have the horses saddled up."

"They can wait a few more minutes."

Henry sighed. "You aren't kidding?"

"Do I ever kid about this?"

~~~

Polly tried to hold her head high when she walked into the barn. She also desperately tried to not feel flushed when everyone ignored the fact that she was much later than expected. She told herself that it wasn't her fault that they'd prepared this outing without giving her notice, but in the end, she just smiled and let Eliseo help her up onto Demi's back.

Tonya and Eliseo settled into their saddles and Eliseo led them all out of the gates and onto the highway.

He held back to ride beside Polly. "I need to talk to you about yesterday," Eliseo said.

"What about it?" she asked. "Because if you're worried I'm going to see some dossier on you, don't. I'm having Ray destroy everything they've collected on you and anyone else here at Sycamore House. The whole thing infuriates me."

Eliseo nodded. "I know you're upset about it. But you shouldn't be. It's okay. We all understand."

"Thanks." Polly rode in silence for a few moments. "But it's not okay. You shouldn't have to understand. It's not like you're working for a top secret government institution. This is Sycamore House."

"And you're in trouble right now. Your friend just wanted to make sure that the people who surround you are safe."

"You're a good guy," Polly said, smiling at him. "But it's still not okay. No matter how they dress it up. So, where are we going this morning?"

They caught back up to Tonya as they turned right onto a gravel road and then into a lane.

"I didn't think you'd been down here yet to explore where Joss and Nate are going to live," Eliseo said. "From what I understand, they're going to start demolishing these buildings this summer. Henry says he wants to start on the foundation in the fall. This is going to be a beautiful place once it's cleaned up."

The ramshackle buildings would soon come down. The old house had fallen in on itself in the middle. There were two outbuildings that were nearly down and an old garage that no longer had a roof. One large metal barn was still standing and in good shape.

"I'm not going into any of those buildings," she said with a grin.

"We checked everything before coming over here," Tonya said. "Yesterday was enough for me."

Polly nodded and turned back to Eliseo. "Doesn't their land back up onto ours somewhere?"

He pointed to a corner. "That's the south pasture you bought last year. We're still clearing rocks and noxious weeds. But by the end of the summer, we'll take the horses and donkeys over to enjoy it."

"I love rural little towns," she said. "Everybody's a neighbor. I wonder what Joss and Nate have in mind for this land."

"It will be fun to see it come together." Eliseo led her over behind the buildings. From that vantage point, they could see for miles. They were on a small rise, giving them great visibility. Crops had been planted and rows of corn and soybeans created patterns on the horizon in front of them. "Depending on the house plan, they're going to have a wonderful view no matter where they look."

"This has all of the advantages of living in town, with all the space of living in the country. I can't believe no one else ever bought this," Polly said.

Tonya rode up beside her. "You people have big vistas out here. Not like the mountains or the Grand Canyon, but there are so many acres between you and anything else."

"You should come back when the corn is tall and the beans are waving in the summer sun," Polly said. "It's a beauty all its own."

Tonya nodded and chuckled. "I'm sure it is. It makes me nervous, though."

"Nervous?" Eliseo asked.

"Yeah. Like wild animals in the woods, snakes and all those other things that get 'cha. As nice as this is, I prefer the city. I understand steel girders and concrete walls."

Polly shook her head. "Never again. Listen..."

Tonya held still and listened. Eliseo just grinned at her.

"What are we supposed to be hearing?" Tonya asked. "There are birds singing and insects buzzing, but what am I missing?"

"You aren't missing anything. Did you hear sirens or car tires squealing? Nope. People screaming at each other in the apartment above you or random white noise that never stops?" Polly asked.

Tonya laughed and shuddered. "Nope. I heard none of those things. And it's kind of creepy. Where's the activity?"

"Let's move on," Eliseo said. "There's coffee at our next stop."

They rode back out and down the gravel, heading to old Ralph Bedford's house. After being attacked last summer, he was back to his old tricks. Eliseo and Jason had spent time with the man, helping him come back to health. If there was one thing Eliseo knew, it was how to restore a person through physical activity. He had a lifetime of it behind him.

He was insistent that Ralph wasn't going to fade away. He'd grown much too close to the man.

"We're going to see Ralph?" she asked.

"He wants to show off his new truck," Eliseo said. "Jason and I helped him choose it. This was as good a day as any."

"That's wonderful," Polly said. It felt good to be outside. The temperature was warm, though the skies were gray. She leaned forward and patted Demi's neck. He raised his head in response.

They turned into Ralph's lane and Polly looked back the way they came, in time to see a familiar pickup truck turn west.

"Did you see that?" she asked Eliseo.

"Hello, Ralph," he said to the man crossing the lawn to them and then turned to her. "No. What?"

"I just saw my pickup truck. I'm sure it was mine."

"There are a plenty of trucks that look like yours, Polly," Eliseo said, swinging down from Nan. Polly still couldn't see how he managed to get up and down from that horse with no help and no step stool. She needed both.

"I'm sure it was mine."

Tonya rode up beside her. "I didn't see anything, but do you want to call the Sheriff?"

"Don't you think we should? If they're out and about driving my truck, they're probably up to something."

Tonya looked at Eliseo. "I'm not comfortable with the thought that they might have been following us."

"They were back far enough that we never would have seen them until they made the turn," he said. "You buzz Ray." He turned to Polly, "Call Aaron."

"That road would lead over to the highway that goes down to Boone," Ralph said. He brought a step stool over to Polly. "Can I give you a hand, Miss Giller?"

She took his hand and smiled. "I'm never going to get you to call me Polly, am I?"

"I try," he responded, with a slight bow.

Polly climbed down and could tell that it had been a while since she'd ridden. The muscles in her legs felt wobbly and she decided to stand still in one place until they didn't threaten to collapse.

Tonya tried to swing herself off Nat's back and ended up on

her butt on the ground. Nat looked down at her, huffed and stepped away.

"Damn it," she said, standing up. "That's further than I thought! I was sure I had it." She looked around, her face red with embarrassment.

Eliseo walked over and clapped his hand on her back. "I shouldn't tell you that the first time I tried to dismount from Nan, I did the same thing. But I did it in the privacy of the barn with no one there to catch me." He turned to Polly. "I was so glad you didn't see that happen. You never would have hired me."

She shook her head with a smile and swiped her phone open to call Aaron.

"Two days in a row?" he asked. "We haven't finished the other site yet."

"No, that's not it. I promise. It's just that I think I saw my truck."

At his silence, she knew she had his attention. "Where are you?"

"I'm perfectly safe. Eliseo, Tonya and I are at Ralph Bedford's house on the horses. But I saw it turn west on the gravel road just north of here."

"Are you sure it's your truck?"

Polly looked at Eliseo and pursed her lips. "Eliseo says there are a lot of trucks like mine, so I'm not a hundred percent positive, but I'd say maybe eight-five percent."

"Do you think they were following you?"

Her heart sank when he said it out loud. It was one thing for Tonya and Eliseo to speculate, but Aaron was too close to her. "Crap. I suppose so. We rode over to Joss and Nate's new place and then down here. Do you think they're keeping that close an eye on me?"

"I don't know what to think. But, I'd like you to stay safe, so pay attention to what your people tell you to do, okay? We'll check for the truck. Thanks for calling."

She tucked her phone back into a pocket and walked over to Tonya.

She was talking to someone on her head piece. She held a finger up and then said, "If they're this close to you, I want to get you home in a vehicle, not on horseback. It's too exposed."

Polly nodded. "Can we stay for coffee?"

"Sure," Tonya said. "We're not in a hurry. Gerry will be here in a few. Eliseo, can we lead her horse back?"

"Unless Ralph wants to ride back with us," Eliseo said. "I'll give you a ride home later on, old man." He smiled at his friend.

"Come on over to the porch," Ralph said. "I have coffee or lemonade." He winked at Polly. "And your Mrs. Donovan sent cookies home with me the other day. She's trying to fatten me up. I'm going to be in terrible shape when you open that bakery. She's a magician."

"Where's your new truck?" Polly asked.

The old truck was still parked in the yard, but its rear left tire had gone flat. The poor old thing looked like it had been lamed and left to die.

"I cleaned out the garage for her," Ralph said. "It only seemed fitting that she have a good home out of the elements. She's awfully pretty."

Polly followed him to the garage and he bent over and pulled the door up. It creaked and groaned and as it rose, she glanced at Eliseo, who was doing everything in his power not to laugh.

Ralph Bedford's truck *was* pretty. It was also bright orange. Polly walked around the side and discovered that it had flames painted from front to back.

"Mr. Bedford!" she exclaimed.

"If you want me to call you Polly, you'd best use my first name. What do you think?"

"I think it's wonderful. Did you buy it like this or have the paint job done?"

"I had it done," he announced proudly. "I've always wanted to do something wild with my trucks, but thought I was getting too old to pull it off. My buddy here told me that I was just old enough to do whatever I wanted. Ain't it pretty?"

"It's wonderful." Polly started to laugh and tried to hold it back.

"I can't believe this. It's really wonderful. At least I will know who is driving this truck when I see it coming down the road."

"Yes you will," he said, a huge grin on his face. "And all you have to do is wave and I'll stop and pick you up. I'll take you anywhere. You think the kids in town will be jealous?"

She laughed again, this time a snort escaping through her nose. "If they aren't, too bad for them." Polly pulled him into a hug. "Do you have any idea how happy this makes me today?"

"Aww," he said. "I'm just a simple man with simple tastes." He turned to grin at Eliseo. "And a flashy truck to show off."

"I told you she'd like it," Eliseo said. "Who wouldn't?"

Polly slipped her hand in the crook of Mr. Bedford's arm as they walked back to the porch. "So. Is there a pretty woman out there who's caught your eye? Because with a truck like that, you're going to have to beat them off with a stick."

He gave her a sly grin. "I don't have a woman yet, but when I drive this down to the senior center in Boone, you can bet your sweet bippy I'll be keeping an eye out for one of them to act interested."

"Of course you will," she said.

CHAPTER SEVENTEEN

Enveloped in the steam and warmth from a second shower that morning, Polly was trying desperately not to be depressed. Gerry had arrived at Ralph Bedford's to take her home. Polly had stopped along the way to the car to hug Demi's neck. He seemed to sense something was wrong and wrapped himself around her, letting Polly hold on as long as she wanted. He was such a good horse.

Mr. Bedford decided that he had a few things he could do in the garden at Sycamore House and was glad to go for a ride. He admitted that it would have been more fun to show off his new truck, but he had plenty of time and when an opportunity like this presented itself, he should grab it by the reins, so to speak.

In the few minutes it took to get home, Gerry and Polly didn't say much. Polly thanked her and then went inside and up the back steps to her apartment. If this didn't get settled soon, she was going to borrow a shotgun and lie in wait for those two men. It was time for their tyranny to come to an end.

She let the hot water roll off her back and thought about different ways she could trap them. Nothing extraordinary presented itself, which frustrated her even more. By the time she was dressed and in the kitchen, the only idea she had was the shotgun and she knew her aim would be bad enough that she'd miss and make more of a mess than things already were.

Henry had expected her excursion to take most of the morning and now here she was, back in the same place, with nothing to do.

Her phone rang. Polly looked at the number and didn't recognize it.

"Hello?" she said.

"Ms. Giller? This is Mrs. Hastings, Rebecca's teacher."

Polly breathed a sigh of relief that it wasn't anything else, and then realized that this probably wasn't good news either. "Hi there. Is everything okay with Rebecca?"

"She's fine. But how are you?"

"I'm okay," Polly said. "I guess I just need to get through this. But what's going on with Rebecca?"

"It's nothing to worry about, but would you consider letting her come home? She's finished enough work for the school year and I'll be honest, she isn't engaged at all. Andrew tells me that her mother is close to dying and I wonder if it wouldn't be better for her to just be there."

Polly felt horrible. She'd been so involved with her own mess that she hadn't paid close enough attention to the little girl who, at this point, was her daughter. Rebecca had been struggling through this last week alone, going through the motions every day because it was expected of her.

"Ms. Giller?"

"I'm sorry. I just realized how unengaged I've been. Of course we'll come get her. I hoped that school would be a distraction from all the time she's spent with her mother. But you're right, it's probably too much for her to handle right now."

Mrs. Hastings waited and then said, "I haven't spoken to her. I wanted to talk to you first, but if you'd like to come get her, I think she'd be glad of that. Andrew, Kayla and I will clean out her desk."

"I'm not sure who will be there to pick Rebecca up," Polly said.

"I don't have a vehicle right now. It will be someone Rebecca knows, though. I'll call Lydia Merritt or ask Sylvie Donovan to do this for me. Please don't let her go with anyone else."

"Absolutely. Just have them stop in the office and I'll be sure that Rebecca knows there isn't any emergency."

"Thank you so much for taking care of her these last few months," Polly said. "We couldn't have done this school year without you."

"She's a good kid and I hope next year goes better for her."

Polly smiled. This was one of the blessings of living in a small town. "Thank you again."

"And please, if anything happens to Mrs. Heater in the next few days, let me know?"

"Absolutely."

They hung up and Polly took a breath, then headed down the back stairs for the kitchen. Sylvie and Rachel were sitting at the long table in the back and looked up when she came in.

"What's up?" Sylvie asked.

"I have a huge favor. Would you mind going to get Rebecca from school? Her teacher just called and that poor girl needs to be here rather than there. I don't have a car and I don't think my bodyguards would let me leave by myself anyway."

Sylvie was already up and moving. "Of course. Do they know I'm coming for her?"

"I told them it would be either you or Lydia. Mrs. Hastings said to go to the office and they'd call for Rebecca."

"I'll be right back. Do you want her to come upstairs to your place or go see her mom?"

"I need to spend time with her, but I've not wanted to intrude on what little time she has left with Sarah. And honestly, I feel like I've been a horrible friend to her this last week. I've been so caught up in my own damned pity party."

Sylvie grabbed Polly into a hug and said, "How about you give yourself a break. Rebecca has been where she wanted to be. She's been where she needed to be. You two have a lifetime ahead to talk about her grief and your fears. Okay?"

Polly chuckled. "You are good for me, Mrs. Donovan."

"Yeah. We don't do heavy emotions at my house," Sylvie said with a grin. "And besides, who's got time for all of that self-flagellation. Moving on ... right?"

"Right."

"Go back upstairs and I'll send her up when we get here. Give her a hug, make her take a nap with the dogs and cats and then let her spend time with her mother when she's ready."

Polly walked with Sylvie into the back hallway. She watched her go out the garage door to the back parking lot and then went on upstairs. Since Han and Obiwan were on the top landing waiting for her, she sat down and leaned against the wall.

Han tried to wriggle into her lap, but he was getting much too big for that. She nuzzled the top of his head and twisted so she could put her arms around Obiwan's neck. Even on the days he smelled most like a dog, he still calmed her.

She shut her eyes and took a few deep, cleansing breaths. Sylvie was right. She and Rebecca had time ahead of them to work out the kinks that had been introduced over the last week or so. They hadn't had time to talk about Polly's kidnapping or even about what Rebecca was going through.

Rebecca wasn't going to want to talk about it for a while. While she was in the middle of caring for her mom, that was all she had the energy to do. When Polly's mother died, her emotions were so chaotic she wasn't able to identify them until several days after the death. Everything was done by rote as they prepared for the funeral. She existed inside herself until the last person had finally gone home. Even then, the abrupt transformation back to a normal life had left her feeling disjointed. For months, the focus of every day had been around her mother. Without that focus, it had taken time for everyone to find their way out of it.

Obiwan sat straight up and gave a happy bark. Rebecca must be home. Polly stayed where she was and waited.

It didn't take long for the downstairs door to open. Polly was shocked at how frail the little girl looked. She obviously hadn't been eating, her eyes were dark and though she'd pulled her hair back into a pony tail, there was little attention given to it. Evelyn Morrow had done her best, but this wasn't a time to expect much.

"Sylvie said you wanted to see me," Rebecca said, coming up the steps.

"I've missed you," Polly said. She patted Han's head. "We've all missed you."

Rebecca bowed her head. "I'm sorry."

"Oh, no, no, no," Polly said. "I'm sorry. I didn't mean anything by it. You're doing what you need to be doing. I just wanted you to know that we love you, even if I'm not with you all the time."

"I know that. Is it okay that I'm home from school?"

Polly patted the floor beside her. "Sit down here for a few minutes." She didn't try to hug Rebecca or touch her. The girl would let her know what she needed. "Mrs. Hastings called this morning and said there was no reason for you to stay there when your heart and mind were here with your mom."

"Oh."

"Rebecca, I'm so sorry. I should have realized that and been the one to help you make that decision."

"That's okay. I can't believe I don't have to go back to school."

"You know that if you want to, you can always go back."

Rebecca shook her head. "No. I'm not paying attention anyway." She looked down again. "I'm so tired."

"I'll bet you are. Would you like to crawl into your bed and take a nap with the animals?"

"Nah."

"I haven't been sleeping either," Polly said.

"Because there are bad men in town?"

"Yeah. Pretty much."

"I heard about it, but you didn't say anything, so I thought you didn't want to tell me."

Polly chuckled. "I suppose I didn't. I figured you had enough to think about."

Rebecca looked into Polly's eyes. "I'm tired of thinking about death all the time. Does that make me a bad person?"

"Oh honey, no. You're fine!"

"I don't want my mom to die." Rebecca bowed her head again, "but I want this to be over. So does she. She's so worn out. Why won't she just give up and die?"

"I don't know why people wait," Polly said. "But when it's the right time, she'll finally go."

"I feel so guilty sometimes."

"Because you want this to be done?"

"Yeah and because I want to play up here with Andrew and Kayla again. I want to feel happy again and go do things with you."

"I get that," Polly said with a sad smile.

"If Mom was going to get better, it would be great, but it's too late for that."

Polly put her hand on Rebecca's leg. "You're awfully wise for someone so young."

"You learn a lot when your mom is dying," she said flatly. "But you know that, don't you, Polly?"

Rebecca sounded so adult. It wasn't fair that she had to go through this, but Polly knew kids all over faced difficult things every day.

"I'm tired and you're tired. What if we went into my bed and just put our heads on the pillows? Do you think we might take a quick nap?"

"You don't think I'm terrible for wanting to be normal?" Rebecca pressed.

Polly stood up and held her hand out to Rebecca. "Honey, I think you're just perfect. You've been dreading this day for the last year or so and now that it's here, it isn't quite as horrible as you thought. But you don't want to draw it out any longer than necessary, right?"

"Yes!" Rebecca exclaimed. "You really do get it."

They walked through the apartment to Polly's bedroom. "This happens. Not just with death, but with other things, too. It's not always this difficult, but it's never easy."

Rebecca hopped up on the bed and kicked her shoes off. Polly shook out a couple of blankets and threw one over Rebecca and then dropped down on her side of the bed and pulled the other up and over her shoulders. They turned to face each other and again Polly was surprised at how much Rebecca had grown up. She kept wanting to call her a little girl, but the 'little' was gone. Rebecca was nearly five foot tall and her face had lost its cherubic qualities this last year. Today she was finished with sixth grade and junior high was just around the corner.

"Kayla was wondering something," Rebecca said.

"What's that?"

"Since we're going to be in seventh grade next year, do you think we could take those babysitting classes this summer and maybe start making money?"

Polly propped her head up on her hand. "Sure, why not? Do you have any information yet?"

Rebecca smiled and nodded. "We did some checking. They have a class on a Saturday in June. It costs twenty dollars, though."

"Let me talk to Stephanie and we'll see what we can do to fund your class. I'd be glad to take you down. Do you think Andrew would want to do this too?"

"He thinks it's silly. He says that he can make enough money here if he needs it."

Polly chuckled. "He could certainly make more money if he put his mind to it. What made you and Kayla think about babysitting?"

Rebecca nestled her head into the pillow and wrapped her arm around Han. She yawned and said, "Molly is so cute and I never get to see her. Ever since Jessie moved out, she's too busy to come by."

"I'm sure she's..." Polly started.

"No, I know she's busy with work and the baby. She probably doesn't have time to think about me."

"Sweetie, that's not true." Polly reached out and brushed a few stray hairs away from Rebecca's face.

"It's really okay. Everybody has their own stuff to deal with. But if I'm certified, when Molly gets older, maybe I can take care of her so Jessie can go out and have fun." Rebecca smiled. "It would be fun to babysit the twins, too. But maybe Kayla and I should do that together for a while. They're a lot to handle."

"They are rambunctious," Polly said.

"Joss brought them over to see me and Mom last week. Cooper had a cut on his forehead from falling down. Joss said he stood up and tried to walk when she wasn't in the room. He fell down and bumped his head on Sophia's foot. Joss said that he's always trying to get into things." Rebecca's eyes fluttered as she tried to stay awake. "He let me hold him on my lap. Sophia only wanted her mom, but Cooper put his arms up to me. It was pretty cute."

"That's wonderful," Polly said. She was so thankful that her friends were making time to reach out to Sarah and Rebecca. While she was dealing with her own stuff, they had her back.

"Mom says I should say 'I love you' all the time to people that I care about, even if they don't say it back," Rebecca said quietly.

"That's where you get your wisdom," Polly responded. "You should say it any time you want to say it."

"Thanks for letting me come home today. I love you, Polly."

"I love you too, sweet girl." Polly watched Rebecca's body relax as Han snuggled into the curve of her tummy. Luke snuggled against the girl's legs and within moments her breathing slowed and she was asleep.

Polly closed her eyes, Obiwan tucked in against her back. She didn't bother looking for Leia, she was on the bed somewhere.

~~~

Henry put his finger to his lips when he walked into the room. Polly had heard him come up the back steps and hoped he'd not yell out.

Han slid away from Rebecca and jumped to the floor while Polly and Obiwan crawled out of bed on the other side. She looked back at the sleeping girl and followed Henry into the living room, pulling the door mostly closed behind her so the cats could get in and out.

They went into the kitchen and she smiled at a bag from Joe's Diner.

"You brought me lunch," she said. "Thank you."

"I didn't know Rebecca was here until Sylvie caught me downstairs. Mrs. Hastings sent her home?"

"That poor girl has hardly slept in the last couple of weeks. Since there are only a few days left before school is out, there's no reason for her to be there."

He nodded. "That makes sense. How's she doing?"

"Better than I could hope for." Polly shook her head and smiled. "She's so normal about this. She is able to deal with the fact that she wants her mother to live, but at the same time she wants this to be over."

"Wow," he said. "How'd she get to that place?"

"I suspect it has to do with Sarah and Evelyn. They're both down-to-earth. Sarah has wanted to be part of Rebecca's grief, hoping that would help her deal with it after she was gone."

"I can't imagine what that would be like." Henry took two styrofoam containers out of the bag. "I got you a tenderloin. Is that okay?"

She leaned over and kissed his cheek. "It's perfect. I'll only eat half of it and Rebecca can have the rest when she gets up."

"How much do you remember about your mom dying?" he asked.

"It's weird," Polly said. "Some things are there in vibrant color. Others are like a dream, right there on the edge of my consciousness, but if I think too hard about them, they're gone. I remember Dad being sad and I remember Mom trying to tell him it was going to be okay."

She smiled and looked out the window. "I forgot about that until just now."

"Forgot what?"

"I was in the room when Mom told Dad that he was supposed to answer any questions I had and not hide anything from me. I remember he laughed and asked her if that meant every question, even when I was in junior high and high school."

"What did she say?"

"She told him that if he wanted to make sure I trusted him, he could never evade my questions or lie to me, even about the difficult things." Polly laughed. "I never did ask him about girl stuff, but Mary was there so I didn't have to."

"Sounds like your Dad figured that one out."

She nodded. "You know, he let me talk about Mom's death and never told me that I couldn't feel something, even if I was mad. I remember one time I was in high school and I asked him if he was angry because she'd died." Her voice trailed off as she remembered.

Henry prompted her. "What was his response?"

"He told me that he wanted to be angry, but couldn't figure out who to be angry at. It wasn't Mom's fault, God didn't do it on purpose, and the doctors had done everything they could for her. He said that he worried sometimes that maybe Mom had come into contact with something on the farm that gave her cancer, but he knew that wasn't true, it was just an illogical fear." Polly rubbed Henry's arm. "He cried a lot right after she died. He didn't think I knew it, but I did. He'd go to bed at night and cry by himself. Sometimes I sat outside his doorway and listened until he fell asleep."

"Did you ever tell him that?" Henry asked. 'You were so young. How did you handle it?"

"It wasn't every night and after a few months, he stopped. It kind of made me feel good to know that he loved her and missed her. Sometimes I cried into my blanket, but it was okay. And no, I never told him. Actually, I forgot about it for a long time. I didn't remember that he'd done that until I was in college."

"Death does a number on us."

"But it's such a normal part of life."

"Only because we haven't figured out how to stop it. You know, most of us would like to live a very long time. Longer than we have."

"I know I do," Polly said. "I have things to do and all of this crap that is happening in my life right now is wasting good time."

"Speaking of that, how was the ride this morning?"

Polly cut her sandwich in half and took a bite. "It kinda sucked," she said around a mouthful of bread and tenderloin. "I think I saw my truck when we turned into Ralph Bedford's lane."

Henry shook his head and set his jaw. "I'm sorry."

"It's okay. I needed to be home when Mrs. Hastings called. It all worked out."

They both turned toward the door to the living room when they heard Rebecca's voice, "Polly? How long was I asleep?"

"Come on in, sweetie. Henry brought lunch. Do you want half my sandwich?"

Rebecca came over to the table and sat down beside Henry. Polly pushed the container over to her and tossed ketchup packets across.

"This smells good," Rebecca said. "Thanks."

"You slept for a couple of hours. Do you feel better?"

"I think so." Rebecca turned to look at Henry and said, "Do you know that I love you?"

Polly's eyes filled and she waited.

"I do know that," Henry said, putting his arm around her shoulder. "And I love you too."

CHAPTER EIGHTEEN

"Since I have extra time today, would it be okay if I went to your office to see Jessie and the baby?" Rebecca asked after lunch.

"Are you sure?" Polly asked. "I know Jessie would love to have you, but it's going to make for a long afternoon."

"Can I use your phone and call her?" Rebecca asked. "If she says yes, can I go? I'll take a book and my sketch pad. I just don't want to..." her voice trailed off.

"Of course." Polly took out her phone and swiped it to Jessie's phone number and handed it to Rebecca.

Jessie was thrilled to have Rebecca's company. Both girls missed spending time with each other, even though there was such a large difference in their ages. Rebecca scurried around gathering her things.

Henry shook his head and smiled. "That little girl knows her own mind. She's not going to be easy to stop once she gets an idea."

"No kidding," Polly said. "Do you mind running her back to your shop?"

"I have some things I should probably check on anyway."

"Thanks for this, then," Polly said. She wanted to complain about the fact that she couldn't take Rebecca herself, but decided she'd done much too much complaining this last week about the things she couldn't do. It was time to completely move past the frustration.

She chuckled to herself.

"What?" Henry asked.

"Oh nothing. I'm just laughing at myself."

"You're sure?"

"Yeah. I'm being a whiny butt in my head. I'll get over it." She looked at two expectant dogs at her feet. "Say, why don't you take Han with you and leave him with Jessie and Rebecca for the afternoon. I'll take Obiwan down to the office with me."

Henry knelt down and patted his knee. Han put a paw on it and leaned forward. When Henry tapped his own cheek, the dog gave him a quick lick and wagged his tail.

"When did you two learn that?" Polly asked.

"We've been practicing all sorts of things. I told you he was going to be my boy." He spoke to the dog. "Of course I'll take you to the shop. Dad said he likes having you visit. I should take you over there every day so that you don't turn into a lazy mama's boy like your big brother."

Polly laughed. "You're such a goofball. Both of you."

Henry stood back up and said, "Do you want me to take Obiwan o-u-t-s-i-d-e before we leave?"

"No," she laughed. They'd taken to spelling words that the dogs recognized and it cracked her up. "We'll figure it out. This is why I have bodyguards living here, so I can go ... there ... when I want to. And I'm feeling just ornery enough to want to."

Rebecca came back into the dining room. "Thanks for letting me go. Will you tell Andrew and Kayla where I am?"

"Absolutely. I know they've been missing you, but one more day won't make a difference."

Rebecca started to follow Henry to the back steps, then turned and ran back to Polly to give her a quick hug. "It's all going to be okay. Isn't it?"

"Yes it will, sweet girl. Go have fun."

Polly watched them leave and then said, "Okay, Obiwan. Let's go downstairs and see what's happening. Lazy mama's boy. What a brat that man is. You don't need any silly tricks to prove to me how smart you are."

They went downstairs and Obiwan followed her into her office and settled down in a corner so he could keep an eye on her and on the door.

Polly pulled the stack of mail closer to her, once again dreading what she might find. She tossed several items in the recycling bin, separated out the bills and then, just as she got to the magazines and catalogs, found a nine by twelve envelope addressed to her. There was no return address.

Her heart sank and she reached into the drawer for a letter opener and the pair of tongs she'd kept. She slit the top of the envelope open and peered inside, but couldn't see past the fact that there was another envelope and a folded piece of paper. She dumped them out onto the desktop and using the two tools, opened the piece of paper.

It was another letter from Joey. She felt the blood rush from her face and behind her, Obiwan whimpered.

"Silly tricks. Whatever," she said to him. "You're more sensitive than most people I know.

He walked over to her and put his head on her leg.

"Do you want to know what this is?" she asked. "It's absurd. Just about the time I decide that I'm able to deal with this crap, something else shows up to remind me how little control I have."

She swiped her phone open and dialed Aaron Merritt.

"How are you doing, Polly?" he asked, tentatively.

"I have another letter. I opened the outside envelope and unfolded the letter, but there's a smaller envelope in here that I haven't opened. I don't want to wait for you guys, because you'll take it away before I can see what's in it."

"But you're going to wait for us anyway, right?"

She huffed. "I probably should have opened it before I called if I was going to do that, don't you think?"

"Good girl. What does the letter say?"

She took a deep breath and started to read:

"Dear Polly,

It is difficult to be so close to you, yet be unable to touch your face and hold your hand. I've thought about no one else but you for these last two years and now that we are in the same town, I think you should finally admit that you have missed me too."

She stopped. "How is one person so insane?" she asked Aaron.

"I don't know. Is there more?"

"Yes," she said. "But I don't want to go on."

She heard a car door slam in the background, then another and another. "What are you doing?"

"We're coming up to get the letter," he said. "Go ahead."

"I'm closer than you realize and hope that you will soon be able to rid yourself of the extra people who have chosen to interfere in our love. I look forward to spending time with the real Polly Giller.

"Please hurry back to me, Polly. I don't want to be the man that is doing these terrible things, but I don't seem to have a choice. All I can think of is you. M tells me that this is the only way to get your attention. Please forgive me. You are the only one who can stop me."

"Polly?" Aaron said softly into the phone.

"It's my fault," she replied.

"We've been over this. You can't take responsibility for the actions and thoughts of an insane man. No matter what."

"All those years ago I could have said no, but I was attracted to his mind, to his interest in history and literature. How did it go so badly?"

Obiwan nudged her elbow and she unconsciously rubbed his head. He sat up, put his paws on her leg and lifted up to sniff the papers on her desk.

"I'll see you when you get here," Polly said, swiping her phone closed. "Get down, Obiwan. I don't think they'd appreciate doggie drool on their evidence." She pushed the contents of the envelope away and sat back.

Jeff showed up at her door and said, "Hey, are you okay?"

She pointed at the letter. "I got another one."

179

"I wondered. Stephanie said she thought you were calling the Sheriff. Is there anything we can do?"

"Nah. They're coming to get this." She pointed at the smaller envelope. "I don't even know what's in that one."

Jeff sat down and Obiwan wandered over for attention. "Where's the other dog?" Jeff asked.

"He went to the shop with Henry."

"That one is all puppy," Jeff said. " I remember when this boy showed up." He bent over and rubbed Obiwan's neck. "He was the cutest pup I'd ever seen."

Polly nodded and glanced at the letter and envelope, then sat up and pounded the top of her desk.

Obiwan looked up and Jeff jumped. "What?" he asked.

"I told myself upstairs to quit being a whiny butt about this. The jerk isn't going to own my emotions any longer. The Sheriff can have it and I'm moving on."

"That's great news." Jeff stood up. "Don't go anywhere. I have something to show you." He patted his leg. "Come on, Obiwan. I have treats for you in my office."

"You're too good to us," Polly said to his back.

He came back and put another piece of paper on the desk in front of Polly, then handed Obiwan a treat.

"What do you think?" he asked. "Sal and Sylvie haven't seen it yet, but I thought maybe you needed a little fun today."

Polly had seen initial sketches of the sign and logo for the coffee shop, but here it was in color. The words 'Sweet Bean' were set into a line drawing of a dachshund.

"They'll love it," she said.

"I wanted this finished so we could advertise. We'll put signs in the window so the curious people will know what we're doing."

"It's great. Thank you." She pushed the paper back across the desk at him.

"No, you keep that. It's yours."

~~~

Polly looked up when she heard voices in the outer office. Stephanie knocked on the door to announce Sheriff Merritt and Marla Lane.

Obiwan wagged his tail at Aaron and as Polly watched, gave Agent Lane a curious look as if he weren't sure what to make of her.

"I'm sorry, Polly," Aaron said.

She didn't respond, but pointed at the envelopes and sheet of paper on the edge of her desk. Agent Lane took several pairs of disposable gloves out of a jacket pocket, handed one pair to Aaron and much to Polly's surprise, handed a second to her. The third she slipped onto her own hands.

"You've already touched this?" she asked Polly.

"Just the outside envelope. I shook everything out onto my desk and used these," Polly held up the kitchen tongs, "to open the letter."

"I see." The woman opened the letter again, slipped it into a clear plastic bag that she pulled from the same jacket pocket and flattened it out. "Is there anything you can see in this letter that gives us good information?"

Polly shook her head. "Just more insane ramblings. That's all I can see."

"Sheriff Merritt," Marla Lane said, "He mentions that he is closer than Polly realizes. Have your men checked the woods behind this place? And what about the barn?"

"The barn is quite active during the day," Aaron said. "Polly's employee is quite familiar with everything happening down there and if someone was hiding, he'd know it."

Using her index finger, Agent Lane slipped the second envelope open. Polly could have done that. The tip of the flap was the only thing sealed shut.

"What's in there?" Polly asked, as the woman peered inside and said nothing for longer than Polly thought necessary.

"It's hair, but it doesn't look like human hair." Marla Lane's brows creased as she peered in the envelope. She held it over to Aaron, who shook his head.

"May I see?" Polly asked. As long as it wasn't another photograph, she could handle this.

Agent Lane leaned over the desk, and bent the envelope open so Polly could see inside.

"It's horse hair," Polly said with a frown. She slipped a glove on her right hand. "May I?"

"Sure."

Polly pulled a hank out and looked at it, then dropped it back into the envelope. "It's not dark enough for the Percherons. We need to ask Eliseo about the donkeys."

She stood up and said, "Am I safe enough if you accompany me to the barn or do I need to contact my bodyguards?"

Aaron smiled at her. "We'll be good. Let's talk to Eliseo."

Obiwan jumped up to follow her and wagged his tail when she headed for the side door leading to the barn.

She held the first gate open for Aaron and Agent Lane, then went on ahead of them. Obiwan bolted for the pasture and ran to greet Nat and Nan who were standing against the south fence line.

"Eliseo?" she called out. "Are you here?"

He came out of the feed room, sweat dripping off his forehead. He drew a handkerchief out of a back pocket and wiped his face, then wiped his hands clean. "I was pulling down hay. How can I help you?"

"This is FBI Agent Marla Lane," Aaron said. "She's investigating the kidnappings. Polly got some strange hair in the mail today and we'd like to check your donkeys. Polly says it isn't dark enough for the horses."

"May I see?" Eliseo asked.

Agent Lane opened the envelope again.

After looking at the hair, Eliseo said, "She's right, it didn't come from the horses. They're brushed often enough that I would have noticed that much clipped off. Let's see what the little boys look like. I'll be right back with them."

He went into the feed room and then came back out and gave a sharp whistle. He handed the bag of carrots to Polly and said,

"You keep them occupied while I check their tails."

Polly sat down on a bench and put the bag beside her. She fed carrot bits to Tom first and then Huck. The donkeys nuzzled her shoulders and pushed their heads under her hands, looking for more. She was glad to oblige.

That was one thing she appreciated about her animals. They were always glad to see her, no matter how long she'd been away. There was no judgment and no expectation, just affection.

"Yes, ma'am," Eliseo said. "It looks as if our boys have had some unexpected grooming. See here?" He held Huck's tail up. "Just a few snips on the underneath of both their tails. It wasn't noticeable from afar."

"When do you think this might have happened?" Aaron asked.

He nodded as Polly fed the donkeys more carrots. They were thrilled to be part of the action. Tom stepped close to Agent Lane, looking for attention. She took a step back, so Polly put her hand on his halter and drew him back with another carrot bit.

"I haven't given them a good brushing since last Thursday or Friday," Eliseo said. "I would have noticed it then." He put his hand on Huck's head. "That was Thursday. They have the run of the place and with the weather so nice, I haven't been locking them in the barn." He shrugged. "It's easier than replacing doors."

"So anyone has access to them during the day?" Agent Lane asked.

"Yes" he said. "I'm not sure what else to say. If I'd thought they were in danger, I would have done something different." He turned his head toward Aaron. "Are they in danger?"

Aaron shook his head. "I don't think so. This was meant to scare Polly, to tell her that they're close enough to cut the hair off a donkey's tail." He chuckled. "That's something I would have liked to have seen. How in the world did they get those donkeys to be so obedient?"

Eliseo patted Huck's head. "You see how quickly they respond to treats." At the word, both donkeys looked up at him. "No, you beggars, you've had enough."

Polly handed him the bag of carrots and leaned in to hug Tom's neck. "You two have to be more careful of strangers," she said. "What am I going to do with you?"

Agent Lane put her hand out to shake Eliseo's. He took it and said, "If you think I need to lock the barn and take the donkeys out to my place, I can call Doc Ogden and borrow his trailer."

"I'm sure they're safe enough," she responded. "Thank you for your time. Miss Giller?"

"Yes?" Polly said.

"Are you ready to go back up to the house? We have other things to look into this afternoon and should be on our way."

The woman spun on her heels and headed back the way they'd come. Polly gave a perplexed look to both Eliseo and Aaron and mouthed "What?" to the Sheriff.

He shrugged and said, "Thank you, Eliseo. Let us know if you see anything else out of place, will you?"

"Of course, Sheriff. But I think we'd all appreciate it if you'd hurry and find these men so we can stop worrying about Polly."

"I'd appreciate it, too. This has gone on much too long for my taste and I'm ready to have my office back."

They looked up to discover that Marla Lane had cleared the barn and was striding up the sidewalk to the house.

"She's intense," Eliseo said.

"But she knows this case," Aaron replied.

Polly pursed her lips. "A lot of knowledge isn't worth a hill of beans..." She chuckled. "Did I just say hill of beans? Who am I? Anyway, she doesn't know the area, she doesn't know Joey and she doesn't know me. I think she could invest more time trying to understand those three things."

"I guess that's why she has me," Aaron said. "Come on. Best not to keep her waiting."

"I'll bet it's great fun riding in the car with her," Polly said as they walked out of the barn. She whistled for Obiwan and he ran over to join them as they walked through the gates.

Aaron smiled. "Oh yes, she's quite chatty." He put his hand on Polly's back as they approached the door. "Maybe I should sic Lydia on her."

"That's just mean."

"A little bit."

Marla Lane was waiting outside the office door for them, gently tapping her toe on the floor.

"Have a good time tonight," Aaron said. "I'm glad Lydia has somewhere to be so she isn't worrying about me while I'm working."

He headed out the front door before Polly could ask what he meant.

She ducked her head in the office. "I'm taking Obiwan upstairs," she said to Stephanie. "Is there anything I should know about?"

"Is everything okay?" Stephanie asked.

"Just another love note from Joey. At least there weren't any photographs this time."

Jeff came out of his office and stood there while Polly talked. "What was in there that sent you to the barn?"

"They cut tail hairs from the donkeys. Aaron says they're just trying to scare me, telling me that they can get close enough to do that. I think he's right. But, it makes me mad. I have bodyguards and they go after my donkeys."

Polly gave him a wicked grin. "Maybe I'll tell Ray that he and Jon should sleep in the barn until this is over. That would teach him to get all up in my business."

She realized from the expressions on the faces in front of her that they had no idea what was going on. She shook her head. "It's nothing. I appreciate them and what they're doing. I'm just testy over the negative attention."

"Come on Obiwan," she said. "Let's get you upstairs."

CHAPTER NINETEEN

Setting the timer on the oven, Polly felt a little righteous, knowing that she'd actually prepared a meal. Obiwan barked and before she knew it, Han was tearing across the floor to greet her. The sound of footsteps on the back stairway announced Henry and Rebecca's return.

Henry gave her an odd look when he came into the dining room and asked, "What are you doing?"

"I'm cooking," she said. "When I decided that I was going to be done feeling sorry for myself, I realized what a slacker I'd been for the last week."

"Okay, but why are you cooking?"

Now Polly was confused. "Because I'm tired of eating takeout. You have to be just as weary of it."

"Ohhhh," he said, looking around the room. "I see. You talk to Rebecca. I'll be right back."

Rebecca gave Polly a knowing smile and kissed the top of Obiwan's head. He'd been waiting patiently for her to give him attention.

"Did you have a good afternoon?" Polly asked.

"It was great. Mr. Sturtz said I should learn how to whittle. He said that there are images in wood and all I have to do is take away the wood that doesn't belong." She laughed. "I told him that was weird, but I'd give it a try."

Rebecca reached down into her backpack. "I made a face. It's weird, but it's a face." The piece she handed to Polly looked almost like Santa Claus, with a beard and a small face under a hat.

"That's good," Polly said. "In fact, that's really good."

"Mr. Sturtz helped me. He showed me how to get the texture in the beard and how to smooth out the little hat."

Polly shook her head. "Rebecca, this is great. Did you know you were going to make this when you started?"

Rebecca shrugged. "Yeah. Kinda."

"Do you want to do more whittling?"

"I might." She dropped her voice to a whisper. "It made him happy to teach me. He says that kids my age aren't interested in stuff like that anymore."

"He probably had a blast with you," Polly said. She turned the piece over in her hands. "Rebecca, this is cool."

"It was no big deal."

Polly handed it back to her. "It's a big deal. I'm impressed."

"Do you think Kayla and Andrew might like doing it? I was thinking we could go over this summer and he could teach us."

"That's a great idea," Polly said. "Bill would love that. How was Jessie and the baby?"

"Molly was inside with Mrs. Sturtz for a while. She says it's too loud out in the shop. Jessie says she thinks Mrs. Sturtz likes having a baby around."

Polly shuddered and then chuckled. At least Marie had Jessie's little girl to play with. Marie Sturtz would never push Henry and Polly to have children. In fact, she would rather they never had children before thinking that she was pushing that on them.

"Isn't it funny how things work out," Polly said.

"What do you mean?"

"Jessie is working there and Marie gets to play with a baby whenever she wants."

"It's a pretty cool setup. There's a playpen in Jessie's office with a bunch of toys. Jessie said that when Molly is crawling and walking, she might have to think about daycare, but for now she gets to be with her baby all the time if she wants to." Rebecca took out her sketchpad. "I drew pictures of the baby when I was there. Do you want to see them?"

"Of course," Polly said.

Rebecca opened the pad and Polly could see Beryl's influence. The pages were filled with different angles as Rebecca worked out the lines of Molly's face. Polly drew her fingers across the nose on one of them. "You're enjoying your time with Beryl, aren't you?"

"Sometimes drawing is the only thing I want to do," Rebecca said, dropping into a chair at the table. "Ms. Watson says that's because my emotions are going crazy and when I draw, they flow out of my fingers onto the page." She looked up at Polly. "People think weird things about art, don't they?"

Polly laughed and gave Rebecca a hug. "I guess they do. They try to put into words things that don't have words."

"But isn't that what art is?" Rebecca asked.

"You're right. It is."

Henry came back into the dining room with a grin on his face.

"Where'd you go in such a hurry," Polly asked.

"Just checking on something."

"You're being awfully cryptic. What's going on?"

"I'm going to take a shower. Today was a messy, dirty day. I'll be back in a few minutes." Henry left before she could ask him any more questions.

"What was that all about?" Polly asked Rebecca. "Do you know?"

Rebecca reached down and picked up her backpack. "I don't know anything. I'm going to put this in my room, if that's okay. I won't need it for school stuff anymore, so it doesn't have to be downstairs."

Polly was distracted by Henry's behavior, "Sure," she said. "Whatever you want. Are you staying up here for supper or eating with Evelyn tonight?"

"Probably up here," Rebecca said and left the room.

Polly didn't know what to make of it all, but knew it would come out when it did. She pulled dishes and silverware out to set the table and arranged asparagus in a casserole dish. She took the chicken and potatoes out, flipped the pieces over and re-set the timer after putting the pans back in.

A loud knock at the front door startled her. She peeked into the living room, to make sure Henry wasn't running to the door. His bedroom door was closed and so was Rebecca's.

"I'll get it," she called out.

She opened the front door to Lydia and Beryl.

"Come with us," Lydia said. "Right now."

"Is there a problem?"

"Oh sweetie," Beryl replied. "There's a huge problem. We're about to have a party and you aren't there. Come on!"

"But I have dinner in the oven."

Beryl scowled at her. "We heard. You've been buying takeout for over a week and tonight you decide to cook. What's up with that?"

"Henry?" Polly called.

He came out of the bedroom, fresh from the shower, his hair still wet and mussed. "Don't y'all get plastered tonight," he said. "We don't have enough beds left."

"You'll take care of dinner?" she asked.

He nodded and waved at her to leave.

Rebecca came out of her room dressed in a swimsuit and carrying a beach towel.

Polly chuckled. "Dare I ask?"

"Come with us," Lydia said. "You're gonna love it."

She followed them downstairs and Lydia said, "Shut your eyes," just before opening the doors to the auditorium.

Polly obeyed and let them lead her in.

"Don't scuffle, pick up your feet," Lydia whispered. "And keep your eyes closed."

It felt like she was walking on plastic and she wondered what they'd done to the auditorium.

Beryl counted out, "One. Two. Three. Open Your Eyes."

The room exploded with "Surprise!"

Polly opened her eyes to a backyard beach party. Three children's pools filled with water had lawn chairs surrounding them. Card tables were covered with sea blue cloths and LED tiki torches were planted in containers around the room. The floor was covered with plastic and canvas drop cloths. Polly looked for sand, but didn't find any and breathed a small sigh of relief. Beach balls, rubber rafts and brightly colored life preservers were scattered on the floor and Polly recognized the inflatable palm tree from Henry's bachelor party.

Two step ladders were spaced apart with a long ladder resting atop them. It was strung with white lights and underneath was a table filled with colorful glasses and a sea blue punch.

At the north end of the auditorium a badminton net had been set up. Stephanie and Kayla Armstrong were batting a beach ball back and forth across it. Rebecca ran over to join them.

"What is this?" she asked as she smiled at a room filled with her friends.

"We decided that since you had a hard time coming out and saying hello to us, we'd bring Bellingwood to you," Andy said, handing her a glass of punch with a bright pink umbrella sticking up out of it.

Jessie was sitting with Marie Sturtz and Henry's Aunt Betty around one of the baby pools. Marie waved and handed Jessie's baby, Molly, back to her mother. She jumped up and came over to Polly.

"How are you, dear? Everyone says you're doing fine, but I'm still going to worry." She took Polly's arm. "You shouldn't have to be trapped inside."

"It's getting better," Polly assured her. "My friends from Boston have come into town and they've made it easier for me to get out and about." She pointed at the card table where Joss and Sal were talking to Gerry and Tonya. Polly was glad someone had thought to invite them. As furious as she was with Ray and as frustrated as she was with everything that was happening, those two girls had done their best to keep her safe and give her a modicum of freedom.

"We're glad they're here." Marie dropped her voice. "You know, Betty tells me that Dick and a few of his buddies were ready to park themselves in their trucks with their shotguns at the ready all around Sycamore House."

"I've heard that," Polly said with a laugh. "But I'd hate for them to get hurt."

"Honey, none of us wants *you* to get hurt. You know how important you are to everyone here, don't you?"

"Thanks Marie. This is a little overwhelming, though."

"Any chance for a party," Beryl said, taking Polly's other arm. "We had fun planning this one. But no one would let me hire a stripper. I even offered to let Henry do it." She shook her head in mock disgust. "Bunch of stinking fuddy-duddies. Now come on, girls. Let's get Polly settled so she can put her feet in the water, drink her very boring, virgin punch and warm up in the glow of sisterly love."

Polly snorted with laughter. "Only you could make it sound dorky. This is wonderful."

As soon as she was seated, someone turned the lights down and the sound system on. The sound of waves washing against a beach provided a background for fifties and sixties beach songs.

"Take your shoes off," Beryl ordered. "We made sure the water was warm enough to be pleasant. If you put your feet in, others will think it's okay."

"You do it," Polly said. "You be the leader."

"Do I have to do everything?" Beryl bent over, took Polly's shoes off and dropped her feet in the pool.

"You are such a freak," Polly said. "But, you're right. It feels good." She leaned back in the chair and took a drink of her punch.

Sylvie opened the side door and stepped in. "Dinner is served. No hurry, just wander in when you're ready."

Polly stayed where she was and watched as women around the room tried to figure out whether to go or not. Betty Mercer, Henry's aunt, finally made up her mind and hitched the baby on her hip and headed for the door. She patted Polly's shoulder as she walked by.

Just as any good crowd of people will do, as soon as one went, the majority of the room followed.

"They're like sheep," Beryl said.

Polly swatted at her. "Stop it, you. I thought we were supposed to have fun. No bad-mouthing my friends."

Tonya sat down next to Polly. "Has Ray talked to you yet today?"

"No," Polly said with a laugh. "Is he scared of me?"

"He did tell us that he'd forgotten what you could be like when you were angry."

"What was he supposed to be talking to me about?"

"We're concerned with what happened this morning."

Polly stopped to think about it. Was that ride just this morning? The day felt like it had been at least a week long.

"Yeah. I figured. Have you heard whether or not anyone else has seen my truck out there?"

"Not yet, but he wants us to be extra vigilant when you're out and about." She glanced around the room. "I'm glad they did this tonight. Does it help?"

"Of course it does." Polly felt her muscles relaxing and turned on Beryl. "Did you spike my punch?"

"Who, me?" Beryl spun around and walked away.

"She's trying to get me drunk," Polly said. "Anyway, I should apologize for being such a baby. The ride this morning was nice and it was wonderful being able to eat at the diner yesterday, and I appreciate being able to walk outside with my dog..."

"But?"

"But I'll try to be better about my limitations. If you tell me I shouldn't go somewhere, I won't."

"Please don't stop asking us, though. Gerry and I think that this morning's near encounter was a fluke. And they didn't get close enough to threaten you."

"But they got to the donkeys."

"They're ducking in and out like little boys who don't want to get caught. They know they can't get close to you, so they're trying to scare you."

"It's working."

"I know, but we're here. We've got your back."

Polly took another drink of her punch, screwed up her courage and said, "I have a strange question for you."

"Okay..."

"The only exposure I have to serial killers is from television and movies..."

Tonya rolled her eyes.

"I know, but they always talk about how serial killers escalate and it gets bad before they get caught. If this Allendar doesn't get caught, how bad is it going to get?"

Tonya thought for a moment and then said, "First of all, television shows have to tell an exciting story and their killers have a huge background built. Secondly, not all serial killers are as smart as Ted Bundy and the few others that make national news. This guy isn't at the top of the list of intelligent killers. He's gotten away with it because he uses people who are willing to be led. He preys on weak-minded fools like this Delancy fellow. He's making mistakes right now. When you escaped, he should have left the area. Even though there are places for him to hide, the FBI and the local police and sheriff offices and the Department of Criminal Investigation ... they're all looking for him."

Polly nodded. "And this is Iowa. At some point, some farmer is going to recognize that he and Joey are out of place, they'll put it together with all of the gossip, and make a call."

"Exactly. But remember, Allendar doesn't want to panic or escalate or do anything that will get him caught. He craves the power he has over Delancy. If Delancy is caught, Allendar will move on until he finds someone else to control. Otherwise, when Delancy tries to break away, Allendar will kill him and then move on."

"So the only reason those two are focused on me is because of Joey - not the actual serial killer."

"That's right," Tonya said, nodding.

Polly looked up when Lydia replaced the glass in her hand with a full one. "Is this one spiked, too?" she asked.

Lydia grinned. "I'm not telling. The line is down, do you girls want to eat?"

Polly stretched and flicked her foot in the pool. "I think I'm fine for now. Maybe I'll just drink my supper tonight."

"Would you like me to bring you a plate?" Tonya asked.

Polly chuckled. "You're my bodyguard, not my maid. But thanks. I'll get something later." She reached her hand up to pull Lydia's plate down so she could see its contents. "What's for dinner, anyway?"

Lydia pulled her plate back up. "You get your own. There are burgers, hot dogs and brats."

"But my feet are so comfy," Polly said.

"Fine. Have mine." Lydia put her plate in Polly's lap, causing Polly to jump up with it in her hand.

"No, I was kidding." Then Polly saw the ornery look on Lydia's face. "You're mean to me. I was going to go later." She handed the plate back and slunk out to the hallway and got in line.

Beryl came up behind her. "I would have brought you a plate."

"Nah. Lydia offered me hers. Who needs that guilt?"

When Sylvie saw Polly, she ducked under the counter and came up with a plastic sand bucket. "You're the only one who looks out of place," Sylvie declared. "Fix it."

Polly put on a pair of yellow over-sized sunglasses and dropped the rubber flip flops to the floor so she could slip her feet into them. She pulled the visor over her head and held up the snorkel. "What am I supposed to do with this ... or this?" She had just put her hands on a rubber ducky.

Sylvie shrugged. "They're yours now. Burger or hot dog?"

"Burger, please. When did you plan this?"

Beryl bumped Polly's shoulder with her own. "No questions. You just enjoy the evening."

Rachel filled Polly's plate with cole slaw, potato salad, baked beans and a roll and Polly went back into the auditorium. Lydia waved and pointed to two empty seats beside her.

"How are you, Polly?" Angela Boehm, the Methodist pastor's wife was sitting with Lydia and Andy.

"Fine, thanks." Polly sat down beside Lydia.

"Angela and her husband are moving this summer," Lydia said with a sigh. "Just about the time I start enjoying a pastor and his family, they move."

"You don't have any say?" Polly asked.

"We always do, but the Conference asked Del to help a church in northwest Iowa. Their pastor died the day before Christmas."

"That's awful," Polly said.

"It's been hard on everyone. His family stayed in the parsonage for the last five months while the kids finished school and his wife came to grips with it all. Two retired pastors have taken care of things during the transition, but now they need someone to come in and offer stability and an opportunity for the church to heal."

Lydia frowned. "I wish they didn't need you and I wish they'd tell us who will be appointed in Bellingwood."

Angela patted Lydia's knee. "All in good time. I'm sure you will love the new family and they will love you, just like we have." She winked at Polly. "But I'm not sure that they'll know quite what to do with you."

Polly laughed. "What do you mean?"

"It isn't every town in Iowa that sports a celebrity quite like you," Angela said with a smile.

Beryl stuck her head forward and whispered loudly. "She means dead bodies."

"I get it," Polly said, wrinkling her nose at Beryl. "Maybe we don't tell them."

"I have a reason for bringing this up," Lydia said. "There are some big renovations the board wants to do at the parsonage. Usually there are only a few days between one pastor moving in and the other moving out. I thought I'd talk to you about letting Del and Angela move into the hotel the week before they're to leave town."

Polly smiled at her friend. "Of course. Whenever you're ready."

Angela nodded. "Thank you. We moved into a town once and

they were still working on the kitchen floor when we got there. Then, the chair of the board told us that the upstairs bathroom didn't work and the attic was leaking. We had to rent an RV for six months before we could finally move in. It was a mess. Del kept insisting that if they would just let us in, he'd do the work." She shook her head. "It probably would have been faster and cheaper if they'd built a new parsonage." Then she laughed. "They built that new parsonage two years after we left. The next pastor wouldn't put up with it."

Polly looked around the room. It was good to listen to people talk about the things that were happening in their own lives. Kayla and Rebecca were sitting in a pool and eating hot dogs, Rachel and Sylvie had come into the room. Sylvie was laughing with Joss and Sal while Rachel had joined Stephanie and Jessie. The three young girls were laughing at the baby's antics.

Jean Gardner had corralled Polly's mail woman, Lisa Bradford, and other women that Polly had met through Lydia or gotten to know in town were at tables around the room, laughing and talking with each other. They were here to remind her that the town was bigger than a terrorizing serial killer, but what they didn't know they were telling her was that life continued no matter what.

CHAPTER TWENTY

"Friends like that make this much easier," Polly said.

"Did you have a good time?" Henry asked. Polly was nestled into his arms in bed. It was late - much later than she'd expected to be up.

"I did. And I like the way they involve everyone in things like this. Did you know that Lisa Bradford's sister works for NASA? That's so cool. And Rebecca's teacher, Mrs. Hastings was here for a while. She has an uncle who used to work in the kitchen at the White House." She turned to face him. "I don't have anyone interesting like that."

"You just don't know about them."

Polly nodded. "That's true. I wonder if I would ever have taken the time to ask Dad about these things if he'd lived longer."

Henry pulled her closer. "I haven't talked to my parents about those things either. We assume they'll live forever."

"But they don't. And then everything they know is gone."

"Maybe you need to talk to your uncle."

She bristled. "It's probably going to have to be lost information, then."

"Polly." His tone was scolding, but she knew he understood. They'd talked through this many times. Her relationship with her father's brother was never going to be easy ... no matter how hard she tried. And she wasn't trying right now.

"Maybe someday." She chuckled and said, "Sal tells me that you might be getting tired of her. Is she bugging you that much?"

"Nah. She's fine. With you out of the picture, she shows up during the day more often, worrying over details, but it's okay."

"How long do you think until the coffee shop is ready to open?"

"I dunno," he said. "We could probably have the coffee shop part of it open in three weeks. Dad's installing the bar tomorrow. Then it's up to her and you to get the rest of the place put together."

"We have a few tables and chairs in the storage unit."

Henry moved out from under her.

"What? Am I too heavy for you?"

"No, my arm went to sleep." He turned to face her. "We can have my guys get those and bring them over. Do you have enough?"

"Enough to get started. What about the bakery?"

"That's going to take more work. It will all be installed in the next few weeks."

"I can't believe we're almost there. This is going to be real."

Henry laughed. "I'm glad it's nearly finished. We're getting busy again. I bid on a new apartment complex out past the winery. Pretty sure we're going to get it. Nate is ready for us to dig in on his place and there's a knick-knacky store that wants us to bid on building out another space downtown."

"So I'm about to never see you again?"

He hugged her close. "I'll be around. And one of these days you'll be so busy, you're going to be the one who's never available."

Polly put her head back on her pillow. "It was nice of people to do this for me tonight, but I'm done with this. I want to go back to helping other people and doing things for them."

"I know that." His eyes fluttered shut.

"I'm sorry. You sleep. I'm still wired so I'm going to read."

"Come here," he said and waited until she turned her back to him before snuggling around her. "You read, I'll rest my eyes."

Polly reflected back on the evening as she thumbed through the pages of her book. She'd stayed to help clean after the bulk of the group was gone. Henry had come downstairs and Len Specek had come to pick up Andy. She smiled at how happy those two were together. Andy giggled like a high schooler when she talked about him.

They were leaving at the end of the week for Spain to spend time with Len's daughter, Ellen, in Barcelona. Andy was both terrified and excited out of her mind. She couldn't wait, but it had been so long since she'd done any traveling, she worried about every small thing. There was nothing to be said to calm her down either. She was going despite her fear and promised to relax once she was solidly and firmly on European soil.

Ellen was planning to spend several days with them and then they were off to Paris. Len promised Andy that they didn't have to hurry to see everything on this trip. Barcelona and Paris were enough. They'd go back again and see any part of Europe she wanted to visit.

Polly hoped they had a wonderful time and returned with pictures and stories. She had no desire to travel to Europe, but if Henry wanted to, she'd go. He hadn't reacted when Andy and Len described their trip. For that, she was thankful. Henry always said he'd like to see the United States before worrying about flying across an ocean. He was hinting at a trip to the east coast in the not too distant future. It would be fun for them to go to the historical places that area was so famous for. The only time she'd done touristy things was when her Dad visited. He'd been shocked that she'd never gotten out to Lexington or down to Plymouth, or even out to the Mayflower.

They were just part of the landscape and something Polly knew she'd always have time to visit. She visited when he insisted and was glad for it, now that she was back in Iowa.

She looked down at the words on the page in front of her. This was one of her favorite books - Asimov's "Foundation." She'd just finished the Robot series. How many times had she read these stories? The copy she had in her hand was one she'd found in a thrift store in Des Moines when she was in high school.

Her dad had said nothing that day, he just offered to carry the bags of books she'd purchased. They'd gone down to watch several of her friends play basketball in the state tournament, but Polly had done research on the best places to buy used books. Everett had said she could choose two stores and that was it. In the first, he struck up a conversation with the owner while Polly wandered in and out of the shelves. They were playing a game of checkers when she arrived at the counter with her first load of books. Her dad had stood, thinking it was time to go and then shook his head when she told him she'd just started.

A tear leaked from her eye as she realized how fortunate she'd been to have him. How many fathers would let their daughter wander a used book store for hours and not complain? They'd stopped for tacos that day. He always made her feel like the time he spent with her was more important than anything else. She missed him.

Polly scooted away from Henry to put her book back on the table beside the bed and turn off the light. When she settled back onto her pillow, Henry whispered. "You were thinking pretty hard."

"Why are you still awake?"

"Your brain was putting out so many waves, I couldn't sleep."

"I'll bet I can fix that," she said, teasing.

"I'll take that bet. If I lose, I win."

~~~

When Polly's phone rang, she jumped, sending both cats to the floor. Henry sat up. "What is it?" he asked.

"Just a minute." She picked up her phone, swiped it open and swore. "It's Evelyn downstairs."

"Hello, Evelyn," Polly said. "What's up?"

"It's time. Sarah asked for you."

Polly breathed deeply and said, "I'll be right there."

"Tonight?" Henry asked.

"I think so. Sarah asked for me." She was already swinging her legs out of bed.

"Do you need me to be there?"

Polly leaned back and kissed his cheek. "Thank you, but no. Maybe take time with Rebecca in the morning after this is over, but we'll be fine for now."

"Don't worry about calling if you need me," he said. "I'll come right down."

Polly found her jeans and pulled a sweatshirt on, then slipped into the flip flops from the party. "You boys stay here," she said to the dogs who, in their confusion, headed for the door.

Han barked and Obiwan sat down.

"Han, come," Henry commanded. The younger dog slunk back over to the bed. Henry said his name again and Han jumped up, then sat at the edge of the bed, watching Polly.

She slipped out into the living room and headed for the main door. Obiwan whined at her once more.

"Okay, you can come. In fact, maybe that's a good idea." She turned to face the bedroom. "I'm taking Obiwan with me."

"Okay," he said.

They went downstairs and crossed the darkened foyer to the addition with the help of the flashlight on Polly's phone. She knocked quietly on Sarah Heater's door and went in.

Rebecca was sitting in a chair beside her mother's bed, holding Sarah's hand. Tears streamed down her face when she saw Polly. Obiwan walked right over to the girl and put his head in her lap, as if he understood what she needed.

Evelyn nodded at Polly, who went to the other side of Sarah's bed.

"I'm here, Sarah," Polly said. "Everything's okay. I brought Obiwan and he's loving on Rebecca right now."

Sarah moved her hand toward Polly. She took it between her

two hands. There was so little energy left in the woman, but Sarah gave her a slight squeeze.

Polly looked at Rebecca, "How are you doing, honey?"

"I'm okay. She's so tired. I told her that it was okay if she died tonight. I don't want her to hurt anymore."

"That's good," Polly said.

Sarah's lips moved and Polly stood and moved closer so she could hear the woman speak. "Love you," the woman whispered.

"We love you, too, Sarah. It's okay for you to go now. Henry and I will always love your daughter. She's safe with us."

Sarah nodded and turned to Rebecca. The girl stood as well and threw her arms around her mother. "I love you, mommy," Rebecca said. "I'll miss you so much, but you have to go now. You can't stay any longer. I know that. I love you."

It broke Polly's heart to see this child be an adult. She'd had to grow up this last year, faster than anyone wanted her to, but Sarah had done a wonderful job with Rebecca. She was still able to love and be happy, even in the midst of her grief and sorrow."

Sarah relaxed and her breath caught. Both Polly and Rebecca held theirs until she took another breath. It went on that way for a few minutes and Polly finally sat down again. Rebecca looked at her in confusion.

"Go ahead," Evelyn said. "This could be a while. Our bodies don't always give up so easily."

Rebecca sat back down and Evelyn stood over her, quietly stroking her hair. Obiwan was lying on the floor beside Rebecca.

They quietly watched and waited. Every once in a while, Sarah stopped breathing, but started again. It was maddening to watch. Polly kept a close eye on Rebecca. She was completely exhausted, her face was drawn. Her shoulders slumped as she watched her mother expectantly.

After an hour passed, Polly stood and wandered around the room, her nerves raw. She couldn't imagine what Rebecca was experiencing. There were a few photographs in the room. She was glad to see that there were some from the last few weeks of Sarah and Rebecca together.

Polly picked one photo up and showed it to Rebecca. It was a picture of Rebecca standing at her mother's side, with bunny ears over Sarah's head. The two were laughing at the camera. These were the moments that Rebecca would want to remember someday.

There were only two photographs of Polly's mother just before her death. Polly was in both of them. Her father had taken them. While it was difficult remembering her mother that way, it was also the last memories she had before the funeral.

In one of the pictures, she was laughing out loud. Polly remembered that moment with great clarity. A college friend of her father's had stopped in to wish them well and told stories of learning to ski. He painted a hilarious picture of his complete failure to learn, tumbling down the slopes, picking up snow as he went. He'd worn blue jeans because he wasn't investing in ski apparel, and she remembered him telling them how they'd gotten heavier and heavier as his legs got more and more tired trying to get down that mountain in Colorado. A forty-five minute run had taken him four hours. He'd told the story in order to entertain them and her father had finally closed the hospital room door because they were all laughing so loud.

That same friend had come to her father's funeral and done the same thing. Mary and Sylvester had invited him out to the house when he'd arrived in town and they'd stayed up late, listening as he told stories about Everett Giller. Polly hadn't laughed so hard in months. At one point, she'd had to stretch out on the floor, her ribs hurt so badly.

"What was his name?" she wondered to herself. Then it came to her. Jimmy McFarlane. She wondered where he was now. She hadn't heard anything more from him since the funeral. That was probably as much her fault as anything. He'd written a quick note to thank them for their hospitality and Polly was so overwhelmed, she'd let Mary respond to that one.

The dress Sarah had worn to the Valentine's Day dance was hanging in the open wardrobe. Polly needed to make sure this was cared for. One day Rebecca would be able to wear it. Then

Polly smiled. The moon stone necklace and earrings that her father had given her would actually make it to another generation. How beautiful would they be on Rebecca with this dress? And what if she was going out on a special date with Andrew?

Polly scolded herself silently. She would not do that to those kids. If they fell in love with other people, that was going to be fine. She stole a glance at Rebecca and wondered how Andrew was going to handle Sarah's death.

He wasn't comfortable spending time here with Rebecca. Kayla had been good about it all, somehow understanding that her friend wanted her to know her mother.

That was one of those things that made Polly's heart ache. When she had gotten to college ... heck, even now, there was no one in her life that knew her mother. Sal had known Everett and that meant the world to her. But no one knew that beautiful woman who had loved Polly. She was thankful that Kayla had gotten to see Rebecca and her mother together, even if it was in this circumstance. Rebecca would want that as she grew older. Just to know that there was someone in her life who could help her remember Sarah.

Evelyn had taken Polly's chair and picked up her crocheting. She was pulling together the granny squares into a blanket that was nearly finished. The squares were bright and Evelyn was using a navy blue as the unifying color. It was so Rebecca.

The fuzzy purple pillow that Andrew had given Rebecca last year was on her bed. Polly's throat caught when she saw two stuffed animals that belonged elsewhere lying beside it. Kayla's stuffed teddy bear named Silver and Jessie's purple horse named Durango had been keeping Rebecca company when the girls couldn't be with her. Polly shook her head. Sometimes friends never ceased to amaze her. She sat down on the bed and picked Durango up.

Rebecca glanced her way and grinned. She whispered, "Jessie said I should keep him for now. She said I needed him more than she did, especially now that Molly is there."

It felt so strange to hear a voice speak. While the room was by no means silent with Sarah's raspy breathing, the normalcy of speech was out of place. Then Polly realized that it shouldn't be, so she said, "And Silver?"

"Kayla gave him to me this weekend. She'll want it back soon. I know she misses it." Rebecca giggled. "She asked about Silver tonight at dinner. I should have just come to get it and give it back."

"I think Kayla will be glad Silver is here with you tonight," Polly said.

"I'm glad you're here," Rebecca replied.

Polly nodded. "I promised your mother I would be and honestly, I wouldn't want to be anywhere else right now." She glanced at her watch. It was nearly two o'clock.

All of a sudden Rebecca gasped. "Did you see that?" she asked.

Both Evelyn and Polly looked up in surprise and then looked at Sarah. Something had definitely changed.

"What did you see?" Evelyn asked.

Rebecca looked down at her hands, "It's going to sound strange," she said.

"Go ahead," Polly prompted.

"I saw her spirit leave. Maybe it was her soul." Rebecca pulled her hand away from her mother and scooted her chair back an inch or two. "She's not there anymore. Can't you feel it?"

Polly walked over to stand beside Rebecca. "I believe you."

Evelyn put her crocheting down and put her hand on Sarah's arm. She touched the woman's face, brushing an imaginary hair away from her forehead.

Rebecca wasn't sure they believed her, because she insisted, "It's like this is just a shell now. And it was so peaceful when she left."

"I'm glad you saw that, honey," Evelyn said. "It will take a few more minutes for the body to realize that no one is there, but your mama isn't in pain any longer."

Polly knelt and took Rebecca's hand. The girl was still processing on what she'd experienced. "I wish you had seen it," Rebecca said. "It was so cool." She turned to Polly. "I know that it isn't cool that she died, but it had to happen and the way it did was like a gift to me."

Obiwan nuzzled their clasped hands and Rebecca slid out of the chair to the floor and wrapped herself around him. "Did you see it?" she asked. "I know dogs see things differently than people do."

She looked up at Polly. "Am I crazy? Did I make it up?"

"No honey," Polly said. "Evelyn knows what you saw and just because we didn't experience it, doesn't make it any less real."

"It was real," Evelyn said, reassuring the girl. "And it's something that you'll keep with you for the rest of your life."

It took another twenty minutes. Polly and Rebecca leaned forward every time Sarah stopped breathing and started again. Polly found herself praying that she would just stop. And finally ... she did. They waited, silently as seconds passed and then as a few more seconds passed.

When it became apparent that it was finished, Rebecca sat back up in her chair. "I feel like I should say something. But I don't know what to say."

Polly patted her knee. "You don't have to say anything at all."

"But it's really over. She died."

"What do you think you should say?"

"That I'll miss her every single day. That when I grow up and have children, I want to be a mom like she was. That I wish she'd had the opportunity to do great things."

Polly nodded.

"But I already said those things to her when she was alive," Rebecca said. "And she told me that she was proud of me."

"I know she was," Polly said.

Evelyn walked toward the door. "You two stay as long as you want. I'm going to call Ben. He knows this call is coming."

Polly smiled. "Thank you, Evelyn."

Rebecca looked at her mother's body. She patted the hand that was lying next to her. "I don't need to talk to this body any longer," she said. "Now I can talk to her wherever I am. Can we go upstairs?"

"Absolutely," Polly said. "Shall we take Durango and Silver with us?"

"Yes please." Rebecca started to walk away and turned back. "I don't want to leave her alone."

"You won't," Evelyn said as she came back into the room. "I'll be here. Go on upstairs and I'll see you tomorrow."

Rebecca rushed toward the woman and hugged her. "Thank you for everything. Mom told me that you were one of her best friends. Did you know that?"

"Oh my dear, thank you. That means the world to me." Evelyn looked over Rebecca's head at Polly, tears in her eyes. "I'm going to miss her something fierce. And I'm going to miss spending time with you, too."

The two held on to each other and finally Evelyn broke away. "Now you go on upstairs with Polly. You need to get some sleep because tomorrow will be a busy day."

Polly handed Durango and Silver to Rebecca and carried the purple pillow. "Thank you so much," she said to Evelyn as she went past her. "For everything and for taking care of this now."

Evelyn smiled at her. "It's my honor. We'll talk tomorrow. After Ben leaves, I'm going to drop into my bed in the next room and you might not see me until late."

"Which is when you might see us. Thanks again."

Rebecca stood in the doorway and looked back at her mother. For the first time in days, there was no labored breathing and no pain in the woman's face. She was finally at peace.

"She's beautiful, isn't she?" Rebecca asked Polly.

"Yes, honey, she is."

CHAPTER TWENTY-ONE

Opening the door to the apartment, Polly felt like she had been completely deflated.

"Polly?" Rebecca asked quietly.

"Yes, honey."

"I don't want to go to my bedroom. Can I just sit out here on the couch for a while? Maybe you guys could leave your door open so the dogs could come out?"

Polly hugged her shoulders. "Let's bring our pillows out. You take one sofa and I'll take the other. If we sleep, great. If not, that's fine, too."

Henry opened the bedroom door. Polly heard the television.

"You weren't sleeping?" she asked.

"No. I was worried about you two."

"She died, Henry," Rebecca said matter-of-factly. "It's finally over."

"Oh honey, I'm so sorry." He strode across the room and gathered Rebecca into his arms. With a great lurching sob, she sagged against him. Henry reached down and lifted her up, then carried her to a sofa, where he sat with her in his lap.

Polly watched as he stroked Rebecca's hair and let her cry. She smiled down at him, her own eyes filled with tears. It was just what Rebecca needed, strong arms to make her feel safe while she fell apart. How had she gotten so lucky as to marry this man?

Obiwan sat down on the floor in front of them and Han jumped up on the couch, trying to insinuate himself in between Rebecca and Henry. After attempting to push the dog away, Henry finally gave up and flashed Polly a grin. He was just a goofy, happy dog, there was no getting around it.

After a few minutes, Rebecca stopped crying and took a deep breath. "I'm sorry," she said.

"Don't be sorry," Henry said. "We're family. This hasn't been an easy time for you and you've been awfully strong."

"I never wanted Mom to know how sad I was. I didn't want her to feel bad." Rebecca stood up and walked to her room. "Will you stay out here with me, Polly?" she asked.

"Why don't you two girls take our bed? You can watch television or sleep or talk. I'll spend the rest of the night on Rebecca's bed," Henry offered.

"But you have to work tomorrow," Rebecca said in protest.

"And I'll sleep wherever I put my head down. Don't argue with me. I'm the man of the family, got it?"

She gave him a little giggle and disappeared into her room.

"Thank you, Henry," Polly said.

"For giving up my bed? You *should* be thanking me. I like sleeping with my wife. But I think Rebecca needs you more than I do tonight."

Polly kissed his cheek. "For that and for letting her sob. That was pretty cool."

He threw his shoulders back. "That's me. Cool. I won't make much noise tomorrow morning when I leave, but I'll take care of the dogs. You two sleep until you wake up." He walked toward the bedroom. "Is Mrs. Morrow taking care of everything?"

Polly nodded. "We'll talk tomorrow."

"Give me a minute to get my things and you two can have the room."

Rebecca came out of her bedroom, dressed in her pajamas. Polly still had the two stuffed animals that had been lent to her and carried them into the bedroom. They passed Henry on his way out. He gave Polly a kiss and hugged Rebecca again, then pulled the door halfway closed behind him.

"He didn't have to do this," Rebecca said, climbing up into the bed.

"He knows that," Polly said. "But he's a good guy and sometimes life is more important than sleeping in your own bed." She put Durango and Silver between them on the pillows. "Do you want to watch television or would you like to talk about things?"

Rebecca looked up at her. "Can we talk tomorrow? I don't want to think about it right now."

"Of course we can. TV on or off?"

"It doesn't matter," Rebecca said with a shrug. "On is fine."

Polly handed her the remote and chuckled as the two dogs tried to decide where they belonged. Han walked around the bed once and put his paws up beside Polly. She patted the bed and he made a half-hearted attempt to jump up, but then walked back to Rebecca's side and looked at her. He finally padded out of the room, turning to look back at them. Henry gave a low whistle and the dog disappeared from the doorway.

Obiwan, on the other hand, jumped up and planted himself between the two girls, his head nuzzling Rebecca's elbow.

"He knows I'm sad," she said.

"I'll never figure out how he got to be so smart," Polly responded "He's always known what was going on with me."

"Do you think I'm going to be this sad for the rest of my life?" Rebecca asked, clicking through channels on the television.

"No, not at all," Polly said. "You're going to have times when your heart completely breaks and with no warning, you'll start to cry. Even if it's fifteen years from now."

Rebecca creased her brows. "Really?"

"Absolutely. Something will happen and you'll wish your mom was there to experience it with you. It's going to take time for the raw pain of all of this to go away, but it will smooth out and every week that passes, you'll be able to think about her in different ways and learn to smile at the memories rather than cry at her loss."

"Do you still cry sometimes about your mom and dad?"

Polly thought about it for a moment. "Sometimes I get sad that Mom missed out on so much of my life. I was about your age when she died. I don't know that I miss her as much as I miss Dad, though. There are times I get wrecked when I think about how much I miss him. And I miss Mary, too. She was there throughout my life." Polly bit her lower lip. "I do cry when I miss them."

Rebecca thought about that, then she asked, "Did Mary ever act like she was jealous when you missed your mom?"

"No, honey. Mary loved my mother. She was my friend and only wanted to make sure that I was happy and healthy. Are you worried that I'll be jealous of how much you love your mom?"

"I think I worry about too many things," Rebecca said. She turned the television off. "Mom told me that I didn't need to worry about you. Sometimes I worry that if I love you and Henry like I love her it isn't fair to her, but she told me that it doesn't matter, that she'd be gone when that happened."

Polly stroked Obiwan's back. "You are one of the most loving girls I know. I think you have plenty of love inside you for all of us. It doesn't have to be one or the other. You don't have to love one of us more than the other."

"But..."

Polly put her hand up. "It's different love. You love me differently than you love Henry or Andrew or Kayla, right?"

"Yes." Rebecca turned on her side and scooted so she could see over Obiwan.

"But do you love any of us more than the other?"

That made the girl think. "It wouldn't be fair if I did."

"It's not about fair," Polly said. "I love you as much as I love Henry, but it's different love. I believe we have the capacity to love everyone with more love than we even realize."

"Okay." Rebecca shut her eyes and Polly wondered if she was falling asleep. "Will they cremate Mom tomorrow?" she asked out of the blue.

Polly wasn't quite sure what to say. "I suppose so. Why?"

"I was just wondering." Rebecca opened one eye to look at Polly. "Would it be creepy if I wanted to see what that looked like?"

"The actual cremation?"

"No!" Rebecca exclaimed. "The remains. Will it just be ashes?"

"If we're going to spread them in the woods and the creek, you'll get to see them then." Of all the conversations she could be having with Rebecca right now, this one was not something Polly was prepared for. The practicality of the event wasn't something she'd considered.

"Okay. That makes sense. When are they going to pick up the hospital bed?"

"Sometime this week. Why?"

"I was just wondering. Are you going to turn that back into a guest room right away?"

Polly raised up on her elbow. "Would it bother you if we did?"

"I don't know," Rebecca said. "I was just thinking about how you should do it really fast so I don't have time to think about it. Is Evelyn going to move back home tomorrow?"

"Probably. Do you want her to stay?"

Rebecca shook her head. "No. We talked. I can go see her any time. She just lives over there in the apartments where Andrew used to live. And she said that she would call and ask to take me to lunch sometimes. We'll still be friends."

"You're a pretty practical girl," Polly said.

"Mom told me that life keeps moving on and that I'm not supposed to get stuck at this point. We talked about death a lot the last couple of weeks. She was cool about it."

"It sounds like you two worked it all out. That's wonderful."

"She made me promise to do three fun things every week until I didn't have to think about doing them. And she made me double triple promise to do three fun things in the week after she died."

"What do you want to do?" Polly asked.

"For one of them, I want to go back for the class party on the last day. Do you think Mrs. Hastings will let me?"

"Of course she will."

"Then I want to go on a horseback ride. Kayla wants to go too. Can I go down and ask Eliseo about that tomorrow?"

Polly smiled. "I'm sure he would love to. What's your third thing?"

"I saved a little money. Do you think that Sal would take me shopping for a new dress for Mom's funeral?"

"I think Sal would be thrilled," Polly said. She reached out and squeezed Rebecca's hand. "You two would have a great day."

"You can come too," Rebecca said. "I didn't mean to leave you out."

"You aren't leaving me out, you're having fun with friends. We'll call Sal tomorrow and set up a time."

Rebecca took in a deep breath and let it out slowly. "I was going to talk tomorrow, but I talked a lot now."

Polly chuckled. "We can talk tomorrow, too. Are you ready to try to sleep?"

"Maybe just for a while."

~~~

Polly woke back up to Henry tapping on her shoulder. She glanced at Rebecca, whose face was peaceful in sleep. Obiwan turned his head, then rested it against Rebecca's side.

"What's up?" she mouthed.

Henry tilted his head to the living room. The cats followed her out and she pulled the door shut. Obiwan knew what he was doing, he'd be fine.

"What time is it?" Polly asked, fumbling for her phone.

"It's eleven thirty," he said.

"In the morning? Why are you here?"

"I got a call from Jeff." Henry picked an envelope up from the coffee table. "He wanted to know if he should call the Sheriff, but I

213

thought you might want to know about this before we did that."

Polly pulled her hand back from the proffered envelope. She gave a deliberate shudder and said, "I don't want to touch it if it's what I think it is."

"Do you want me to just call Aaron?"

She nodded and dropped down onto the couch. "Go ahead. I'm too fuzzy to even think straight. Is there any coffee left in the kitchen?"

"I just started a fresh pot. It will be ready in a few minutes. Are you sure you don't want to look at this first?"

Polly put her hand up to take it from him. "I don't. Every time one of these comes in, I'm terrified of what I'll find in it." She grimaced. "But if I don't look, that FBI lady will take it out of here and I'll never see it again." She turned it over and then back over again and again. "Has anyone seen Ray or Jon this morning? Do they know about this?"

Henry chuckled. "I think Ray is keeping his distance."

"Good for him," she said. "What about the rest of 'em? Are they around?"

"No. I talked to Jon this morning and told him that you would probably be in all day with Rebecca. I would have let you sleep, but I thought that if the Sheriff needed to start moving on this, you wouldn't want to make him wait."

Polly turned it over again and slid her finger under the flap. "This almost makes me sick to my stomach. I'm so worried about that other girl he kidnapped."

"I'll get coffee. You decide whether you're opening it or not." Henry left Polly alone with the envelope.

She finally opened it and dumped the contents onto the table in front of her. Sure enough there was a white envelope and a photograph, both of which were upside down. Now what was she supposed to do?

"My tongs are downstairs," she said. "And so are the gloves they gave me."

Henry came back with a steaming hot cup of coffee. He reached into his pocket and pulled out the gloves. "Nope. I'm a smart boy."

She grinned. "You really are. Thank you."

The first thing she did was to turn the photograph over. She glanced at it and flipped it upside down again.

"My phone is in the bedroom. Would you call Aaron? She's dead."

"Oh Polly, I'm sorry," Henry said, sitting down beside her. He put his arm around her shoulders. "I know that was your biggest fear."

"Does this mean they've taken someone else too?" she asked.

"We have no way of knowing that. Let me call Aaron."

While he made the call, Polly opened the envelope and took out the handwritten letter.

"I'm so tired of killing, but he says that I won't get better until I finally have you. Please make this stop, Polly. You are responsible for all of this and you are the only one who can help me. If you ever loved me, you will join me so we can be together forever.

"By the time you get this, we will start again. They don't know the right things to say to me. They don't know about our time together or the way that you loved me. They don't know anything, even though I try to tell them. He says this is the only way I'll get better. Please help me, Polly."

She gently put the paper back down on the table and sat back, pulling a pillow up to cover her face. She wasn't sure whether she wanted to cry or scream, but the pillow was the right thing for either choice.

"Is there anything I can do?" Henry asked.

"Find him and string him up," she said. "I just want this to be over. I don't want any more girls hurt because Joey has some sick and twisted idea we should be together. He tells me this is my responsibility."

"Polly..." he started.

"I know, I know. Taking responsibility for an insane man's actions says nothing for my own sanity. I get all that, but at some level..."

"No. You just can't do that to yourself."

"Too late," she said flatly. "I'm so tired."

"Of course you are. You haven't slept well for the last week and then last night you were up with Sarah and Rebecca. You must be exhausted."

"Is Aaron coming over?"

"Alone. He told your FBI lady that she didn't need to ride with him to pick up an envelope. At least you won't have to deal with her, too. I called Ray. Do you mind?"

"Of course not. I said what I needed to say to him. He's still my friend. Is he coming up?"

Henry nodded as a knock sounded at the front door. "That's him."

"I'll get it," Polly said, standing up. She put the pillow back on the couch and ran her hand through her hair. "I probably look like hell."

"You're fine. Stop worrying."

She opened the front door to find both Ray and Jon standing there.

Jon stepped in first, "We're sorry to hear about your friend's death," he said. "If there's anything we can do to help you get through that, just let us know."

"Thanks," Polly said. "Come on in."

Ray hung back. "Are we okay?" he asked.

Polly took his hand "We're fine. Would either of you like coffee? It's fresh."

Jon nodded. "I'll get it," he said. "Ray?"

"Sure. That sounds good. Is this it?" Ray asked, pointing at the table. He put gloves on, turned the pieces right side up and took quick pictures of the items and then peered at the photograph. "They put her in your truck again."

"That's no longer my truck," Polly said. "I will never drive that thing again, no matter what anybody does to clean it or paint it or whatever. I don't want to see it again. Ever."

"Would you look at the picture again?" Ray asked. "This time, avoid looking at the girl and the truck. Do you have any idea where this might have been taken?"

She took a deep breath and steeled herself, then put her hand out for the photo. Polly looked at the background of the photograph and tried to place herself wherever it might be. "I don't know," she said and held it out for Henry to look at. "It could be up on the Boone River. It kinda looks like Tunnel Mill." Then she glanced at Ray. "You know that place. I took you there on Saturday."

"Do you think so?" he asked.

"I don't know for sure," she said with a shrug. "It wouldn't hurt to check it out again, though."

"Do you feel up for a ride?"

Polly was startled. "Today? Ummm, no. I have a little girl in there who just lost her mother. I'm not leaving her today."

As if on cue, the bedroom door opened at the same time another knock sounded on the front door.

"I've got it," Henry said.

"Polly?" Rebecca called out quietly.

Polly jumped up and ran over to her. "You're awake."

"What's going on?" Rebecca rubbed her eyes and peered at Ray and Jon. "You're the two guys who are staying in the rooms above my mom." She stopped. "I mean..."

"It's okay," Polly said. "These are my friends, Ray and Jon Renaldi."

Aaron Merritt strode into the room, looked around and changed his entire stance once he realized that Rebecca was there. Rather than greeting the men, he walked across to her and said, "I'm very sorry to hear that your mother died, Rebecca."

"Thank you, Sheriff. Why are you here?" Rebecca asked. "Is something wrong with what we did for Mom?"

"Oh no, honey. Everything is fine there," he said. "I'm here to talk to Polly about something completely different."

"Is this about the bad guys who kidnapped her?"

"I'm afraid so," he said, looking at Polly.

Rebecca followed his eyes. "Did something else happen?" Then she looked at Ray and Jon. "You're here to keep Polly safe, right?"

Jon smiled and said, "We sure are. And any other pretty girls that live with her."

Polly rolled her eyes and watched Rebecca take that in.

The girl lifted a corner of her upper lip for just a moment and then said, "Girls like you, don't they."

Everyone in the room laughed. Jon got a sheepish look on his face as it turned bright red.

"She got you, brother," Ray said. "Right between the eyes. This one won't put up with fake niceties."

"Good for you," Polly whispered. "We need to talk about some things. I'd rather you didn't have to hear it. Do you mind?"

Rebecca nodded. "Can I watch TV?"

"Sure. It won't take very long. I'll be in soon."

CHAPTER TWENTY-TWO

Ray waited until Aaron had left and said, "Polly, I hate to admit that I'm buying into the idea that you're the only person around who will find a body, but if that's true..."

"Stop it. I'm not leaving Rebecca today," she said, standing back up and crossing her arms. "Don't you guys get it? Her mother died this morning."

He sat down and looked up at her. "I do get it, but there's a girl out there whose mother wants to know what happened to her."

Polly snarled at him. "That's not fair."

Jon put his hand on Ray's shoulder and pushed him back on the sofa. "She's right. That isn't fair. None of this is Polly's fault, even though that jerk keeps trying to push responsibility on her. The last thing she needs is for us to reinforce that. Leave her alone."

"I'm sorry," Ray said. "He's right. Really, Polly. I'm sorry. This has me frustrated. Why can't we find these guys? It isn't like they know the area."

Polly sat back down. "They don't know the area, but I remember Joey remarking about how easy it was to hide out here.

"'pAnd he was right. There are a million wooded acres and abandoned houses and barns. There are gravel roads and fields they can get lost in. Not to mention the state parks and protected areas. All they need is a map and as long as they don't stay in one place, no one would ever find them."

"They'll make a mistake," Henry said. "They practically did when you were at Ralph Bedford's and saw your truck. They think that no one will recognize the background of their photographs, but so far, it's been simple enough for both you and Sylvie to pick out their locations. It's going to happen. They'll get caught."

Jon nodded. "Joey's starting to panic. He knows that killing these girls is wrong. He killed the first one because he was all caught up in the frenzy of the moment. But this last one bothered him. He's going to be the one who makes the mistake. We just have to hope that he makes a mistake in public rather than in private with this guy who will kill him and move on."

"I don't want him dead," Polly said, dropping her head and shuddering. "That would be awful. I don't want him bothering me again, but I certainly don't want him dead."

Ray put his hand up and nodded at her bedroom door.

Polly turned and saw Rebecca standing there. "What's up, honey?"

"This is bad, isn't it?"

"What do you mean?" Polly asked.

Rebecca pointed at Ray and Jon. "This. It's worse than just kidnapping you and you getting away. No one told me anything, but it's really bad, isn't it."

Polly looked at Henry. He gave a slight shake of his head and then shrugged his shoulders.

"How much have you heard?" Polly asked her.

"That some guy named Joey killed two girls and someone else wants to kill him. Who's Joey?"

"He's an old boyfriend of mine," Polly said. "He should be in a mental hospital, but he escaped. He wants to take me away with him because he thinks that I should be his wife."

220

Rebecca walked over and stood beside Polly. "And the other man?"

Polly set her jaw. She didn't want to put this on Rebecca today. How much could one young girl process? "He's a known serial killer. But he doesn't kill just anybody. He kills men like Joey after he manipulates them into murdering other people."

"Joey wants to kill you?" Rebecca's voice squeaked.

"I think that in the deepest part of Joey's heart, he doesn't want to, but this other man has made him believe that he does."

Rebecca shut her eyes and thought about it, then put her hand on Polly's shoulder. "Mom wouldn't believe this if I told her. Do you remember that day you chased the man before we went to see her in the hospital?"

Polly smiled. She did. All she'd wanted to do was get a license plate. She was sure he was involved with the death of one of the men who had been hired by the winery to grow their grape vines. When Rebecca told Sarah about the escapade, Polly had worried that the woman would be afraid to let her raise her daughter. Since then, so many other things had happened. Sarah had finally just accepted that Polly's life was anything but normal.

"I will always keep you safe. You know that, right?"

Rebecca smiled at her. "You'll try. I should take self-defense classes if I'm going to live here. I'll need them."

Both Ray and Jon laughed. "You're a smart girl," Jon said. "Living with Polly could get exciting. I think Henry's hair has gotten grayer since we arrived."

"No, I think he's rubbed more of it off the top of his head," Rebecca said. "He has to worry about Polly every day and every night."

"I'm sitting right here!" Polly exclaimed.

"Did you find the first girl they killed?" Rebecca asked Polly.

"Yes, honey, I did."

Rebecca tilted her head toward Ray. "He wants you to go out with him so that he can find the other girl, doesn't he."

"How did you know that?" Ray asked.

"Because that's what you do. You fix things. That's why you're

still here. But Polly won't go because she's worried about me."
Rebecca patted Polly. "I'm fine."

"I know you are, but..."

"If you call Sal, she could take me to Ames. She'd feel sad for
me and get me ice cream and everything."

"Wow, are you too bright for your britches," Henry said.

Polly looked over at him. "I think we're in trouble."

Rebecca shrugged. "Mom always says that as long as I'm polite
and respectful, I don't have to be a stupid girl. So I'm not. Do you
want to call Sal and see if she's free? If she's not, I could go
downstairs and help Sylvie and Rachel in the kitchen until Kayla
and Andrew get here. You don't need to babysit me. I'm fine."

"Are you sure?"

Rebecca glared at her. "Would I say I was fine if I wasn't?"

"Yes," Polly said. "You would."

"Well I am. I know that I'm going to cry when I miss Mom, but
right now I'm okay and I don't feel like sitting up here moping."

Polly shook her head. "Okay. Take a shower and get ready. I'll
call Sal and then do the same. We'll come up with a plan."

Rebecca went into her room and shut the door.

Ray stood up. "Are you sure you're ready to raise that one?"

"I think she's going to raise herself," Henry said. He looked at
his watch. "I hate to leave you alone, but I'm going to take off if
you don't need me. Dad and Len are moving the bar into the
coffee shop today." He bent over to kiss Polly's cheek. "Take care
of yourself and text me, okay?"

"I promise," she said.

"Call me when you're ready to go," Ray said. He and Jon went
out the front door.

Polly sat back on the sofa, exhausted. She'd slept, but the last
hour had worn her out. Rebecca walked through to the shower
and Polly followed her with her eyes. She was handling her
mother's death better than Polly expected, but at some point, you
could only cry so much.

Henry came back out of the bedroom with Han. "I'll take the
dogs outside and send them back up. Are you going to be okay?"

"I'll be fine. Thanks for coming home. I'm glad you were here."

He nodded toward the bathroom. "She's a pistol. All of a sudden she has more confidence. What happened?"

Polly took a deep breath. "I don't know. Maybe she's been in a holding pattern for so long, not knowing for sure where she was supposed to land or who she was supposed to be with, and now that it's over, she can settle in."

"I can't imagine going through what she's been through, but she certainly seems to be handling it."

"I wonder how much of it's because she had her mom there with her through the entire process ... until this morning. Sarah helped her figure out how to handle it all."

He put Polly's phone on the sofa beside her. "Here's this if you want to call Sal. What do you think she'll say?"

"Sal was there through Dad's death and Sylvester's and then Mary's death. She always knew just how to take care of me and what to say when it needed to be said. If there's anyone I trust with Rebecca today, it's her."

"Kiss me," he said, bending over. Their lips met and he put his hand at the base of her neck, holding her close. When they broke apart, he said, "I missed you last night."

"I missed you too. One of these days things will go back to normal."

"That's a curse 'round these parts," Henry said with a laugh and a southern twang. He walked into the media room, calling for the dogs while Polly swiped her phone open to call her friend.

~~~

Polly watched the world pass by from the window of Ray's Jeep. She was almost depressed. It was one thing to stumble across a body, but to go out with the intent of finding one wasn't something she wanted as part of her life.

Sal had been thrilled to take Rebecca shopping. She told Polly that no one wanted her at the coffee shop and she was in between writing projects, so in essence, all she was doing was annoying

Mark and bugging her dogs. A trip out of town would be the perfect remedy. When Polly tried to talk about how to pay for Rebecca's dress, Sal just laughed at her. Polly chose to let it go.

"This way, right Polly?" Ray asked as he signaled for a right turn.

She nodded.

"He's not looking at your head," Jon said from the back seat.

"Sorry. Yes. Right turn here and follow the sign where the highway goes north," she said.

"What's wrong?" Ray asked.

"It's nothing. I'm just not excited about deliberately looking for a body. Especially this poor girl."

"I know," he said. "But as soon as she's found, her family can start dealing with it."

Polly sat up and turned to look at him. "Why did you press me so hard to come out today?"

He shook his head.

"Come on. Did you and Aaron talk about this?"

Ray huffed out a breath.

Jon sat forward and said. "Yes. We knew that picture was going to come. It had to come. Aaron talked to us about getting you out to look for her before the FBI could move in. That's why he came up. He's giving us ... well, you ... time to try to find her. That way, when they tell her family that she's dead, they won't have to do it with just a photograph."

"Okay, then," she said. "Let's do this. The turn should be right up here."

"I remember this now," Ray said. "So, if it was Aaron's idea, you're on board?"

Polly scowled at him. "Not really. But kinda. I needed to hear why it was so important for me to get out. Especially today. It makes more sense now. He should have said something to me."

Ray drove down the road to the river and pulled into the parking area. "Where do you want to start?" he asked.

"I have no idea," Polly said. "I never do this with the intention of finding someone. I generally just stumble on them."

Jon got out of the back seat and opened her door. "Let's take a walk, then."

"I feel like a ghoul," Polly whispered to him.

"Shhh," he whispered back. "We won't tell anyone."

They walked down to the river and she looked around, poking in bushes and kicking at brush. They walked back into the hillside until the brush was too dense and then paced the perimeter of the parking area.

"There's nothing here," Polly said. "I'm sorry."

"You have nothing to be sorry about," Ray told her. "We hoped it might work, but it's okay."

"We could try a couple of other sites," Polly said. "The next one down the river is an active campground, so nothing there, but if we go west another mile after that, there's another bridge. I think there's a dirt road leading down to the river."

He shrugged. "Might as well give it a shot. We have time before I told the Sheriff I'd call."

They got back in the Jeep and he turned it around and drove out, then headed in the direction Polly pointed.

"If you could just sense the bad guys like you do dead bodies, we could be done with this whole thing," Jon said, pushing on Polly's shoulder.

"Are you guys ready to head back to Boston?" she asked.

"No," he laughed. "That isn't what I meant. This is a mini vacation for me. You live a slower life than you did in Boston. We would have had more trouble keeping up with you out there."

"Yeah," she said with a chuckle. "I was such a busy girl. Work, work and more work. All those nights clubbing and partying. You would never have been able to keep up with me."

"It was more than you do here. You're almost boring."

She swung as far as the seatbelt would let her move. "This is not my normal life. I'm stuck inside because of a couple of psychopaths. I am not boring. And I love my life. Every bit of it."

"Leave her alone," Ray said. "It isn't like you are some great playboy. For all your mouth, you're over at Mom's house more often than not."

"That's just because she cooks for me."

"Uh huh ... you're a mama's boy."

"She'd like to see *you* more often," Jon said.

"I'm there every Sunday unless I'm out of town. That's enough."

"Boys, stop it. The turn is just down this hill. You don't want to miss it," Polly interrupted. "Though I'm surprised to hear that Jon isn't out every night trying to find his next girlfriend." She turned and smirked at him.

"I wish," he muttered.

Polly grabbed the door handle as Ray negotiated the path leading to the river. Signs announced that it wasn't maintained and they weren't kidding. The middle was washed out and had it not been dry, this would have been a very foolish thing to do. Ray pulled off onto a level area and said, "Well. That was exciting. I'm glad we have the Jeep. At least I know we'll get back out."

Cars flew by on the bridge overhead as Jon opened Polly's door again.

"I'm not sure where to begin," she said. "I haven't ever been here before."

Ray started forward. "Let's check the river first. We can wander the rest of this later. I can't tell if any of these tire tracks are recent, but if people fish from here or get off the river with their canoes, we couldn't tell the difference."

Polly stumbled and reached forward to balance herself, brushing against his back. He stopped and offered his hand.

"I've got it," she said. "It was just a rock in the way."

"You're still angry with me, aren't you?"

"No. I'm not angry."

"You don't trust me, though," he said.

"Nope," she said, pursing her lips together. "I don't."

"You know I'll keep you safe."

"I trust you with that, but I pretty much think you're slime."

"I was just doing my job."

"Uh huh, that's what the Nazi soldiers said. You can justify whatever you have to justify. You should have talked to me, but you didn't trust me." She caught her foot on a branch and stopped in her tracks, trying to hold on to her balance.

"You might want to watch where you're going," he said.

"You might want to shove it where it will hurt," she replied.

They reached the water's edge and she looked across the river and then up along the banks on both sides. Polly stood still for a few minutes, trying to see everything in front of her at once, then she decided to take it more slowly and scan the area in sections. When she realized there was nothing there, she turned to the bridge abutment.

"I'm just going to slide behind here," she said. "I'll be right back. I want to look on the other side of the river."

"Jon?" Ray said. "Go with her."

"How long are you going to punish him?" Jon asked as they crawled through the brush.

"I thought I was over it," she said. "I don't think I'm really that mad."

"Then what was that about?"

"Sometimes he is such a big brother. All helpful and stuff. I think it ticked me off." Polly started to laugh. "I'm an independent cuss, aren't I. Dad always said that was going to get me into trouble. I drive Henry crazy with it, too. Why should I let someone else do what I can do?"

Jon jumped down to a clearing and held out his hand. Polly took it and jumped down beside him.

"That wasn't so difficult, was it?" He bowed at the waist.

"So it's just Ray that annoys me," she said, laughing. "I'm horrible. I'll apologize when we get back."

"Do you see anything?" he asked, gesturing out at the river.

Polly took her time and scanned sections of this side of the bridge. She looked back into the field behind her and didn't see anything. With a sigh, she said, "No. Nothing. I feel so bad."

"Stop it. The day isn't over yet."

"But Ray is right. That family should have their daughter back."

Jon clambered back up the little hill and then held his hand out to help Polly pull herself up. She grabbed the exposed roots of a nearby tree to give herself extra momentum and when it pulled out of the sand, she and Jon both tumbled back down.

"Damn it," he said.

"I'm so sorry! I tugged on it and thought it was strong enough. Are you okay?" Polly crawled over to him.

"No, I wasn't swearing at you. I ripped my shirt."

"Seriously?"

"It was one of my favorites," he said with a whine.

"Are you two okay over there?" Ray called.

Jon winked at her. "Polly ripped my shirt. She's getting frisky. I think this is starting to get to her."

"If she's going after you, she's lost her mind. Have you found anything?"

"We'd let you know if we found anything." Jon rolled his eyes. "He big-brothers everyone."

Polly picked at the hole in his shirt. "Are you sure you didn't get hurt?" she asked. "I shouldn't have trusted that root."

He brushed her hand away. "I'm fine. Stop it. But I'll let you go first this time."

She pulled her way up the hill and then put her hand out for him.

"I think I'll do this one on my own," Jon said. "Go on ahead. I'm right behind you."

Polly climbed back through and stopped to wait for Jon. She leaned against the bridge. "This feels like an old fairy tale. Billy Goats Gruff and the trolls under the bridge."

"We're the trolls?" Jon asked.

She shrugged. "Something like that." Polly dropped her head and ran her fingers back through her hair.

"You okay?" Ray asked.

"I'm fine. And I'm sorry I was so prickly. I'm really not mad at you."

He nodded as Jon stepped in beside her.

"We okay here?" Jon asked.

Polly looked back the way they came. "I can't believe she's not here. I have no other idea of where to look. We might as well just go back to Sycamore House. I'm useless."

She took a deep breath and stretched her neck, rolling her shoulders. "Damn it, no I'm not," she said.

"What?" Ray asked.

"Look up there. We were looking at the river. She wasn't in the river. They put her in plain sight. I just needed to look up."

At the top of the hill, tucked in under the bridge, they saw the body of the young girl who had been kidnapped.

Jon pulled Polly into a hug. "I can't believe you found her."

"I thought that's why we were here," she said.

"But you really did it."

Ray was walking back up the road, looking at the face of his phone. "No signal," he called back. About halfway up, he stopped and made a call. Then he came back down. "That was Aaron. They'll have everyone here in a few minutes. I told him that I'd stay if you two want to head back. Once those vehicles get in here, we'll never get out."

"I can stay," Jon said.

Ray smiled. "No. I can talk to your friendly FBI agent with authority. You two go back and clean yourselves up. You're a mess. Someone will drop me off later."

Polly hugged him. "Thanks for everything. And I suppose, thanks for believing in me."

"We had to find her. You were our best bet. No one else would have found her under there. Now go, before people start arriving."

CHAPTER TWENTY-THREE

Waking to both telephones ringing and the town's sirens sounding, Polly and Henry sat straight up. She tried to make sense of the noise assaulting her. Something inside her clenched. This was bad news.

"What time is it?" Henry asked, fumbling for his phone on the bedside table. He flipped the lamp on and stared at his phone. He seemed just as fuzzy and foggy as she felt.

"I don't know. What's going on?"

"Answer your phone."

She saw that it was a call from Lydia. "Hello?" she said. Henry was talking to someone else on his own phone. Even before Lydia responded, he was out of bed and pulling on his pants, while listening to whomever was on the other end of the call.

"Honey," Lydia said. "Someone torched the coffee shop. That's what the siren is. I thought you'd want to know."

"What?" Polly stammered. "They torched the coffee shop? What time is it?"

"It's after midnight. They're calling out the fire trucks and the volunteers."

Henry was in a shirt when Polly jumped out of bed. "I have to go, Lydia," she said. "I'll talk to you later.

"Lydia?" he asked.

"They have a scanner. She wanted to make sure we knew about the fire. Wait for me. I'm going with you."

He started for the door and turned around. "What about Rebecca?"

"I'll wake her up. She doesn't have school tomorrow. But you aren't going without me."

Polly pulled her jeans and a t-shirt on and slipped into a pair of flip flops before running into Rebecca's bedroom. "Honey?" she said quietly.

"What are the sirens about?" Rebecca asked.

"Can you get up and get dressed quickly? The coffee shop is on fire."

Rebecca jumped up and out of bed. "What should I wear?"

Polly turned her bedside lamp on and said, "I don't care. Jeans and a sweatshirt. Put your shoes on. Henry's waiting."

"Who would set fire to the coffee shop?" Rebecca asked, pulling a pair of jeans out of her drawer. She opened another drawer and drew out a sweater, then sat down on the floor and put her shoes on, lacing them up as quickly as her fingers could move.

"I have no idea. I just want to get downtown and find out what's happening.

Rebecca jumped up and looked around her room. "I don't need anything else, do I?"

"No, I think you're good to go. Come on."

Rebecca's hair was mussed and she was rubbing her eyes as they walked through the living room. She'd had a busy day and Polly had been so thankful when she'd fallen asleep after dinner. The trip with Sal had been successful and while Polly was cleaning up the kitchen, she'd modeled a pretty black dress with white polka-dots. She was smiling as she spun, the skirt lifting in the breeze she created. Sal had given her a much needed distraction.

The dogs were running back and forth from room to room,

trying to figure out why everyone was in such a rush. Henry finally picked Han up and put him on one of the sofas. Obiwan sat down and watched as they rushed around.

Rebecca grabbed up her backpack as they headed out. "I might want to draw," she said. "I haven't ever seen a fire before. Is that okay?"

Henry nodded and took the pack from her. "Let's just hurry," he said.

They all ran for the back stairs and down to the garage. Henry opened the garage door as they jumped in and put their belts on.

"We should have just walked," he said. "They probably have the street blocked off."

"Get us as close as you can," Polly said. "We'll walk from there."

He backed out, turned, and drove out of the driveway to the highway, then headed for downtown. People were coming out of buildings and he was right, police cars were blocking Washington Street. Henry pulled into an alley and waited for Polly and Rebecca to jump out and join him. They walked a block and were stopped by Bert Bradford, standing in front of a police car with its lights flashing.

"You can't go any closer," he said, watching the activity up ahead and not paying attention to who he was talking to.

"Bert. It's me. This is my project and Polly's building," Henry said. "You have to let us through."

"Sal's building," Polly muttered.

Henry scowled at her.

"Look, take the alley to the back of the pizza place," Bert said conspiratorially. "Devin's still there. He'll let you in."

"I'll call him," Polly said, taking out her phone as they ran down the sidewalk to the alley. Henry took Rebecca's hand as Polly dialed.

"Hello?" Devin said.

"Hey, it's me, Polly. I'm with Henry and we can't get close. Will you let us in your back door?"

"Come on up. Sal and Mark are here already. I called them after I called the fire department."

Polly wanted to ask more questions, but she knew she was slowing Henry down. She swiped the call closed and ran to keep up with him and Rebecca, glad to see the light from the inside of Pizzazz. Sal was holding the door open as they ran up the steps to the dock and inside.

Sal's face was white with shock and it looked as if she'd been crying. As soon as they were inside, she took Polly's arm, leaning against her for support.

"What the hell?" Polly asked, as they walked through the kitchen to the front of the building.

"I think it was Molotov cocktails," Devin responded. "I saw a couple of guys loitering around while I was cleaning up and then I heard glass breaking and all of a sudden there were flames inside the building. It took me a couple of minutes to get back to the phone, so I didn't see where they went. All I could think was that I had to call someone."

Henry had dropped Rebecca's backpack on a table and walked to the front door. He opened it and the sounds of equipment and people rushed in.

"Where are you going?" Polly asked him.

"I'm going out. You stay here. I'll be back."

Before Polly could focus on the activity outside, her phone rang again. Sylvie was calling.

"Hey Sylvie," she said.

"Where are you? Do you know about the fire?"

"Yeah. I'm in Pizzazz."

"Can I get there?"

"We came in the back door. Call me as you get close and someone will let you in."

"Has the whole building burned down?"

Polly stepped closer to the window. It was hard to see around the trucks and the mass of people, but it looked as if the building was still standing.

"I think it's good. Devin saw it happen, so he called right away."

"How's Sal?" Sylvie asked, then spoke into the background.

"They're at Pizzazz. We just have to go down one more block. Quit your whining."

Polly chuckled. "Who's whining?"

"Andrew. He didn't want to get out of bed. But we never have this much excitement in town. I think everyone is out here tonight."

Sal turned and walked back to the table where they usually ate pizza every Sunday evening. She dropped into a chair and put her head in her hands. Mark sat down beside her, stroking her hair. He looked up at Polly and mouthed, "Help me?"

"I'm going to try to take care of Sal," Polly said. "How long until you're here."

"We're just crossing the street."

"Mark?" Polly asked. "Could you let Sylvie and her boys in? They're coming down the alley."

He looked relieved to leave Sal in her hands.

"He'll be at the back door," Polly said and swiped to end the call. She sat down beside her friend. "Are you okay?" she asked.

"Why would they burn down my building?" Sal asked in a faint voice.

"I don't know. But we'll deal with this."

"I can't start all over again."

"Don't say that. You can do anything you want." Polly reached out and took Sal's hand. "This isn't the end. I promise."

"Everything's gone," Sal wailed.

Polly spoke quietly, but firmly. "That's not true and you know it. We haven't moved any of the furniture or appliances in. It's just a building. It was insured and it will all work out. We don't know what's going on and that makes this a terrible time for you to be over dramatic. No one knows what to do for you."

Sal looked up and twisted her lips into a pout. "If this isn't a good time for drama, when will it be a good time? Huh? Tell me that, will you?"

"I love you to pieces, Sal Kahane, but this is ridiculous. At least wait until it's over to fall apart."

"You're not very nice."

"Because I won't put up with you feeling sorry for yourself? Especially when we don't have any answers?" Polly shook her head. "I'm sorry, but you need to get over yourself. Now buck up. Sylvie's here and she's less nice than I am about pity parties."

Sal sat up and took a breath as Sylvie rushed in. Jason and Andrew were right on her heels. As soon as Andrew saw Rebecca, he rushed over to sit with her. Jason hung back, watching to see people's reactions.

"Mark told me what happened," Sylvie said. "Can you see in the building yet?"

"I can't," Polly replied. "Don't you think it's good news that we haven't seen flames shooting up into the sky?" She turned to Sal. "And isn't it great news that there wasn't anyone living in the upstairs apartments yet? At least we know that no one is going to lose everything they own and no one is hurt."

"Little Miss Pollyanna," Sal said, mockingly. "Always finding the good in everything."

"Sal Kahane," Sylvie snapped.

"What? My building burned down and she wants me to be happy about it."

"I don't want..." Polly started.

"Stop being selfish," Sylvie interrupted. "We're all in this in one way or other. You haven't even started making payments on the building and I know that it's well insured. Nothing of value has been lost, people are safe. So stop moping around like your world is ending."

"Shit," Sal muttered. "Sorry."

Sylvie walked away and up to the front of Pizzazz. "Hey," she said. "I think it's over already. And here comes Henry."

She stepped back when he came in the front door. "What does it look like over there?" she asked.

"It wasn't as bad as it could have been." He walked over to Devin and put his hand out. Devin shook it. "If you hadn't seen it happen, it could have been much worse. They got here in plenty of time to save the building. We need to make decisions about what to do next, but what could have been devastating just isn't."

Sal had gotten up and come up to join them. She hung back, unsure as to what to say. Finally Mark spoke up. "You think the structure is sound after that?"

Henry nodded. "Whoever did this tossed four Molotov cocktails in through the glass windows. They were idiots, too," he said with a small laugh. "They actually went out and bought four bottles of vodka. It would have been cheaper to use gas, but they used the good stuff."

Rebecca had been watching everything and Polly could tell she had a question.

"What's up, Rebecca?" Polly asked.

"Why would a cocktail burn a building?"

Henry smiled. "A Molotov cocktail. That's different than a mixed drink. With this, they stuff a piece of cloth down into a bottle filled with something flammable. Then they light the cloth and throw it wherever they want the fire to start. The liquid spreads when the glass breaks and the fire takes off."

"Oh!" she said. She and Andrew started whispering back and forth and she went back to her sketching.

Henry watched for a moment, caught Polly's eye and gave her a wink. Then he continued. "The fire was getting going when the first truck arrived. It scorched the floor and did a number on Dad's bar. They hit one of the posts up high and the fire traveled up. I'm not sure about how sound the ceiling is now. We'll get in there to check as soon as it's safe." He turned to Sal. "We might want to talk about opening up the ceiling and getting rid of the apartments. It depends on what you want to do though."

She stayed silent as he spoke, nodding and listening.

"Bad water damage?" Sylvie asked.

"It's not good," Henry responded. "There's going to be a lot of cleanup before we can get started again. The walls are a mess. Jerry will need to come up and tell me what's going on with wiring. But those things will all happen. The good news is that the damage was minimal and it can all be fixed."

"How far in did the fire get?" Polly asked.

"The wall between the coffee shop and the bakery will need to be replaced and the kitchen needs to be dried out. It will be fine. At least that's what they're telling me. No one is going in right now. They'll keep an eye on it tonight, just to make sure nothing else pops up, but for now the crisis is over."

One of the trucks pulled out as city workers came in with saw horses and netting. They closed off the sidewalk and street around the building and people began gathering in front of Pizzazz.

"I should re-open," Devin said. "I could sell a lot of pizza."

Mark laughed. "With no cook or servers?"

"You're family," Devin said. "It's your job to help me out in times like this."

"Fine then," Mark said. "I'll call on you the next time I have to deliver a calf at two thirty in the morning."

Devin shook his head and mocked his brother-in-law. "Fine then. But you can tell people that if they want, soft drinks are on the house."

Polly followed Henry back outside as he made his way to the perimeter that had been set up.

"I can't believe it isn't any worse," she said.

"It's bad enough. This is going to push back the opening date by a couple of months. But Sal looked like she was ready to fall apart and I knew I had to give her good news."

"What about the ceiling and the apartments. Do you think they'll have to come down?"

He nodded. "Unless she was counting on those as income, she should just let us strip them out. I'm absolutely positive that the floors will be deemed unsafe once the inspector gets through in there."

Polly took his hand. "Going into business with her might have been the worst decision I've made so far."

"Why's that?" he asked.

"She has no confidence in anything and she was coming unglued. It's just a building and there wasn't anything in it."

"I love you, Polly," Henry said. "But sometimes you are too pragmatic for your own good. This was the first investment that Sal has ever made. She's pouring her entire soul into it. Then for no good reason, she saw it fall apart. How did you expect her to react?"

"Like a grownup," Polly said. "She was acting like a baby. Even Sylvie yelled at her."

"Sylvie's as bad as you are. Maybe even worse. She doesn't put up with people who don't have a strong backbone."

"Are you telling me I'm going to have to apologize to Sal for yelling at her?"

He looked at her and grinned. "Did you really yell at her or do you think it's worse than it was?"

"I don't know," Polly said. "I'm tired. I want to go back to bed. I want to sleep through a whole night without someone waking me up for a crisis."

"You go on back to Pizzazz. I want to talk to a couple of these guys over here before we head home. I'll be there in a few minutes."

Polly dropped his hand and started back across the street. Jason and Sylvie were outside talking to a group of people. Henry's parents were on the other corner with a different group and she waved to them. Marie put her hand up to stop the conversation, but Polly shook her head. She'd talk to them tomorrow.

My goodness, she was tired. She wasn't ready to go back inside and deal with Sal, so she leaned against the corner of the building and watched as the community gathered and dispersed. The excitement was over for the evening and tomorrow morning was going to come whether they slept or not.

"Don't scream or I will tase you," a voice said in her ear. A hand reached around and grabbed her forearm, wrenching it behind her. He grabbed her other arm and held them together. "We're going to walk away from here very quietly. If you make a scene, I will take you down and he will start shooting. You don't want people to be hurt tonight, do you?"

"Did you do this?" she hissed through her teeth.

"Pretty smart, huh? It got you out of that damned building and away from your bodyguards."

"Joey?" she asked.

"It will all be okay. Just come with me and don't do anything stupid. I *will* use the taser. I don't want to have to drag you."

They'd moved further away from the main street lamps. It got darker as they went along.

"Why are you doing this?" she asked.

"Because it's the only way I will ever be happy. It made so much sense when he fully explained it to me. There is only one person who will be able to satisfy everything I need. That's you. I will have you all to myself."

"Oh Joey," she moaned. "You are so wrong. Why did you kill those girls?"

"Because they weren't you." He sounded surprised that she didn't understand that.

"Why did you take them in the first place?"

"I had to do something when you ran away. What else was there?"

Polly shut her eyes as he slowly walked her deeper into the darkness. Trying to talk to or reason with him was useless. He was as insane now as he ever had been. She tried to drag her feet, leaning her weight on him to slow him down.

All of a sudden, he released her arms and she heard him drop to the ground. Polly spun and saw Jason standing over Joey, fury on his face.

"Jason," she cried. "What did you do?" She looked around desperately, trying to see if Allendar had noticed. It terrified her that he might open fire on the people still gathered.

"You were gone," Jason said. "I saw this guy walking with you and I realized it was the man who kidnapped you." His breath caught as he spoke, emotions threatening to overwhelm him. "I wasn't going to let him hurt you again. I told you that someday I would be strong enough to protect you."

She put her hands on her temples and clenched her fingers in her hair. "Grab his arms," Polly said. "We have to get him off the street. He has a partner who threatened to start shooting if I didn't go with Joey. They're the ones who started the fire."

Jason looked at her in confusion, but obeyed and put his hands under Joey's armpits. They dragged him into the alley and Polly directed him behind a dumpster. She took out her phone and dialed the one man she needed.

"I'm downtown, Polly. I know there aren't any dead bodies from the fire. Tell me you haven't found another one."

"Come to the alley behind Pizzazz," she said quietly. "Jason just knocked Joey out when he was trying to take me."

"He did!" Aaron said. "Good for him. That boy's brain is growing into those muscles he has."

"Aaron, Joey told me that Allendar has a gun and threatened to shoot it into the crowd if I didn't go with him. I don't know if he's here or not. They're the ones who started the fire. They did it to draw me out."

"I'll be right there. Keep him quiet."

"He's out for now," Polly said. "Hurry."

"I'm with Ken Wallers. We'll get everyone sent home. I'll be right there. Tell Jason to sit on him if necessary."

"Got it."

CHAPTER TWENTY-FOUR

As Jason bent over and patted Joey Delancy's pockets, Polly stopped him. "Don't touch it," she said.

"Why not? It's just a taser."

She patted her own pockets and couldn't come up with anything that would protect the taser from Jason's fingerprints. "Just don't touch it. Who knows what they need for evidence. The Sheriff said you could sit on him, though."

He stood back up and placed himself between her and the prone body on the ground. "He won't hurt you again, Polly."

"You made sure of that. Thank you."

"Did he say there was someone else who would shoot up the people on the street?"

"He did, but now that I think about it, that wouldn't happen. If his partner saw him go down, he's on the run. From what I understand, this guy needs someone else to do his dirty work. All he does is play mind games until he's tired of the weak-minded fool that he's manipulating."

They heard running on pavement and she stepped backward as both Ray and Jon Renaldi entered the alley. Ray was livid.

"What were you thinking - running out of Sycamore House without us?" he asked.

"Ray," Jon said, putting his hand on his brother's arm.

Polly squared her shoulders and stepped forward again. "Don't push me tonight, Ray. What was I thinking?" She paused to make sure he was listening. "I was thinking that my building was on fire, that everything my friend had invested was going up in flames, that my husband's work was threatened. That's what I was thinking. I was thinking that this is Bellingwood and I'm part of the community. That's what I was thinking."

This time he took a step back. "I'm sorry," he said. "I've been pushing you pretty hard. You're right. So, who put him on the ground this time?"

"You know Jason Donovan, right?" she said.

Ray shook Jason's hand. "You did this?"

"Yuh."

"Good job. He hasn't moved?"

There was a squeak from the ground as Joey turned his head. "Didn't dare," Joey said. "Easier to play dead."

Jon took Joey's arms and zip-tied them behind him, then hauled him to his feet. "At least Polly didn't kick you this time." He turned Joey and headed for the back steps of Pizzazz and pushed him to sit down. Joey sat and looked up at them.

"Where's Allendar?" Ray asked, looming over Joey.

"I don't know. He said he'd meet me when I had her."

"Where have you been living?"

"Here and there." Joey shook his head. "I don't know where he is."

"Where's the girl?"

Joey looked up, rolled his eyes at them and then dropped his head.

"Where's the girl?" Ray asked again. "Is she alive?"

Joey sat there, not saying a word, not reacting

"Look, you little prick. We aren't law enforcement. We can do anything we want to you and there's no one to stop us," Ray said, menace filling his words.

"Ray," Polly said quietly.

"No," he hissed. "You don't get to stop me this time. He's killed two girls and threatened you. This guy's life is worth nothing." Ray spat on the step beside Joey, making the man jump.

"Let me try," she said again.

"He won't talk to you. He's a scared little baby. I'll bet he wants his mommy." Ray stepped back as he taunted Joey, making room for Polly to move in.

"Joey, you have to tell us where she is. Don't make this worse on yourself. Please tell me." Polly reached in and lifted Joey's chin with her finger. "Look at me, Joey. Tell me where she is."

"Why did you run away?" he asked, his voice whiny. "You made me kidnap those girls and then kill them. I'm not a killer."

"No you're not," she said, continuing to hold his chin. "Tell me where to find her."

He turned his head away from her and dropped it again. "I had to do horrible things. He wouldn't do anything. I had to do it all. He made me touch dead bodies and..." Joey looked up again. "Why didn't you stay, Polly? I just wanted to be with you. We're meant to be together."

"I'm here now," she said. "Look at me and tell me where she is." Polly felt a hand on her back and stood up to see Aaron and Henry standing there.

"Joey, you have to tell me," she said again.

"I can't go back to that hospital. They'll know I failed. I told everyone that I was going to get you back and that I'd be free."

"I promise you won't go back there," Polly said. "I promise."

"Really?" He looked at Aaron and then at Ray.

Both men nodded. "You won't go back to Boston," Ray said.

Somehow that brought relief to Joey. "I don't know how to tell you where she is, but I can take you." He leaned into Polly. "Your truck and clothes are there too."

"Where's Allendar?" she asked. "Help us find him and end this tonight."

"He won't go back," Joey said. "He doesn't care about the girls. He only cares about me."

Aaron walked away and took out his phone, then, using two fingers, beckoned Ray to join him.

"Don't move," Ray said warningly to Polly.

Henry started to step forward, but Polly gave him a slight shake of the head. She didn't want to aggravate the situation with Joey any further.

"Come on, Jason," Henry said. "Let's leave this to them. We'll find your mom. She wondered where you'd gone." He took Jason's arm to lead him back out onto the street.

"Are you sure you'll be okay?" Jason asked Polly.

She gave him a hug. "You were my hero tonight. I've watched you grow up for nearly three years, but I don't think I realized just what that meant. You were amazing."

He turned away, embarrassed, and followed Henry out of the alley. Polly watched them turn the corner and suddenly felt exhausted. She sagged and Jon took her arm.

"Are you okay?"

"I'm so tired. These emotional late nights are wearing me out."

"At least this one is nearly over."

"Is it?" she asked.

Aaron and Ray came back to join them. "If the only person in this whole scenario that is important to Allendar is Joey here, we're going to use him to draw the man out."

"Oh, Aaron," Polly said.

"We'll keep him safe. I have two vehicles coming in now. You go on home and let us do our job tonight."

Ray took Joey's arm and stood him up.

"Don't make me leave, Polly," Joey said, reaching for her. "Please take care of me."

Her heart went out to him. He was so pathetic ... so easily manipulated. She no longer saw the man that she had thought she loved three years ago, but his familiarity tugged at the part of her that remembered their time together.

"I'm sorry, Joey. There are so many things that are more important than you right now. You have to go." Polly turned away as Aaron and Ray led him down the alley.

Stu Decker opened the driver's door and FBI Agent Marla Lane stepped around from the passenger side. Polly didn't feel any satisfaction or joy as they put Joey in the back seat. Aaron got in the driver's seat and closed the door. She felt tears run down her cheeks as she realized that this was mostly over for her.

"Are your friends inside?" Jon asked, pointing at the back door to Pizzazz.

"I suppose," she said. "But I don't want to see anyone tonight. I just want to go home." She started to cry as she took out her phone. "Let me call Henry. He'll come get me."

Jon stood silently as she made the call.

"Henry, where are you?"

"I'm in Pizzazz. Do you need me to open the back door?"

"Can you just get the truck and come get me? I don't want to see anyone. I don't want to have to talk about this or explain why I'm crying. I just want to go home and go to bed."

"We'll be right there. Are you safe?"

"Jon's with me."

"Give me time to get to the truck. You're fine, honey."

"I know. Thank you."

Jon reached out to take her arm. "You are fine," he said. "I can't believe what you did here tonight."

"I didn't do anything. I just talked to a man that I used to know. He thinks he's in love with me and he'd do nearly anything to make me happy." Polly shook her head. "I can't believe they're using him as bait to catch Allendar. He's been through enough."

"Polly, he killed two young women because they weren't you," Jon said with disgust.

She dropped her head. "I know. But that's because he is so weak. I wasn't surprised that he was so easily manipulated by a psychopath. Anyone that knows Joey wouldn't be surprised."

"At least it's over for you," Jon said. "We'll stick around until Allendar is caught, but you're nearly rid of us."

Polly grinned at him. "I wish you two could have come to Iowa just for fun."

Henry drove in with Rebecca in the back seat.

"You know that we'd never have thought to do that, Polly. I'm just glad we had a reason and that you're still safe at the end of it." Jon opened the front door of the truck and waited as she climbed in. "I'll be right behind you," he said. "Our car is down the street."

"I'm just going to go upstairs and go to bed," Polly said. "Text me when you get to your room and I'll talk to you tomorrow."

"Good enough. Get some sleep, everyone."

Polly pulled the door shut and sagged in her seat. "I'm exhausted. Take me home and put me to bed." She craned her neck to look at Rebecca. "How are you doing, honey?"

"I'm good. Is it really over?"

"It is," Polly said. "The police have Joey and they're going after his partner."

"What about the girl who was kidnapped?"

"He's taking them to her. It's time for us to go home, sleep until tomorrow and then finish preparing for your mother's memorial service."

Rebecca huffed a small chuckle. "That seems like it was so long ago. A lot's happened today."

"How are you doing with that?" Henry asked as he turned into their driveway.

"It's okay. I cried when I went to bed. It felt strange not to be downstairs in her room. In fact, it feels strange not to have to do anything or worry about her. I wonder how long I'll still think that I should check on her?"

"It might be a few weeks," Polly said. "Did you talk to Evelyn about that?"

"She said that caregivers feel a sense of loss not only because they lost someone who was close to them, but also because their schedules have changed and they have free time again. I think she's right."

"If anyone would know, she would," Polly said.

Henry pulled into the garage and they unbuckled and climbed out of the truck as the door came down.

"Are you going to be able to go back to sleep?" he asked Rebecca. "We messed with your schedule tonight."

"I might read a book, but I'm pretty tired," Rebecca said. She hefted her backpack out and Henry took it from her, then held the door open as they went inside. Rebecca opened the door to the upstairs and started up the steps.

"Obiwan and Han must be sleeping," she said. "Good for them. It's late."

Polly looked at Henry. His brows furrowed and he said, "Rebecca, stop."

She crested the top step and turned to look at him. "Why? What's up?"

At that moment, an arm grabbed her wrist and the man pulled her against his body.

"Come on up, Mr. and Mrs. Sturtz," he said.

Polly shuddered as she realized that she recognized the voice. He had been so calm when she was blindfolded and tied to a bed. She wondered if that was his normal demeanor.

"Go ahead," she said to Henry. She used his body to block her actions as she swiped her phone open and called Aaron. "You're Marcus Allendar, aren't you?" she asked loudly, hoping to cover Aaron's usual witty repartee at the beginning of their phone calls. She slipped the phone into her back pocket, thankful that technology had gotten to a point where this was even possible.

Henry must have realized her intentions because he stamped his feet up the steps and shouted, "What in the hell are you doing in my house?"

"Calm down, Mr. Sturtz," Allendar said. "We all know why I'm here. I've been following your wife all week. That is, whenever she had enough bodyguards to protect her so she could go outside. You know, your boyfriend and I were in that old house across the street there." He pointed toward the front of the building. "They say it's on the market, but no one paid any attention to us when we were there."

He held his gun close enough to Rebecca that she had a hard time moving without brushing against it. When they got to the media room, he shoved her onto the couch and she scrambled to put as much distance between herself and Allendar as possible.

"Go on," Allendar said, waving his gun at Henry. "Sit with your little girl. She's had a rough week, so I hear. She probably wants to have an adult around who will take care of her. I'm not about to hurt a child, don't worry. I just want time with Polly Giller. From what I understand, the sun rises and shines on this woman. What's so damned special about you that you screwed young Joey Delancy up so bad he ended up in a psych ward?"

Polly shook her head. "Where are my animals?" she asked.

He rolled his eyes. "As much as they want to tell you that we all kill and torture small animals, that isn't my thing either. They're safe in one of the bedrooms. I found your treats and they followed me in." He shrugged a shoulder. "They got a great many treats, so you'll either have very uncomfortable animals or your husband will find a big mess to clean up after we leave."

"Why do you want Polly?" Henry asked.

"I want to see what it will take to make her mine," Allendar said. "Delancy was mine after the third session. His mind was weak. But this one might take a very long time to break. It will be a joy to watch her try to stay strong. We'll see what happens when we remove everyone from her life. What will it take for her to depend on me when she knows that she will never see any of you again ... when there is no more hope ... when her life is only worth something because I say that it's worth something?"

"You'll never break Polly," Rebecca said defiantly. "You shouldn't even try."

He nodded, raising his eyebrows. "You might be right. But it's going to be so much fun to dig into that mind."

Polly knew that they had to keep him here long enough for Aaron to arrive. "Can I pack a bag? Just some clothes and a few things?"

"You're going to come without a fight?"

"I assume that if I don't, you'll threaten Rebecca and Henry, right?"

Allendar was impressed. "I guess so. Sure," he said. "Pack a bag. I'll come with you to make sure that you don't do anything stupid."

Polly rolled her eyes in front of him and looked pointedly at Henry. He gave her a slight nod and put his arm protectively around Rebecca.

"This way," she said. "You figured out which bedroom was mine, didn't you?"

"I did. Very nice, by the way."

"How did you get in?" she asked.

"I left Delancy downtown, but figured he'd fail miserably when it came to getting you off by yourself. He's taking the FBI to where the girl is, right?"

"Yes he is," she said. "Everyone thinks you're going to try to kill him, so they're watching for you."

He smiled at her, showing perfect white teeth. This man was a showoff. "Good for them. That will give us just enough time to get on the road. Where would you like to go first? I was thinking about Montana and then maybe we'll make our way down to Arizona for the winter. I don't like extreme temperatures."

"You didn't tell me how you got in here."

"You were in such a hurry to get to the fire, you didn't notice that the garage door didn't go all the way down. I triggered it back up and you forgot to lock your back door. Started feeling safe inside the four walls of your building, didn't you."

Polly opened her drawers and started taking clothes out. He stopped her by placing his hand on hers. She was surprised at how dry and warm it was. Her hands were cold and clammy.

"Not too much," he said. "You aren't going to need clothing unless we're on the road."

"What?"

"You don't think I'm going to leave you any dignity, do you?" he asked. "That's the first thing I'll take away. Just pick out an extra pair of pants and a t-shirt. You don't need any extra bras or panties. But if you soil yourself in the car, we'll want an extra wet until we can wash them." He cackled at the thought of it and Polly shuddered.

She took out a pair of soft jeans and a t-shirt, hoping someone would get to her before she actually had to leave the building with this man. He'd left Henry with a cell phone and she prayed that Aaron could hear what was happening and was on-site. It was the only reason she was able to remain calm at all, hoping that everything would come together while she was dragging her feet in the bedroom.

Something must have shown on her face. "Why are you so calm, Polly?" he asked, brushing her cheek with the gun. "Do you think that they're coming to rescue you? Did you believe that I wouldn't have a cell phone jammer on me? Any calls you or your husband have tried to make since you got here have been blocked. No one knows I'm here. No one knows that you're in trouble. Go ahead. Take your phone out of your back pocket. Look at it. You'll find that you're all alone."

Polly hesitated.

"Go ahead," he said. "You might as well learn right now that I'm a step ahead of you. Take out your phone."

She drew it out of her back pocket and swiped it open. It went right to the home screen. There was no call to Aaron, there was no signal at all."

"Now give it to me," he said. "You won't be needing it any longer."

Her heart clenched up and she felt her throat constrict. This couldn't be happening. She handed him the phone and he dropped it on the floor of the bedroom and crushed it under his foot. "There. That should take any temptation away. It's time for us to leave. Bring your measly belongings and come with me."

Polly didn't move.

"I said 'Come with me,'" he ordered, his voice low and menacing. "Don't make me threaten your family."

She dropped to the floor. "Please don't do this," she whimpered. "Just leave. We won't tell them you were here. Just go."

Allendar reached down and grabbed her upper arm, forcing her to stand back up. "Oh, Polly, Polly, Polly. I'm going to do this and so many other things to you. Every time you resist, I will punish you." He slapped her cheek.

Tears sprang to her eyes and she immediately raised her hand to her face. He pushed it away.

"There will no longer be any comfort for you. You aren't allowed to even care for yourself. I am the only one in your life who will give you anything. It's going to take time for you to understand just how much that entails, but one day you will be exactly the person I want you to be." He smiled at her and then caressed her cheek.

Unconsciously, she flinched and pulled back.

He slapped her again, harder this time. "I told you not to resist. You must start learning these lessons. Oh, you're going to be spectacular! Now, let's go. We'll leave by the front door. I think that you won't be allowed to say goodbye to your husband and the little girl. We'll let that pain be the next lesson in your journey."

Allendar pushed her forward and placed the gun at her neck. "If you want to live, you will walk quietly through the living room to the front door and down the stairs. The car is parked in the lot. I'll tell you which one it is when we're outside. Don't make a peep or there will be hell to pay."

Polly's mind was trying to come up with a way to stop this man from taking her, but right now she had nothing. She didn't want him to hurt Henry or Rebecca, but knew that wasn't what she needed to focus on. The gun at her neck kept her moving forward and even though she'd laughed about taking self-defense courses, she'd done nothing about it, figuring that the worst that could happen to her had already happened. She had no idea how to take this man down.

He pushed her across the living room and she didn't dare look back toward the media room, concerned that he might go ballistic. She didn't mind getting slapped around. If he thought that was going to break her, he was nuts. She'd been through much worse.

The moment she opened the front door, though, all hell broke loose.

Obiwan charged out of the front bedroom, followed by Han, both dogs barking and screaming. The noise startled Allendar enough that he didn't see Jon and Ray Renaldi standing just outside the door. Jon swept his arm down, crushing Allendar's wrist. The man let out a scream and dropped the gun.

Ray picked up the gun as he bent forward and sacked Polly in the stomach, carrying her down, back and out of the way of the chaos and into the living room. Men and women wearing FBI jackets stormed up the steps and wrenched Allendar to the floor.

Henry stood in the doorway of the front bedroom. Ray gave Polly a hand, helping her to stand and then nodded. Henry ran forward and took her into his arms.

"I love you, Polly, I love you," he whispered, holding her tightly.

"He said he jammed the phones," Polly said. "How did you tell them he was here?"

"Nothing like some good old fashioned conversation," Henry let her go, but held on to her hand. "Rebecca ran downstairs to get Jon. She told him everything and he took care of the rest. All we needed for you to do was buy us some time."

"I was doing my best, but that was when I thought Aaron was on the other end of my phone call."

"It was all we needed," Aaron Merritt said, walking up the steps with Rebecca. "This girl is a smart cookie. When Henry's phone didn't work, she found Jon and showed him where the phone was in the kitchen."

Rebecca stopped in front of Marcus Allendar and looked him up and down, then lifted her lip into a snarl and stepped past him. "She would never have broke," Rebecca said and ran to Polly for a hug.

"Oh, she already was," he said with a laugh. "She was going to be my best creation yet."

FBI Agent Marla Lane took his arm and led him down the stairs, looking over her glasses at Aaron.

"What was that?" Polly asked.

"I made her promise to leave you alone. That I'd take your statement tonight."

"What about the other girl? Did you find her?"

He nodded. "She's safe. Stu took her to Boone to the hospital. Her parents and husband will meet her there."

Obiwan and Han were both standing at her feet. "Why did you send them out?" she asked Henry.

"Because I figured they would create so much chaos, that man wouldn't be able to focus on whatever it was that Jon and Ray were doing outside the door."

Ray laughed. "I couldn't believe it when I heard the noise, but it worked out perfectly. Thanks."

"Thank you," Polly said and stepped forward to hug him. "For everything," she whispered. "Just thank you."

He kissed her cheek. "You know I'm coming back in a couple of years just to hang out here in the quiet of Bellingwood."

"You think this is quiet?" she asked.

"I think it could be if you don't have a serial killer trying to kidnap you. It's the perfect place to hide from the world for a week."

"Come on, brother," Jon said. "She needs to give a quick statement to the Sheriff and then she needs sleep. You can talk to her about your future vacation plans tomorrow."

They left and Aaron said, "I'm not going to spend any time on this tonight. You people have had a rough couple of days and I want you to sleep. Will you promise to all be ready to talk to me and Stu tomorrow? Tell us everything that happened here tonight?"

Polly put her hand on her chest and said, "I promise."

Henry and Rebecca both nodded.

Aaron put his hand on the front door handle. "Do you promise to try to get some sleep? Lydia will talk to Sylvie and Jeff tomorrow and tell them to keep things quiet for you until you're alert again. Then call me and we'll set up a time to hear your story."

Polly nodded and Henry walked over and shook Aaron's hand. "Thanks for everything," Henry said.

"Sleep. We'll talk tomorrow." Aaron started to shut the door and then poked his head back in. "We'll take care of locking up.

Don't worry about anything."

"Okay," Polly said. "Thanks."

After he was gone, Henry sat down beside her. "I don't think I can fall asleep. What about you two?"

"No way," Rebecca said.

Polly drooped. "I'm so tired, but I'm afraid I forgot how to sleep. Maybe a movie to dull our minds?"

"Star Wars?" Rebecca asked with a laugh.

CHAPTER TWENTY-FIVE

"Really? I'm free to be out on my own?" Polly had spent the better part of the last two weeks feeling like she was under siege. Now she was free again. She could make her own decisions about coming and going.

Henry had taken them to Aaron's office in Boone to give their preliminary statements. Agent Lane informed her that she would need to be available if they required more information.

Now that they were back in Bellingwood, Henry wanted to spend time at the coffee shop, assessing the worst of the damage in order to design plans for reconstruction.

"This is the first time I feel like I can leave home without worrying about you," he said.

"Should we go out tonight? By ourselves?" Polly glanced at the media room where Rebecca, Andrew and Kayla had settled in with the animals. "And Rebecca too. She's part of us now."

"How about the new Mexican place?" he asked.

A knock at the front door caught their attention.

"Sure," Polly said. "You head out the back door. You don't need to get caught in any of this."

Henry winked at her, gave a little wave and left the room before she got to the door.

Tonya and Gerry stood there with smiles on their faces.

"Come in," Polly said. "I want to thank you for all you did for me."

"We don't have time. Ray got us on a flight out of Des Moines. We'll be home in time for a long weekend and then we're off again on Monday," Tonya said. "I just wanted to say thanks for your hospitality and for the entertainment."

Gerry interrupted. "We're sorry we weren't here for the excitement last night, but I'm glad you all are okay."

"Thank you for giving me some freedom, though," Polly said. "I feel like you spent your time here for nothing."

Tonya reached out to shake her hand. "It was good downtime for us. We've been running a tough year and next week things get nuts again. Bellingwood is a nice place to be."

"If you ever need a place to hide from the real world," Polly said. "Let me know. There will always be a room for you."

"We might take you up on it," Gerry said. "Take care of yourself."

Polly watched them go back down the steps and breathed a sigh of relief. They were great girls, yet she was happy to see them leave.

"Who wants to go for ice cream?" she called out as she headed for the media room.

"You don't have a car," Rebecca reminded her.

That stopped Polly for a second and then she said, "It's a beautiful afternoon, the sun is shining, it's only a few blocks away and we can walk. Are you up for it?"

Both Andrew and Rebecca looked at Kayla. "Will your sister let you go with us?" Rebecca asked.

"You run down and ask her," Polly said. "Meet us in the kitchen. You two," she pointed at Andrew and Rebecca. "Grab your library books. We're going to stop in and say hello to Joss on the way. Come on, all of you, get moving. I'm free and I want to see the world!"

Polly hugged Obiwan and kissed the top of Han's head as the dogs looked up at her from their comfortable spots on the sofa. "You two stay here. We'll be back after a while and then I'm taking you on a long walk wherever we want to go." She went down the back steps and ducked her head in the kitchen.

"Sylvie. Oh Sylvie!" she sang out.

Sylvie came in from the auditorium. "What are you up to? You look more sane than you did last night."

"I am. I've had some sleep. The bad guys are in jail and I'm free. Can I take your son up to the library and the General Store for ice cream?"

Sylvie pursed her lips and was about to say something, then thought better of it. "Sure. He can have ice cream."

"You were going to tell me it would spoil his dinner, but we both know better than that, don't we," Polly said.

"You're right," Sylvie acquiesced.

"Your boys are lucky," Polly said. "You are such a great cook, they don't hate eating your meals."

"Yeah. You just keep thinking that."

Kayla came into the kitchen. "Stephanie said I could go. Will we be back by five or should she come get me?"

Polly thought through the whole process, knowing that Kayla's things were still upstairs. She said to Sylvie, "It's never easy, is it."

Sylvie just smiled.

"Go take your things to Stephanie and tell her she'd better meet us at The General Store when she's done with work."

Kayla threw her head back and sighed loudly. "I'm going to deserve ice cream after all of this walking," she said dramatically and went out to head up the steps.

Polly chuckled. "I love kids at this age. Their filters are pretty thin."

"Speaking of thin filters, have you talked to Sal since last night?" Sylvie asked.

Rebecca and Andrew came rushing into the kitchen. "Are you ready to go?" Andrew asked. Then he looked at his mom. "Did she ask if I could have ice cream?"

Sylvie stared at him.

"Mom," he said. "Would it be okay if I went to the General Store with Rebecca and Kayla and Polly for ice cream? I know that dinner is coming and I promise to eat reasonably." He rolled his eyes to Polly. "We're going to the library, too. Can I go?"

It was all Polly could do not to laugh out loud, but she maintained her composure.

"Yes you may. But just ice cream. No candy or chips or anything else. Got it?" Sylvie said.

"Yeah! Come on, Rebecca. Let's find Kayla and tell her to hurry." They ran out the front door of the kitchen.

"So?" Sylvie asked.

"Sal hasn't talked to me yet. But then I've been out of it today. I slept late and we just got back from Boone."

Sylvie nodded. "You two need to work this out sooner rather than later."

"We'll be fine. You worry too much," Polly said.

Rebecca stepped in from the back hallway and said, "We're ready to go."

"I'll talk to you later, Sylvie, and really... don't worry." Polly ignored the look Sylvie gave her and followed the kids out the back door. It felt odd to not have another vehicle here for her to drive. She wondered how long it would take before she begged Henry to take her out looking for one.

She watched Rebecca walking along with Kayla and Andrew, then smiled when Kayla started skipping down the driveway. She couldn't hear what the kids were saying, but Rebecca handed Andrew her bag of books and took Kayla's hand. The two girls skipped to the highway, looked both ways, ran across and then started skipping again.

Andrew slowed down enough for Polly to catch up. "No skipping for you?" she asked, putting her hand out to take Rebecca's bag.

"That's okay," he said. "I'll carry it." His voice sounded so dejected she put her hand on his shoulder.

"What's wrong?"

He heaved a huge sigh and said, "Look at them. They're being girls and I'm not a girl. You won't catch me skipping."

They waited for a car to go past and then crossed the street. When they got to the sidewalk, Polly said, "You should try it. It's kind of fun." She skipped a few steps and stopped to wait for him.

"No," he said. "I put up with enough because I have girlfriends. I don't need to give the guys another reason to be dogging me."

"Is it really bad?" Polly asked.

He shrugged a shoulder. "Sometimes it can get bad. Mom says that it's because they're jealous."

"She's probably right, you know. Are there boys you want to hang out with in your class?"

"Maybe." Andrew crossed his arms in front of him, a bag in either hand. "But I think they only want to be my friend so they can come to the barn. And I don't like those big horses."

"But you like Tom and Huck. Why don't you invite those boys to come over after school?"

"Last day tomorrow. Duh," he said, rolling his eyes at her.

"Okay. Invite them this summer. Eliseo and Jason will show them around."

Rebecca and Kayla had already run up the front steps of the library and were waiting at the front door for Andrew and Polly.

He put his foot on the bottom step. "You always have an answer for everything. You just don't know how it is."

"I don't think it's as hard as you're making it," Polly said. "Race you?" She ran up the steps and stopped in front of the door.

Andrew looked up at her from the bottom step. "That wasn't fair!" he whined. "I didn't know we were racing."

"Gotta be prepared, buddy boy. Come on. Get up here. Let's get this show on the road," Polly said.

Rebecca and Kayla both looked at her as if she'd gone nuts.

"Yeah, yeah, yeah," Polly said. "I might be a little loopy. It's been a long week and I'm finally free. Deal with it. I'm paying for the ice cream."

Andrew handed Rebecca her bag of books when he got to the top of the steps and they went inside.

Joss was at the main desk and smiled when she saw them. "What are you four doing out and about today?"

"We're returning books and then we're going to the General Store for ice cream," Rebecca said.

Joss nodded and said, "I heard from a reliable source that the flavor of the day is mint chocolate chip." She put her hand out to take their bags.

Polly said, "You guys go look for more books. Don't take too long, though."

The kids took off and Joss looked her up and down. "You look like you're in pretty good shape after all your excitement last night. It's all over town, you know."

"How much?"

"Let's see," Joss lifted her index finger and began ticking off the events. "The fire. Jason took down your old boyfriend with some kind of ninja move and then the serial killer guy was at your house when you got home and the dogs were the big heroes there. Did you get any sleep?"

"A few hours. I'm hoping that tonight is calmer. Rebecca needs to rest. That poor girl hasn't yet dealt with what has been piled on her these last two days. It's been non-stop. We fell asleep watching movies last night. Henry carried her to bed and then tucked me into the couch."

"How's he doing?"

Polly shook her head. "I have no idea. We've barely had time to talk. He was wonderful last night. Smart enough to send Rebecca downstairs to find Jon and then he snuck into the front bedroom and released the dogs when I opened the door. Joss, I thought I was going to have to leave with that awful man just to keep them safe. He'd jammed our cell phones and I didn't think anyone knew what was going on. I was scared to death."

"And you're here in the library this afternoon with three kids," Joss said. "I don't know how you do it. The craziest things happen to you and you just keep going."

"What's my other option?" Polly huffed. "Curl up into a ball and cry? Huddle under blankets and make everyone take care of me? Whine around town about how awful my life is?"

Joss scowled at her. "When you put it that way... But most people I know would do any or all of those rather than just deal with it and move on."

"I have too many other things to do. That's just a waste of my time." Polly glanced around. "Speaking of other things, are you coming to Sarah's memorial service Saturday morning?"

"I'll be there with the kids. I'm not sure if Nate will be able to get away from the pharmacy. He'll try."

"Having you there will be enough. Sylvie's making lunch. It's going to be simple. Sarah wanted us to focus on Rebecca's life. Rebecca is her memorial."

"Are you spreading her ashes on Saturday?"

Polly shook her head. "No. Rebecca and I will do that sometime on the spur of the moment. Whenever she's ready, she's just going to tell me and we'll go out and sit on the bank of the creek and talk about Sarah while she lets them go. Until then, I told her that the box could stay in her room."

"What if it takes a while?"

"I guess if it takes her a couple of years to let go of that last remnant of her mom, that's fine." Polly smiled. "She's got her own mind, that's for sure. Henry and I don't really need to raise her, we're just going to guide her along while she raises herself. Sarah did a wonderful job. It's pretty amazing."

"You think it will be that easy?" Joss sounded surprised that Polly was so naive.

"No I don't," Polly said with a chuckle. "She's going to be a royal pain in the hind end when we won't let her do things her way or when we demand that she listen to our opinions, but she's smart - smarter than anyone realizes. She'll figure it out. And if she doesn't, well then, I guess I'll deal with it."

"Just like you deal with everything else," Joss said, glancing behind Polly. "Here they come."

"Would you believe Kayla has never read a Harry Potter book?" Andrew demanded, slapping the book down on the counter. "Can you believe it?"

"Why's that?" Joss asked.

"I don't know," Kayla said. "I didn't read much before we came here."

"Your two friends have checked this book out several times," Joss said. "They need to let you have fun reading it by yourself. Don't you dare spoil any of the mysteries for her, got it?"

Andrew nodded emphatically and put a stack of paperbacks beside Kayla's book. "What are these about?" he asked.

Polly picked the top book up and looked at him. "What made you pick this up?"

"Is it the television show that Mom watches sometimes?"

She turned the book so Joss could see. "Perry Mason books?"

"There's a ton of them back there. No one ever reads them anymore. Can I?"

The two women looked at each other and Joss asked, "Are you done with the young adult books?"

"Nah, but these look kind of fun. They're just mysteries, right?"

"Okay," Joss said. "Give 'em a shot. It would be nice to see them in circulation again. Tell your friends if you like 'em. What do you have, Rebecca?"

"Mom told me about the Black Stallion books. I've never read those. We talked about it when she watched the Percherons. Now that she's gone, maybe it's time for me to read them."

"I'm sorry for your loss," Joss said, reaching out to touch Rebecca's hand. "She was a wonderful mother and a terrific woman."

Rebecca pulled her hand back and dropped it to her side. "Thank you," she said quietly.

"Let me check these out and you can head for the General Store," Joss said. She quickly moved through the books and put them in the bags Andrew and Rebecca had been carrying. When she handed Kayla's book to her, Rebecca opened her bag so that she could drop it in.

Polly gave Joss a gentle smile as they left and when they got to the front door, she held it open for the three kids. She took a deep breath once they were outside.

"Ice cream now?" she asked.

They walked down the sidewalk and crossed the street to the General Store, then went inside. A table was open and Andrew ran to sit down in a chair.

"What do you want?" Polly asked. "I'm having a hot fudge sundae with nuts and whipped cream and a cherry on top."

"Can I have a banana split?" Andrew asked with a huge grin on his face.

Polly laughed at him. "What would your mother say?"

"She'd say I was going to spoil my dinner. Can I?"

"What if I split it with you?" Rebecca asked him. "Then it wouldn't be so bad, would it?"

"You're a smart girl, Rebecca," Polly said. "What about you, Kayla?"

"That sounds good, but I don't have anyone to split it with."

"Do you really want one?" Polly asked her. "Because I think I know how we can work this out."

Kayla's eyes lit up. "Yes!"

"I'll be right back. The three of you sit here and don't move." Polly went up to the counter and when the young girl who was taking orders stopped in front of her to ask what she wanted, Polly leaned in and said. "A hot fudge sundae with nuts, whipped cream and a cherry for me and then I'd like you to make up a double banana split for three kids to share. Make sure there are plenty of cherries and spoons and fun stuff for them. I don't care what it costs."

The girl smiled and nodded. "I know just what they want. We'll bring it over in a few minutes, okay?"

"Thanks," Polly said. She pulled napkins out of the dispenser and went back to the table to join the kids. "Banana splits are coming. You had better not get me in trouble, though." These kids weren't going to be able to eat that much ice cream and get through dinner. Sylvie would probably kill her and Stephanie would never let her take Kayla out again, but she just couldn't find it in herself to feel guilty. If three kids were who she was going to celebrate her freedom with, they were doing it in style.

She watched Rebecca try to laugh and joke with Andrew and Kayla. Something about Joss's comment had changed her demeanor. "Are you okay, Rebecca?" Polly asked.

Andrew and Kayla stopped talking to watch what was happening.

"Yeah," Rebecca said. "I think so. It's just weird to have people talk about Mom in the past tense. They're going to do that a lot, aren't they?"

"Well, she is gone," Polly said.

"She's not gone. Saying she's gone is like you're saying she's coming back. She's dead. She's never coming back."

"Right..."

Rebecca had started to wind up and then immediately she forced herself to calm back down. "It's weird, that's all. They're going to say nice things about her and expect me to do what? Cry for them?"

Polly glanced at Andrew and Kayla. They were completely at a loss as to what to say.

"Maybe we should talk about this later tonight," Polly said. She watched Rebecca fold in on herself and knew she'd handled that one badly. "I'm sorry," she said quietly. "I don't know what to tell you. People have different ideas about how to handle death. You and your mom talked about it and you've thought about it and I'm guessing she answered your questions and when you needed to cry because you knew how much you were going to miss her, she held you and talked to you. Right?"

Rebecca nodded.

"I miss my mom, too," Kayla said simply.

Polly put her hand on Kayla's back, thankful that enough time had passed and they had gotten to know each other well enough that the girl didn't flinch quite as often. "I'll bet you do."

"I didn't get to tell her goodbye before she died. You were lucky, Rebecca."

Andrew squirmed uncomfortably in his seat and Rebecca looked across the table at her friend, then blinked as she tried to regain her composure.

"I'm sorry, Kayla," Rebecca said. "I was being selfish. This is just so weird for me."

"No one here knew my mom and we didn't even get to have a funeral."

Polly's heart broke. Why hadn't she thought to do anything for Stephanie and Kayla? It had been such a strange time for them. Stephanie had gone back to Ohio to talk to the prosecutors and when she got back to Sycamore House, life just moved on.

Rebecca stood up and took Polly's hand, pulling on it, asking Polly to follow her. She drew Polly out the front door and said, "I know we haven't talked about this, but I think we should ask Stephanie and Kayla to be part of the service on Saturday. It won't add any more people, so we don't have to plan for it, but they need to say goodbye to their Mom, too, don't you think?"

Polly felt tears squirt out of her eyes as she reached out and pulled Rebecca close. "You are an amazing little girl. I am awfully proud of you. You don't have to do this if you don't want to, though. No one else is even going to think of it, so there's no pressure."

"I want to. It's the right thing. Kayla's right. They didn't get a funeral and they should have one."

"You wreck my heart sometimes, Rebecca. I think the world of you."

"Mom would want me to do this."

"Yes she would." Polly gave her another squeeze and said. "I think I see the ice cream coming. Are you ready for this?"

"Thanks, Polly," Rebecca said.

"I love you, sweetie."

CHAPTER TWENTY-SIX

Dancing in anticipation, Rebecca stood at the main doors into the auditorium between Henry and Polly.

"People are going to think I'm strange," she said.

Henry put his hand on her back. "You're in good company. Since the day Polly got here, she's stirred the community up. They never know what to think when she's around."

"You guys are okay with this, right?" Rebecca asked.

"Honey, this is awesome. Your mom would love it."

"I let everybody do the sad funeral thing, but now it's time to party. Is that really okay? Mom didn't want us to be sad."

"It's just fine," Polly assured her.

They'd had a rather somber memorial service at the Methodist church. Stephanie and Kayla tried to refuse to be part of it, but after spending time with Reverend Boehm on Friday afternoon, they'd agreed that it might be good to celebrate their own mother's death. The service had been fairly standard, as memorial services go. Hymns, a message of hope and each of the girls took a few moments to talk about how much their mothers had meant to them. There had been very few dry eyes in the church and Polly had been pleased with the number of her friends that had attended. Many of them had grown to know Sarah and Rebecca over the last year and a half and they were there to celebrate the life of a woman who had loved her daughter more than anything.

Rev. Boehm had agreed to hold the congregation for an extra ten minutes so Rebecca, Henry and Polly could get back to Sycamore House first. Rebecca had checked the auditorium one last time and pronounced it ready to go. Sylvie, Rachel, Hannah and Stephanie were in the kitchen putting the finishing touches on the meal.

The front door of Sycamore House opened and Polly wasn't at all surprised to see Lydia and Aaron come in, followed by Andy and Len Specek and Beryl Watson.

"That was a beautiful service, Rebecca," Lydia said, hugging the girl. "You are very lucky to have spent so many years with your mother."

"Yes I was," Rebecca said. "She was great."

Aaron put his hand on the crash bar to open the door, and Rebecca stopped him. "Just a few more minutes," she said.

He looked at her and then at Polly, confusion creasing his forehead.

"Just wait," Polly echoed, winking at him.

The foyer began to fill with people and Rebecca slipped away. Polly waited and chatted with her friends until Rebecca flung open the doors and Cyndi Lauper's "Girls Just Want to Have Fun" blasted over the speakers in the auditorium.

"What is this?" Lydia asked.

Beryl started to laugh and grabbed her friend's arm. "It's a discotheque! I don't think I've ever been to a funeral luncheon quite like this one."

Murmuring and surprised laughter accompanied the guests entering the auditorium.

They'd spent all day Friday decorating the room. Jon and Ray had stayed through mid-afternoon, catching an early evening flight out. Before he left, Ray handed Polly a flash drive and told her that was every bit of information he'd collected on the people that surrounded her. There was nothing in there that was a threat to her or her friends and family. He hinted that there were things she might want to know in the future, but for now, it was unimportant. Polly didn't know what to do with the drive, so she tucked it away behind the junk in a drawer in her desk. Now all she needed to do was forget that it even existed. It had been good to see them and Polly appreciated everything they had done. When she tried to talk to Ray about payment, he took her aside, his grip on her arm tight.

Ray was angry that she'd asked again. He'd done this because they were family and he thought she understood that. Polly nodded and then in a moment of seriousness, he asked if she would consider helping him out sometimes when he needed to have a quiet place for his employees to run away to. That had surprised her. Why would he want to send people to the middle of Iowa? There was nothing here for them to do ... no ocean beaches or mountains or resorts. He'd smiled ... a bit patronizingly and told her that she didn't know what she had here. But, if she would make Sycamore Inn available when he needed it, he'd consider the debt fully paid. Polly agreed. It was a simple enough request and she would be glad to do that for him.

They'd helped in the auditorium before leaving, covering the windows to limit the afternoon's light. Henry and Eliseo had hung disco balls from the ceiling and installed black lights around the room. Neon tablecloths and party ware, balloons, and streamers filled the room. There were glow sticks on the tables and even Sylvie's punch glowed.

It took a few moments for people to find a seat in the room and the noise settled down when Rebecca took the stage with a microphone. Jeff turned down the music, which at this point was playing "Boogie Wonderland."

"Thank you for coming to celebrate my mother's life," Rebecca said. "We talked for a long time about what we would do today and one day she said that she missed out on the disco era. She loved to dance. This might be different than you'd expect..." Rebecca paused for effect and gestured around the room. "But it's what she wanted. Mom always said that even if I missed her, I should remember how much fun we had and that today would be one last hurrah and nobody could stop us."

Rebecca took a deep breath and bent down to pick a glow stick up from the floor. She snapped it and said, "So let's party like it's the seventies. Lunch is ready, just head out the door to the kitchen line and please laugh and have a good time." She raised her glow stick. "Thanks Mom."

Jeff took the microphone from her and lifted her down from the stage. Rebecca's face was beaming when Polly and Henry got to her side.

"Was I okay?" she asked.

"You were great," Polly said. "I'm proud of you and I know your mom would be, too."

"Did you see Mrs. Hastings is here?"

Polly looked around. "I think some of your classmates and their families are here with her, too. That's pretty cool."

"Have you seen Andrew?"

"He's over there with a couple of boys from your class," Polly said, pointing to the cake table. Sylvie had used tonic water to add a glow to the frosting on cupcakes and it was wild seeing them reflect the black light.

"Can I go?"

"You can do whatever you want today," Henry said to her. "We'll take care of the weird adults."

"Thanks." Rebecca handed him her glow stick and started to walk away, then thought better of it and took it back. "I might get lost in the dark," she said with a laugh.

He took Polly's hand and drew her close. "Do you think she'll ever get back to being a kid?"

Polly watched her rush up to Andrew and his friends, bobbing in time to the music. "She's working on it. We just need to keep crises away from her for a while. Can we do that?"

He stepped back and gave her a look of incredulity. "We? What's this 'we' stuff? You're the one who brings excitement to this relationship. I'm just trying to hold on."

"Help me, then?" She leaned forward and gave him a kiss on the cheek.

"Polly, can I talk to you for a minute?"

She turned at the sound of Sal's voice. "Sure, what's up?"

"Away from all of this. I need to talk to you."

Henry squeezed her hand and she left him to follow Sal out the back door into the hallway behind the stage.

"I need to apologize to you," Sal said. "I can't believe I was so out of control the other night. You and Sylvie tried to tell me to stop it, but I couldn't get over myself. I don't know when to stop. You know I love you, don't you?"

"Of course I do," Polly said. "You don't have to apologize. You were stressed and things were falling apart. I understand."

"But I never heard from you again. I figured you would at least call to yell at me."

Polly took Sal's hand. "Honey, I'm sorry. My life has been so nuts the last couple of days, I haven't had time to do anything but move from one thing to the next. Thursday was crazy busy with trying to sleep and talking to the FBI and then yesterday we spent the whole day decorating and getting ready for today. I'm so sorry."

"No. I don't want you to apologize. That's my job," Sal said. "I should have called you." She gestured back to the auditorium. "I should have been here to help. I was being all self-centered and whiny and you needed me."

"It's okay. Henry said you've been at the coffee shop. Are you handling that any better now?"

"I think so," Sal said. "He tells me that it's going to be okay. We can't save the apartments, but that's probably better anyway. I don't want to be a landlord."

"Maybe they did you a favor," Polly said with a laugh.

"The next time I act like silly self-centered Bunny Farnam will you promise to beat me upside the head?" Sal asked. "It just hit me that I've been doing that for the last couple of days and now, here I am dragging you away from Rebecca just so you'll tell me that you don't hate me."

"Stop it. I love you to pieces. Come on. Let's go back in and dance."

"That little girl is certainly lucky to have you."

"She's pretty amazing."

"Yes she is. You're going to have your hands full as she grows up."

"Yes, I am," Polly said, opening the door. Earth, Wind and Fire was playing over the speakers and she couldn't help herself. She grabbed Sal's arms and spun her into the room, then twirled up against her. "This is the best music ever," Polly said. She pointed to Lydia. "Look at her."

Lydia was dancing around Aaron as he held two plates of food. When she slid up and down his side, Polly laughed out loud. "You'll never see that happen again," she said.

Sal's eyes were huge. "I can't believe I'm seeing it now! There's Mark, looking lost. He's been worried about us. I should tell him that things are fine."

"Go take care of your man," Polly said. She danced her way to Henry, who was talking to Nate and Joss. "Wanna dance, big boy?" she asked.

"This was a great idea," Joss said. "I think you and Rebecca both needed a party to toss off the stress of the last few weeks."

Henry looked around the room. "You know, I think that everyone here needed this to toss off the stress of the last couple of weeks. We've all been on edge, worrying about that serial killer... not knowing where he was or if he would grab Polly out from under us. This is good. It's just different enough to break apart any leftover tension."

Evelyn Morrow approached Polly, holding two glasses of punch. She handed one to Polly and the other to Henry. "I heard Sarah and Rebecca planning this," she said with a smile. "It's grand that you sent Sarah off with such a big party. It would have made her happy. That woman wanted the world for her daughter. I'm glad you two can offer her a wonderful life."

Polly shook her head and looked across the room at Rebecca, who had found a seat at a table with Kayla and Mrs. Hastings.

They were talking animatedly and Rebecca was drawing on the tablecloth. She laughed and glanced around the room, taking it all in, then returned to the conversation. "I think Rebecca is going to find a way to make her own way in the world. Henry and I will just make sure she's safe and loved."

"Are you two planning to have children of your own?" Evelyn asked. "You have a great deal to offer a big family."

Henry took Polly's hand and they looked at each other. He spoke up. "We're not planning on having children in the normal way. At least not right now. But I'd have to guess that Rebecca is just the first child who will end up in our family. How does that sound?"

Evelyn smiled and reached down to put her hand on their clasped hands. She lifted their hands so she could hold them in hers. "That sounds exactly right for you. Rebecca has no idea what she's started, does she?"

"I don't know what tomorrow has in store," Polly said. "But I do know that I'm going to miss having you here. It's been a joy."

"Thank you for caring for Sarah," Evelyn said. "You all made it easy to give meaning to her final months. I'll miss the everyday excitement that happens here." She gave Polly a wicked grin. "But I don't think I'll miss treating your friends when they're nearly run over or worrying about whether some madman is coming after you. Those gave me a few nights of unsettled sleep."

"You're welcome to come by any day," Polly said. "In fact, I'm sure Rebecca would be glad to see you as often as possible."

Evelyn nodded. "It will be important for her to see me for a few months. Then, as her life gets going again, she'll need me less and less. I'll call next week and see if there's an opportunity for lunch."

"Please do," Polly said. "And thank you again."

Evelyn moved off and Polly caught Jessie waving at her. She was sitting at a table with Bill and Marie Sturtz. Bill's sister and her husband were there as well. Marie was holding the baby and looked up with a smile when Polly and Henry joined them.

"That looks good on you, Mom," Henry said.

"I like having this little one around," Marie replied. "If being a grandma means that I can love on a baby and not worry about the hassle of raising the child, I think that's the best job ever." She rubbed Molly's nose and then looked up in shock. "I'm not pressuring you. Please don't think I meant anything by that."

Polly felt Henry breathe deeply beside her.

"Good," he said under his breath.

She sat down beside Jessie. "I haven't had any time in the last couple of weeks. How are things with Molly?"

"It's good," Jessie said. "I'll be glad when Rebecca and Kayla can babysit. I'm ready to get out of the house by myself one of these days, but Marie tells me not to be in a hurry. She's right. Molly won't be a baby very long."

Polly felt a horrible desire to tell Jessie that she'd watch the baby while Jessie went out, but the truth was that scared her to death. She knew there was no way she'd feel comfortable taking care of a baby for several hours. Marie was so natural with Molly and as Polly watched, she had no urgent desire to hold the little girl.

The first night in the hospital after the birth, a nurse had put the baby in Polly's arms. She kept waiting for some overwhelming nurturing sensation to flow over her and ... nothing. But she watched Jessie's face every time she held her daughter and saw the power of a mother's love settle in.

Lydia whispered into Polly's ear, "You don't have to feel guilty, dear."

Polly stood up and grabbed Lydia's hand, pulling her away. "How do you do this?" she asked. "How do you know what's going on in my head?"

"It's all over your face." Lydia took Polly's hands in hers. "You are an incredible woman. You've handled so many things these last two weeks that would send nearly everyone here over the edge of sanity and yet you're worrying because you don't want to be a mommy to babies. Give yourself a break. Jessie has a healthy and happy baby because you helped her pull her life together. Marie has a baby at her house for that same reason. Rebecca is having the best time today celebrating her mother's life because you helped make their dream come true for today. Look at the lives you have touched. You've given people jobs when they needed to work, you've encouraged your friends to be more than they ever could have imagined, and you've given people freedom to be themselves. And you do it without reservation, without judgment."

"It's no big deal," Polly said.

"Oh my friend, it's a huge deal, but you will never ask for anything back for all that you've given. But I'm going to be right here beside you to remind you that you are special just the way you are." Lydia pulled Polly into a hug and she could feel the woman's chest rise as she began to sob. "I am so thankful that you are safe. I've been absolutely terrified that something horrible would happen to you with those awful men in town. I haven't been able to talk to Aaron about it because I've been so scared."

She and Polly held on to each other as Lydia cried into Polly's shoulder. Then Lydia said, "So don't you ever feel guilty for living your life the way you want to live it. You hear me?"

"Yes mom," Polly said. "I hear you."

Lydia pulled away and then swatted Polly's shoulder. "And don't call me mom. You make me feel old. Even though you could be my daughter. Don't do it."

Polly gave her a quick hug. "I'll be good. Thanks."

She turned back to find Henry and saw Doug Randall stride across the room to her.

"Hey Doug," she said.

"Did they tell you?" he asked.

Polly grinned. "Tell me what?"

"I'm getting a dog. I get to pick him up after work on Monday."

"A puppy?"

"Yeah. He's a cute little thing. He's a mix. I think he's got bits of everything in him, but he has this big ole nose and you should see his feet. I think he'll be a big dog..."

Polly half-listened as Doug continued to tell her about his new dog. Life did just keep moving on, no matter how much it felt as if things had stopped for her. Babies were growing, lives were changing, and kids were getting older. She was entwined in the lives of everyone in this room in one way or another. It seemed that every time she turned around, the list of her friends grew exponentially.

Music played in the background, she wasn't even sure what she was hearing now. Doug was talking about his trip to the pet store yesterday, Marie and Jessie were laughing over the baby, Rebecca was chasing Kayla on the dance floor, Sylvie and Rachel were sitting down together to eat, Beryl had thrown her head back in laughter, Joss leaned over to say something to Cooper, and Sal was whispering to Mark. All around the room, people were alive and happy to be here.

This was life. This was her life.

THANK YOU FOR READING!

I'm so glad you enjoy these stories about Polly Giller and her friends. There are many ways to stay in touch with Diane and the Bellingwood community.

You can find more details about Sycamore House and Bellingwood at the website: http://nammynools.com/

Join the Bellingwood Facebook page:
https://www.facebook.com/pollygiller
for news about upcoming books, conversations while I'm writing and you're reading, and a continued look at life in a small town.

Diane Greenwood Muir's Amazon Author Page is a great place to watch for new releases.

Follow Diane on Twitter at twitter.com/nammynools for regular updates and notifications.

Recipes and decorating ideas found in the books can often be found on Pinterest at: *http://pinterest.com/nammynools/*

And, if you are looking for Sycamore House swag, check out Polly's CafePress store: *http://www.cafepress.com/sycamorehouse*

Made in the USA
Lexington, KY
06 July 2015